Other *Leisure* books by Raymond Benson:

A HARD DAY'S DEATH
SWEETIE'S DIAMONDS

RAYMOND BENSON

DARK SIDE OF THE MORGUE

A Spike Berenger Rock 'n' Roll Hit

LEISURE BOOKS NEW YORK CITY

A LEISURE BOOK®

March 2009

Published by

Dorchester Publishing Co., Inc.
200 Madison Avenue
New York, NY 10016

ISBN 10: 0-8439-6198-8
ISBN 13: 978-0-8439-6198-0

The name "Leisure Books" and the stylized "L" with design are trademarks of Dorchester Publishing Co., Inc.

Printed in the United States of America.

10 9 8 7 6 5 4 3 2 1

Visit us on the web at www.dorchesterpub.com.

For Max

LINER NOTES

There is no such thing as Chicagoprog. Chicago never had a progressive rock movement (as far as I know), although I'm aware of one band called Pentwater that existed in the seventies. The bands and musicians cited within as Chicagoprog acts are entirely fictitious. A few real Chicago-based bands are name-checked in the manuscript. All of the club venues are real. The band Chicago Green appeared in Spike Berenger's previous adventure and is also real. More information about them can be found at www.chigreen.net.

The author wishes to thank Dave Case, Michael A. Black, Dean Zelinsky, James McMahon, J. A. Konrath, Robby Glick, Kathy Tootelian, and the City of Chicago Police Department for their help in the preparation of this book.

THE CHICAGOPROG FAMILY TREE (PAGE 1)

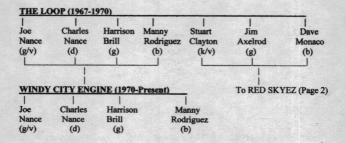

THE LOOP (1967-1970)

| Joe Nance (g/v) | Charles Nance (d) | Harrison Brill (g) | Manny Rodriguez (b) | Stuart Clayton (k/v) | Jim Axelrod (g) | Dave Monaco (b) |

WINDY CITY ENGINE (1970-Present)

To RED SKYEZ (Page 2)

| Joe Nance (g/v) | Charles Nance (d) | Harrison Brill (g) | Manny Rodriguez (b) |

Note: Jim Axelrod and Dave Monaco were rotating members of The Loop with Harrison Brill and Manny Rodriguez between 1969-1970.

Key: g = guitar
      v = vocals
      k = keyboards
      b = bass
      d = drums

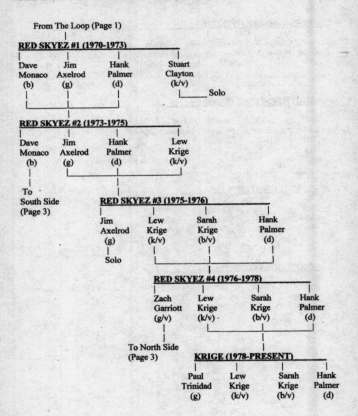

From The Loop (Page 1)

RED SKYEZ #1 (1970-1973)

Dave Monaco (b)	Jim Axelrod (g)	Hank Palmer (d)	Stuart Clayton (k/v)

Solo

RED SKYEZ #2 (1973-1975)

Dave Monaco (b)	Jim Axelrod (g)	Hank Palmer (d)	Lew Krige (k/v)

To South Side (Page 3)

RED SKYEZ #3 (1975-1976)

Jim Axelrod (g)	Lew Krige (k/v)	Sarah Krige (b/v)	Hank Palmer (d)

Solo

RED SKYEZ #4 (1976-1978)

Zach Garriott (g/v)	Lew Krige (k/v)	Sarah Krige (b/v)	Hank Palmer (d)

To North Side (Page 3)

KRIGE (1978-PRESENT)

Paul Trinidad (g)	Lew Krige (k/v)	Sarah Krige (b/v)	Hank Palmer (d)

THE CHICAGOPROG FAMILY TREE (PAGE 3)

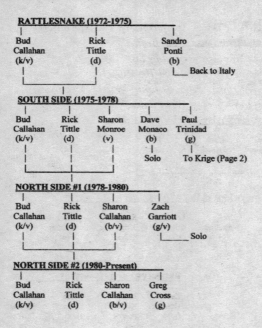

RATTLESNAKE (1972-1975)

Bud Callahan (k/v)	Rick Tittle (d)	Sandro Ponti (b)
		└── Back to Italy

SOUTH SIDE (1975-1978)

Bud Callahan (k/v)	Rick Tittle (d)	Sharon Monroe (v)	Dave Monaco (b)	Paul Trinidad (g)
			Solo	To Krige (Page 2)

NORTH SIDE #1 (1978-1980)

Bud Callahan (k/v)	Rick Tittle (d)	Sharon Callahan (b/v)	Zach Garriott (g/v)
			└── Solo

NORTH SIDE #2 (1980-Present)

Bud Callahan (k/v)	Rick Tittle (d)	Sharon Callahan (b/v)	Greg Cross (g)

TRACK LISTING

1. Too Old to Rock 'n' Roll—Too Young to Die *(performed by Jethro Tull)*
2. Wouldn't It Be Nice? *(performed by The Beach Boys)*
3. Taxman *(performed by The Beatles)*
4. We Are Family *(performed by Sister Sledge)*
5. King of Pain *(performed by The Police)*
6. Hey Joe *(performed by The Jimi Hendrix Experience)*
7. What To Do *(performed by Status Quo)*
8. Witchy Woman *(performed by Eagles)*
9. Jumping Someone Else's Train *(performed by The Cure)*
10. Cops and Robbers *(performed by Bo Diddley)*
11. Photographs and Memories *(performed by Jim Croce)*
12. Old Time Rock & Roll *(performed by Bob Seger & the Silver Bullet Band)*
13. Assassin *(performed by Motörhead)*
14. Would I Lie to You? *(performed by Eurythmics)*
15. Long Time Gone *(performed by Crosby, Stills & Nash)*
16. Taken by Surprise *(performed by The Outfield)*
17. Living Dead Girl *(performed by Rob Zombie)*
18. Angel of Death *(performed by Thin Lizzy)*
19. The Voice *(performed by Ultravox)*
20. Walk on the Wild Side *(performed by Lou Reed)*
21. Voyage 34 *(performed by Porcupine Tree)*
22. Ain't Wastin' Time No More *(performed by The Allman Brothers Band)*
23. Down In It *(performed by Nine Inch Nails)*
24. Doctor Doctor *(performed by UFO)*
25. Down With the Sickness *(performed by Disturbed)*
26. Soul Sacrifice *(performed by Santana)*
27. In My Time of Dying *(performed by Led Zeppelin)*
28. All the Madmen *(performed by David Bowie)*
29. Brain Damage *(performed by Pink Floyd)*
30. Lucky Man *(performed by Emerson, Lake & Palmer)*

"Rock 'n' roll—the most brutal, ugly, desperate, vicious form of expression it has been my misfortune to hear."
—Frank Sinatra

Chapter One

Too Old to Rock 'n' Roll:
Too Young to Die
(performed by Jethro Tull)

Joe Nance had blood on his hands.

He hadn't realized it until he threw his guitar pick into the crowd and waved good-bye. Two streams of liquid crimson trickled down his palms and over his wrist. It meant he must have played a good show.

Nance turned to his bandmates and nodded.

Let's get the hell out of here!

The crowd of two hundred or so fans shouted for a second encore but Nance wasn't having it. He was sixty years old, tired, and hungry. The rest of the members of Windy City Engine were roughly the same age and just as weary and famished. The gig was done. Time to chill out.

Nance led the other three guys off the stage and through the door to the dressing rooms. Martyrs' was a small club on the North Side of Chicago, not far from Wrigley Field. It was a pleasant enough venue and the owner was friendly to classic Chicagoprog bands like the Engine and North Side.

As lead guitarist and vocalist, Nance had led Windy City Engine since 1970. For a band that had been around so many years, it was important to maintain a solid, professional live show to give them longevity. In

1

fact, most of their current income came from constant gigging. They made very little money from CD sales. Except for a few of the classic albums from the seventies, the rest of the band's catalog was rare and out of print. Their last studio album of original material was already ten years old. It, too, was out of print. Nance and the rest of the band had to face it—they were a nostalgia outfit and they just barely made a living at it.

Charles Nance, the band's drummer and Joe's brother, noticed the blood as they slogged into the green room.

"You all right?"

Nance nodded. " 'Course." He examined his fingertips and cursed. There were thin slices in the skin. "Damn it. This is gonna hurt like hell tomorrow night."

"We could rearrange the set so you just play keyboards."

"Are you kidding? The fans'd freak out."

It was true. Although Nance occasionally played keys, people went to see Windy City Engine expecting him with a guitar around his shoulder.

"Yeah," Charles said, "I guess you're right. It'd be like going to see Santana and watching Carlos shake maracas for the whole show."

Manny Rodriguez, the bass player, and Harrison Brill, the rhythm guitarist, collapsed into easy chairs. They already had cold beers in their hands.

"I'm gettin' too old for this shit," Brill muttered.

Charles laughed. "Come on, Harrison, you're never too old to rock 'n' roll."

"Yeah? I'm sure old enough to *die*. I've got heartburn like a son of a bitch."

"My back was hurtin' again tonight, too," Rodriguez added.

Charles rolled his eyes. "You guys. What's wrong with you? Don't be such old men! Come on, that was a great gig we just played. The audience loved it."

"What audience there was," Joe said. "That was the smallest crowd we've had in a long time."

"Well, it's raining. Kept people away."

"Didn't keep 'em from going to see the Cubs."

Charles shook his head. "Well, boo hoo. You guys are pathetic. You should be happy we're still playing at all. I'm going home. I'll see you in Milwaukee tomorrow."

The drummer grabbed his gig bag, saluted the other guys, and left the room.

"How come he's always so cheerful?" Rodriguez asked.

Joe Nance cleared his throat, spit into a paper cup, and replied, "I don't know, but it's always made me want to puke. When we were growing up he drove me nuts. My little brother never got mad, never got upset, and never was in a bad mood. Sometimes I just wanted to kick his ass."

Nance went into the bathroom and ran cold water over his bleeding fingers. He washed them with soap, wrapped them in a paper towel, and then took a leak. When he was done, he went back into the green room, where Ray, the club's owner, was waiting. He had a stack of cash in his hand—a very small stack.

"Here's your take of the door, Joe."

"Thanks, Ray."

"Not many people tonight."

3

"I guess not."

"Probably the rain."

"That's what we figured. Where's the first aid kit?"

Ray nodded toward the white box attached to the wall and handed over the money. He left the room as Nance stuck the wad into his bag. Making payroll was going to be tougher this month.

"How many roadies we got now?" Nance asked as he retrieved some Band-Aids.

"Three," Rodriguez answered. "You know that."

"We might have to let one go." He managed to apply two bandages to his fingers and then said, "I'll see you tomorrow night in Wisconsin."

"Bye, Joe," the other two spoke in unison.

When the band's leader was gone, Rodriguez and Brill looked at each other and sighed.

"You get the feeling Joe's gonna cut loose pretty soon?" Brill asked.

"Yeah. But I've been feeling that for ten years."

"What'll you do if he does? We both know there's no Windy City Engine without Joe."

"I know. I guess we'll do what the guys from Red Skyez do—we form splinter bands, play sessions, you know. I wish Zach needed a bass player. I'd probably leave the Engine myself."

"Zach Garriott doesn't need you, partner. Trust me."

"Screw you, too!" Brill finished his beer. "How come Zach Garriott's the only musician in the Chicagoprog scene who made it big?"

Rodriguez shrugged. "I don't know. Because he's good?"

Brill grunted and stood. "Well, I'm out of here. I thought it was a good show. See you tomorrow night."

"Yeah, I'm leaving, too. Bye, Harrison."

The two worn-out musicians gathered their stuff and shuffled out of the club without saying another word to each other.

They couldn't know that the demise of Windy City Engine was closer than they imagined.

Charles Nance drove his '03 Toyota Highlander south on Damen to North Avenue, took the right turn, and then made a left onto Claremont. He lived in a prewar town house that was desperately in need of repairs and fixing up, but since he was a divorced man of fifty-eight with a limited income from music, he didn't care much about appearances. He was simply happy that he still made a living in the band with which he'd been playing since he was a teenager. It was all he ever cared about and he was sure that his brother, Joe, felt the same way. He knew Joe got tired of never making good money, but in Charles's opinion, Windy City Engine was doing very well for a band that had been around for four decades. They were gigging and he was playing drums for a living! That was all that mattered to Charles Nance. Just put him behind a drum kit—anywhere, anytime—and he had a smile on his face. He knew, though, that many of his contemporaries were ready to throw in the towel. Not him. As far as he was concerned, if the band could afford a couple of roadies to unload, set up, strike, load, and carry the equipment from gig to gig without the band having to do it themselves, then they were doing all right.

Nance slid the SUV into his driveway and parked in front of the separate garage. He'd lived in the pocket east of Humboldt Park and west of the Kennedy

Expressway since the early eighties and it suited him just fine. It was quiet, the neighbors were friendly, and he wasn't far from his brother. Charles was a man of few complaints.

He got out of the vehicle and took a deep breath. The rain had ceased, so the late April night air was pleasantly cool and moist. It was the time of year he enjoyed the most. Seeing that Chicago realistically had at the most only a month or two of spring and fall, three months of hot summer, and nearly six months of winter, residents had to relish what good weather they could get. Charles had a good mind to sit out on his back deck, smoke a joint, have a beer, and listen to the crickets before turning in.

But as he stepped toward the front porch, he noticed that the side gate to his fenced backyard was ajar.

That's odd, he thought. He hadn't remembered going through the gate anytime recently.

He took a few steps toward the gate and peered into the darkness behind the house. He wasn't worried about burglars because he had an airtight security system in his home. Nevertheless, it was possible for someone to enter the backyard through the unlocked gate if they wanted.

"Someone there?" he called.

Silence.

He shrugged, pulled the squeaky gate closed, and turned toward the front porch once again. Charles bounded up the wooden steps, removed the keys from his trouser pocket, and stood at the door to unlock it.

The side gate squeaked again.

What the . . . ?

Charles looked beyond the wooden rail that lined

the porch and saw that someone was standing just outside the gate. He couldn't see who it was, but the dim moonlight revealed the intruder to be a woman wearing a floppy hat. She had shoulder-length blonde hair and she wore a trench coat—the kind private detectives from the old film noir flicks favored.

"Who are you?" Charles asked. "What are you doing in my backyard?"

The figure remained still and silent.

Charles took a step toward her, the rail of the porch between them. "I asked you a question, miss."

The woman raised her right arm and there was no mistaking the glint of black metal in her hand.

"Hello, Charles," the woman said. "Remember me?"

She had a low, throaty voice. One that he recognized. Charles's eyes went wide and he gasped.

The blonde hair . . . the floppy hat . . . !

The handgun recoiled twice. The shots were not as loud as one might expect. They were more like two firecrackers that teenagers might set off during the days surrounding the Fourth of July.

Charles felt his chest explode with a fiery pain that he didn't think was possible for a human being to experience. As he stumbled backward, he managed to blurt out a name.

"Sylvia . . . !"

And then he crashed onto the porch.

Whether Charles Nance was too old to rock 'n' roll might have been debatable, but he certainly wasn't too young to die.

Chapter Two

Wouldn't It Be Nice
(performed by The Beach Boys)

"You're a good friend," Ann Berkowitz said as she patted his hand.

"I'm your son, Mom," Spike Berenger retorted, but kindly so. "I appreciate the sentiment anyway."

"You're my son? I thought my son lived in Texas."

Confusion clouded the old woman's eyes. It broke Berenger's heart to see her in this condition. Alzheimer's was a terrible, cruel disease. Berenger had recently noticed that his mother's memory and recollections were becoming more and more obtuse with time.

"I lived in Texas a long time ago, Mom. I live in the city now."

"The city?"

"Manhattan. New York."

Mrs. Berkowitz, who had kept the name of her second husband, looked around her room. "Am I in New York?"

"Yes, you're on Long Island. Isn't this a great apartment? You're very lucky. Most people have to pay a fortune to live in a place like this."

As a matter of fact, Berenger *was* paying a fortune for his mother to live in Franklin Village, an assisted living establishment in Hempstead. Her room was in the special locked wing known as "the Neighborhood," which kept dementia patients from wandering out of the building.

"And your other son Carl lives in California," Berenger added. "Look, here are our pictures." He pointed to the framed family photos of the two brothers, shot a year earlier when Carl had come to visit. The picture sat next to another one taken long ago in Austin, Texas, when the boys were small. "And that's us when we were little. You remember?"

Ann Berkowitz smiled and had tears in her eyes. She nodded, but Berenger knew she really didn't recall those years. Her doctor had told him that Alzheimer's patients often faked answers to questions they weren't sure about. The poor woman didn't remember Daniel Berenger, Spike and Carl's father. She did, however, remember Abraham Berkowitz, the man who had been Spike's stepfather for a number of years until his untimely death. Particularly painful were the times when Berenger's mother didn't remember that he was her son, like today. She knew he was an important friend, someone who cared about her, and a person who came to visit often . . . but somehow the blood-relation concept didn't always gel.

"Wouldn't it be nice if we had a picnic?" she said, incongruously.

"Oh, that reminds me . . . look, Ma, I brought you a present." He pulled a CD out of his shoulder bag. "The Beach Boys. You like them."

She took the CD and examined the cover. "They look like nice young men."

"They are. They sing good, too. Here, let me put it on the player." Berenger opened the jewel case and placed the disk in the portable CD player he had bought her. She no longer knew how to operate it, so Berenger made it a point to play some music for her whenever he visited.

As the music began, Ann Berkowitz's eyes lit up. It was said that an Alzheimer's patient's appreciation for music was one of the last things to go. The woman swayed in her chair as The Beach Boys sang "California Girls."

"I remember this song!"

"I figured you might. The Beatles and The Beach Boys—they were always your favorites."

The ring tone on Berenger's cell phone blasted out the opening riff from King Crimson's "21st Century Schizoid Man." He quickly pulled it from his belt and answered it.

"Berenger."

"Spike, don't forget we have that IRS audit this afternoon." It was Rudy Bishop, the co-owner, with Berenger, of Rockin' Security, Inc.

"Oh, geez, Rudy, I forgot. Okay, I'll be there in an hour or so."

"He'll be here in a couple of hours, so you've got some time."

"All right, I'm on my way."

"Another thing. Zach Garriott called."

"Really? Mr. Shredder?"

"Yep. He wanted to speak to you. I told him you'd call him back when you got into the office."

"Any idea what he wanted?"

"Nope. He called from Chicago, though."

"Okay, Rudy." Berenger hung up and addressed his

mom, who was in bliss with the music. "Mom? I gotta go now. I'll be back next week, okay?"

"Okay, dear."

"You enjoy the music, okay?"

"Okay, dear."

He stood, leaned down to kiss her on the cheek, and then left the room. It was best to make good-byes short and sweet.

Berenger signed out on the visitor's sheet and then went outside to the parking lot, where he'd left his 2005 Nissan Altima SL. The car had held up nicely and he figured it was nearly time to trade it in and get something newer. Since he lived in Manhattan, he rarely used the car except to make trips out to Long Island or for business.

Zach Garriott, Berenger mused. What a coincidence.

The CD he currently had in his car was a European sampler mix of music related to the same genre from which Garriott had emerged. Berenger's Italian friend, Sandro Ponti, sent the disk to him from Rome. Ponti was once part of the same Chicago underground music scene, something Berenger knew as "Chicagoprog." Zach Garriott had played lead guitar with a Chicago-based prog band called Red Skyez in the late seventies. Sandro Ponti had played bass with a Chicago-based prog band called Rattlesnake in the early seventies. When Rattlesnake broke up, Ponti moved back to Italy, but the rest of the band members formed a new group. For a while it was called South Side, but since most of the members lived in the city's opposite side, they permanently changed the name to North Side. Zach Garriott was their guitarist for a few years before breaking

11

out on his own and becoming the only well-known, supersuccessful musician to come out of the Chicagoprog scene. As for Ponti, he still gigged with various bands in Italy.

Berenger started the car and headed toward Manhattan. The music on the sampler consisted of several new Italian progressive rock acts. Berenger had always been a prog rock fan, and he was happy that the genre had seen a resurgence in popularity during the nineties that had continued into the new millennium. He and Ponti had met in Italy several years after the Rattlesnake era and had got along well. Every now and then, Ponti sent him a sampler of stuff he was listening to and Berenger reciprocated. It was what serious music fans did for each other.

The sampler contained new music by some classic seventies Italian prog bands like PFM and Banco Del Mutuo Soccorso, but there were several new acts as well. One track featured a female singer whose works reminded Berenger of Kate Bush. She had a strong voice and the song was intricate, complex, and hauntingly beautiful. So far it was the best cut on the CD and Berenger played it a couple of times. The singer didn't sound Italian—Berenger wondered if she was English or American. He grabbed the jewel case and noted that the track listing identified her as "Julia Faerie." He'd never heard of her. When next he communicated with Ponti, he'd have to ask for more of her stuff.

Typically, though, as he merged onto I-495 toward the city, he quickly forgot about it.

The Rockin' Security office was located in a brownstone on East Sixty-eighth Street between Third and

Second avenues. Rockin' Security was the number-one security business in the world of rock music. With branches in L.A. and London, the firm had a database of security personnel that could be called in for a single gig or a major tour at a moment's notice. Bodyguard service was a specialty. Berenger also had a private investigator license, which was a Rockin' Security service that wasn't advertised openly. The PI cases were always the most interesting jobs but they didn't come around as often as he'd like. All in all, the partnership of Rudy Bishop and Spike Berenger worked like a dream. As long as Bishop handled the money and the dealings with Uncle Sam and let Berenger handle operations, it was a fabulous gig. Of course, a lifetime ago he had dreamed of being a rock star himself. For a while in the late seventies, his prog band, The Fixers, did pretty well for themselves. But the overblown style of progressive rock went out of fashion when punk and new wave hit the scene, and by 1980 The Fixers couldn't keep up. Berenger became a music manager for most of the eighties and then formed Rockin' Security in the nineties with Bishop.

Berenger entered the building's ground floor, which held Bishop's office, the conference room, and other administrative areas. Melanie Starkey, the office assistant, looked up and smiled. She was a twenty-nine-year-old feisty redheaded babe who spoke with a thick New Jersey accent. Even though she preferred to be called Mel, most of the time everyone called her "Ringo" because of that darned last name. Starkey equals Starr equals Ringo. Who wouldn't automatically think of The Beatles' drummer?

"Hi, Ringo," Berenger said.

"Hey, Spike. How's your mom?"

" 'Bout the same."

She made a *tsk-tsk* sound and looked at him with sympathy. "It's hard, I know."

"Yeah."

He started to climb the stairs when Melanie stopped him. "Hey!"

"What?"

"Have you lost weight?"

Berenger blinked. "I don't think so. Why?"

"You look like you have."

"Uh, well, thanks, I think."

"I guess all that workin' out you do upstairs is payin' off."

Berenger was surprised by her comment because his bulky physique hadn't changed in years. No matter how hard he worked at it, he never seemed to get rid of that extra twenty-five pounds that had attached themselves to him in his forties and never let go.

"Thanks, Mel. You wanna go out on a date?"

She snorted and said, "I wasn't *fishin'*, Spike. You're a good-lookin' guy but you're just not my type. Besides, it's not cool to date the boss. Sorry!"

"Okay, you're fired. Now will you go out with me?"

"You wish."

He laughed, but as he ascended, he studied his likeness in the reflective paneling that lined the circular staircase. There was no doubt about it—he was simply a big ol' hairy bear of a man. The long salt-and-pepper hair he had worn in a ponytail since coming out of the army reached to the middle of his back. His facial hair was slightly darker but the gray and white patches complemented his blue eyes.

14

Berenger went all the way to the operations room on the third floor, and that's where he found most of his team.

Danny Lewis was a smart-aleck kid from Harlem who was perhaps the brainiest hacker Berenger had ever known. He was twenty, half Caucasian, half African American, and had no loyalties to either race. He called himself a "mix," hence the nickname "Remix." Lewis was the firm's tech guru, hacker, systems analyst, programmer, and streetwise geek. And damned good at what he did. He was also the practical joker of the group and could be counted on for the more eyebrow-raising shenanigans.

Tommy Briggs was Berenger's contemporary. At age fifty, Briggs used to be a field agent for the FBI and had held the job for nearly twenty years until he decided to give it up one day and work for Rockin' Security. Briggs maintained a good relationship with the bureau and had pals on the inside. He knew people in just about any federal government organization one could name. If a piece of information could be obtained from an archival or electronic source, Briggs usually found a way to access it though the good-old-boy network.

And then there was the inimitable Suzanne, his number two. Originally from California, Suzanne Prescott was thirty-nine, had short dark hair and deep brown eyes, and possessed the most interesting history of the entire bunch. In the eighties she was a Goth devotee, sporting the classic black clothes, dark makeup, and pale white skin. After doing a bit of maturing she traveled the Far East for a few years and came back a student of Eastern philosophy, martial arts, and Transcendental Meditation. After the love of her life overdosed in the midnineties, Berenger and Prescott had a brief love affair, *brief* being the operative word. But they remained friends and several months later Berenger asked her to work for him.

"Fearless leader!" Remix cried when Berenger entered the room.

"Hey, guys. 'Sup?"

His team members sat at computer workstations, pretending to look busy.

"I'm buried by all this work you left me," Remix said. "I can't even see the sunlight, man. I'm starving and dehydrated and I've gotta take a leak and—"

"Okay, okay, enough." He addressed Briggs. "Anything happen while I was out?"

"Nope."

"Nope," Prescott echoed.

"That's good, I guess. I heard Zach Garriott called."

"The Shredder? Really?" Remix asked.

"Yeah, really. I guess I need to go call him back."

"I don't think he has any openings in his band, Spike. So get that right out of your system. And besides, you ain't half as good as he is."

"Thanks, Remix. Oh, I'm gonna need you in a while. We've got this IRS auditor coming to see Rudy and me. You think you could do one of your specials on him and keep him occupied for a while? Make him, uhm, comfortable while he *waits*?"

Remix's eyes brightened. "The IRS? Holy snowballs, Batman! I've always wanted to take a crack at one of them!"

"Just don't kill him. That's against the law."

"But you don't particularly want to go through with the audit, is that the idea?"

"You got it."

"Leave it to me, bossaroo."

Prescott rolled her eyes as if to say, "Uh oh. We're in trouble."

"Say, Spike, Tommy and I want you to settle an argument for us," Remix said.

"What's that?"

"It's not important, Spike," Briggs grumbled.

"What?"

Remix cleared his throat. "Pink Floyd's album. Is it THE *Dark Side of the Moon*, or just *Dark Side of the Moon*?"

Berenger winced. "Remix . . ."

"No, man, I wanna know! Tommy here bet me a dollar that the album title is *The*-less. I say it's supposed to have a *The* on it."

Berenger looked at Briggs. "Is this a real discussion you guys have been having? On company time?"

"Hey," Briggs answered, "all I said was that the *The* was dropped from the title when the album was released on CD. Back in seventy-three, when the vinyl record came out, it did have a *The* on it. But now it doesn't. Look at the spine of the CD. There's no *The*. Pink Floyd and everybody else constantly refer to the album as just *Dark Side of the Moon*. Having to say THE *Dark Side of the Moon* is . . . well, awkward. Don't you think?"

Berenger stared at his two teammates. "I haven't really thought about it with such intensity, guys. But to answer your question, Tommy's right. The original album had a *The*, but I always called it *Dark Side of the Moon* without the *The*. It sounds better that way."

Remix grunted in disgust.

"You owe me a dollar, Remix," Briggs commented.

Berenger left the room and made his way down to the second floor, which belonged to him and Prescott. Besides their separate offices, the level contained a recording studio and gym exclusively used by Berenger.

He went into his office, sat at his desk, and dialed Bishop.

"Bishop."

"Rudy, I'm here."

"Good. The auditor'll be here any minute. You had me sweating bullets."

"Rudy, I told you not to worry. Besides, Remix is gonna take care of him for us while I call Zach Garriott back."

"Remix? Oh, no . . ."

Berenger chuckled and hung up. He went downstairs just as Melanie buzzed in a thin man in his thirties who wore a conservative suit that Berenger thought shouted I AM AN IRS AGENT!

"Ringo, call Remix and have him come down and make our guest comfortable. Rudy and I will be with him in a minute."

Melanie's eyes bulged as she gulped, but she made the call.

The man approached the desk and spoke with a comically nasal voice. "Hello, I'm Milton Morgan with the Internal Revenue Service and I have an appointment with Rudy Bishop."

"Just a moment, sir," Melanie said with efficiency as she punched buttons on her desk phone. She was doing her best not to laugh. "Remix? Could you come down here? There's a Milton Morgan from the IRS here."

Berenger ducked into another office and waited. After a moment, Remix came bounding down the stairs. Morgan's eyes widened when he saw the dark-skinned young man with out-of-control dreadlocks and piercings decorating his face.

"Hi, there. I'm Danny Lewis, Mr. Bishop's executive secretary."

Melanie snorted again, because Remix was speaking with a phony British accent, as if he were a sophisticated black Londoner from the City.

"Mr. Bishop and Mr. Berenger will be right with you. I'm going to show you into our conference room where you can wait for a minute or two. Can I get you something to drink? Ringo here makes superb coffee."

Morgan nodded. "Coffee would be nice, thanks. Cream and sugar, please."

Remix led the man into the adjacent conference room. "Please have a seat and I'll return in a moment." He shut the door and ran into the kitchen. He poured a cup of coffee and then removed a piece of paper from his pocket. It had been folded into a receptacle for a white powder he had hastily procured from his office. He mixed in two spoonfuls of the powder, and then put the box away. Remix then added the cream and sugar.

"Here you are, sir," Remix purred as he brought the spiked coffee into the conference room.

"Oh, thanks very much."

"You're welcome. Mr. Bishop and Mr. Berenger will be with you shortly."

Remix turned, left the room, and locked the door behind him. As he started up the stairs, Berenger caught his eye. Remix gave him a thumbs-up and winked.

Berenger noted the time on his wristwatch and then walked into Bishop's office.

"Where is he?" Bishop asked. A man in his late forties, Rudy Bishop was a nervous type who couldn't keep still. At the moment he was compulsively tapping the end of a ballpoint pen on the edge of his desk.

"In the conference room. We have time to make that call."

Bishop half smiled and slid his phone across the desk as Berenger sat in the chair on the opposite side. Bishop gave him a piece of paper with the phone number written on it and Berenger dialed.

"Hello?"

"Is this Zach Garriott?" He shot Bishop a look and indicated the tapping ballpoint pen. Bishop immediately shoved the pen into his shirt pocket and attempted to be motionless.

"Yes?"

"It's Spike Berenger."

"Spike! How are you, man?"

"Okay! Nice to hear your voice. It's been a while."

"Yeah, it has. What's it been, three or four years since I saw you in New York?"

"I think so. I heard you called?"

The timbre of Garriott's voice changed from exuberance to solemnity. "Yeah, I did. You heard about Charles Nance?"

Berenger frowned. "No. What about him?"

"He was murdered, man. Shot and killed a few nights ago outside his house!"

"Oh my God!"

Berenger had met Charles Nance a few times. He

knew the man's brother, Joe, slightly better. Their band, Windy City Engine, was one of Berenger's favorite underground prog outfits out of Chicago.

"It's the third one in two months, man, and we're getting spooked!" Garriott said.

"Wait. What do you mean, it's the 'third one'?"

"You haven't heard? About the Kriges? Or Dave Monaco and Hank Palmer?"

"No."

"Where you been, Spike? Someone's killing off Chicagoprog musicians right and left. It's like open season on us, man. You gotta come help us out. I mean it, man! Get out here as soon as you can!"

"Wait, wait, slow down, Zach. Back up. I'm in New York. We don't see news from Chicago unless it's pretty big stuff."

"Yeah, well that figures. If Sting or Elvis Costello got bumped off, it'd be international news. But kill some unknown, underground has-been musicians that hardly anyone listens to anymore, and it just ain't news."

"Zach, will you tell me what's happened? Take a deep breath and start at the beginning!"

Berenger heard Garriott breathe slowly and with force, and then the man said, "Okay. About six weeks ago, Lew and Sarah Krige were shot outside their house in Evanston. Did you know them?"

"No, I never met them. But I know who they are. They were members of Red Skyez. Lew Krige took over from Stuart Clayton when he left the band in the early seventies, right?"

"Right. Well, anyway, they were shot and killed. Then, about three weeks later, Dave Monaco and Hank

21

Palmer were on their way out of the Double Door and were shot. They had just played a gig there and were headed for their cars. Blam, blam! Both of 'em dead."

"Jesus!"

Dave Monaco and Hank Palmer were also former members of Red Skyez. Monaco, a bass player, and Palmer, a drummer, had gone on to other bands and session lineups in the midseventies and beyond.

"And now Charles is dead. We're all freakin' out, man."

"I'll bet. What do the police say?"

"They don't say nothin'! They're runnin' around in circles. Hell, they haven't even admitted that all three murders are connected. They need some help, man, and that's why I called *you*. You're the best in the business, Spike. We need you."

"Do the police have any suspects? Anything at all?"

"Only that a witness reported seeing a woman with blonde hair and a big hat leaving one of the scenes. And if it's who I think it is, Spike . . . well, you're not gonna believe this, but she's a goddamned *ghost*!"

"What do you mean, Zach?"

"I mean what I said! The killer has been dead for thirty-five years!"

Chapter Three

Taxman
(performed by The Beatles)

Berenger and Bishop told Garriott they'd phone him back. They sat in their chairs for at least a minute before anyone moved.

"So, is he doing too many drugs or something?" Bishop asked.

"I have no idea. Zach always struck me as pretty smart. He's made a decent career for himself."

"So did Hendrix. So did Janis Joplin. So did—"

"Yeah, yeah, I know." Berenger picked up the phone and called the operations room. "Suzanne? Hey, would you or Tommy go on the Internet and find all the stories you can about recent shootings of musicians in Chicago?" He gave her the victims' names.

Ten minutes later, Remix brought down a small stack of printouts. As Berenger suspected, the news items were not front-page news. Charles Nance received a page-two story, but the other two incidents were considerably smaller. Lew and Sarah Krige were shot in front of their home in Evanston, just as Garriott had told them. Police suspected robbery or a drug transaction gone bad to be the motive, although nothing from the house seemed to be missing. A witness described a woman with shoulder-length blonde hair and a broad, "floppy" hat leaving the scene. Marijuana was found in the house, adding weight to the drug scenario. The Kriges were in their late fifties and were once members of the band Red Skyez before striking out on their own with the band simply called Krige. Friends and colleagues said the couple had kicked around Chicago for nearly three decades and never found great success, although they made a living and seemed relatively happy.

Dave Monaco and Hank Palmer were also former members of Red Skyez. When that band split up, Palmer followed the Kriges and played drums for their group. Monaco joined the band South Side for a while but struck out on his own in 1978 to play with a variety of musicians and lineups in Los Angeles. He moved back to Chicago in the late nineties and played one-off gigs with various former members of the Chicagoprog scene. On the night of the shooting, Monaco and Palmer had done a show at the Double Door club with musicians not related to Chicagoprog. The duo was shot at point-blank range in the street as they left the club. Once again, a blonde woman in a large hat was seen by a couple of witnesses.

No one saw what happened to Charles Nance. He was shot outside his home in Chicago and his body was discovered the next morning by the newspaper delivery boy. Again, police chalked it up to a possible robbery attempt. There was no mention of the previous murders.

"I don't get it," Bishop said. "Isn't it obvious that these shootings are related?"

"Maybe the police are keeping the evidence close to the vest. They're not going to release some information if it can help catch the killer . . . or killers."

"So what do you think?"

Berenger shrugged. "It's intriguing. I have to admit that I'm interested more because I'm a fan of the music."

"How well do you know all these musicians?"

"Not well. I know Zach the best. I've met all the guys in Windy City Engine. Joe Nance and I are fairly friendly. I knew some of the crew in Red Skyez."

"What about Stuart Clayton?"

Berenger made a face. "Met him once. A long time ago. I think it must've been when his first solo album came out. Nineteen seventy-nine? He's a strange duck."

"I'll say. Didn't he spend time in a mental hospital or something?"

"I don't know about that. He had a stroke or a heart attack, I forget which. That was in the early seventies. Withdrew from everyone, became a recluse. No one thought he would continue in music, but then he put out that solo album. And he put out another one, what, ten years or so later? I guess I'll have to talk to him, too."

"Is he, like, coherent?"

"I have no idea."

After a pause, Bishop shrugged and said, "It's up to you, Spike. You don't have to ask me. If you want the case, we can do it."

"I think I do. We don't have anything pressing right now, do we?"

Bishop shook his head. "Just Rod Stewart's alleged blackmail attempt, which I think is bogus, and that business with Iggy Pop's dogs. Oh, and Willie Nelson says that some very expensive herb was stolen from his ranch in Texas, but I don't think we should get involved in that."

"I'll bet it's not stolen. He probably just forgot where

he stashed it. What happened with Debbie Harry and her landlord?"

"Lawsuit was settled."

"That's good. I didn't particularly relish the thought of her hiring me to go through the guy's garbage just to find a stinking receipt."

"We also have a couple of tours coming up. Need security teams and all that. But you can organize those in your sleep."

"Who's touring?"

"Crosby, Stills, Nash, and Young are doing another protest show."

"What are they mad about now?"

"Beats me. That's their shtick."

"They beat you with a shtick?"

"Oh, shut up."

"Sorry."

"And Penn and Teller want to tour the Middle East."

"Penn and Teller? Since when are they a rock 'n' roll act? One of 'em can't even talk, much less sing."

Bishop threw his hands in the air. "Hey, they called us and we took the job, all right?"

"Fine. So you can spare Suzanne and me for a few days?"

"I guess so. But what's all this about a ghost being the shooter?"

"I don't know. I'm gonna call him back." He picked up the phone and dialed the third floor again. "Tommy? Get ready for a team meeting in a half hour. Tell everyone to pull up all the background info on these Chicago killings, the victims, and the history of the Chicagoprog bands. I'll be up in a bit."

Berenger hung up and redialed Garriott with the speakerphone on. "Zach?"

"Yeah?"

"Spike again. Rudy's here, too."

"Hi."

"Listen, I think Suzanne and I will come out to Chicago tomorrow and check this out. Are you the one hiring us?"

"Yeah. The other guys can't really afford it. I'll foot the bill."

"Fine. I'll have Rudy fax you a contract and we'll get started. I'd like you to let the other members of Windy City Engine know I'm coming and that I want to talk to them. North Side is still around, aren't they?"

"Yep. Bud Callahan and his crew are still gigging."

"Okay, I'll want to talk to them, too. But I gotta warn you, Zach. If the police aren't cooperative with me, there may not be a lot I can do. I can sniff around and do what I do best as an investigator, but without having some hard facts about the three killings at my fingertips I don't know how successful I'll be."

"I understand."

"Is there something you hope to accomplish other than finding out who killed Charles and the others?"

"Yeah. I want to make sure the rest of us—including yours truly—aren't targets!"

"Zach, why do you say this is the work of a dead person? Do you have information that you're not telling us?"

"I can fill you in on that when you get here, Spike. Maybe we're just too freaked out. I know, it doesn't make sense, but the other guys believe it, too. I think it's best if Joe tells you about it."

"Okay. Keep calm and keep your eyes open. I'll call you as soon as we hit town."

"Thanks, Spike."

Berenger hung up and sighed. It was then that he and Bishop noticed the sound of pounding coming from down the hall.

"Oh, shit, the IRS guy!"

Berenger jumped up and ran to the conference room.

"Let me out of here! Can anyone hear me?" Morgan yelled from behind the door.

Berenger fumbled with his keys and finally got the door unlocked. Morgan burst out, his face a mask of sheer terror. "Where's the washroom?" he demanded. Berenger pointed the way and the man ran as if his trousers were on fire.

Melanie exchanged looks with Berenger and she stifled a laugh. After a few minutes, they heard the toilet flush and the washroom door opened. The man's face was pale and damp.

"Are you all right?" Berenger asked him.

Morgan shook his head. "I don't know. I guess." He rubbed his stomach. "Tummyache."

"Sorry about that. I have no idea how that door got locked." Berenger held out his hand. "I'm Spike Berenger."

Morgan shook it. "Milton Morgan."

"Do you feel like having the meeting?"

"Sure, I'm here. We might as well. I think I'm all right."

"Okay. Rudy and I will join you in the conference room. Can I get you anything?"

"No, thanks."

"More coffee?"

"Uhm, *no* thanks."

Morgan returned to the conference room. A minute later, Berenger and Bishop entered carrying stacks of manila folders, accordion files, and ledgers. Bishop introduced himself and then indicated the piles of paper. "I think this is everything. Were you planning to go through all of this stuff now?"

The IRS agent took one look at the massive amount of paper and his pallor went from white to green. As soon as Berenger and Bishop sat at the table, the man's bowels rumbled loudly. His eyes grew wide and he stood. "Uhm, excuse me again. Sorry!" He ran back down the hall and slammed the washroom door closed behind him.

Bishop looked at Spike, shook his head, and whispered, "What was it? Laxative?"

Berenger neither nodded nor shook his head.

"You guys are terrible!"

"Don't look at me!"

Five minutes later, the taxman returned, looking even paler than before.

"Gentlemen, I think I do need to cancel our meeting today. We'll have to postpone it. Is that all right?"

"Oh, that's too bad," Bishop said. "I'm sorry you don't feel well."

"I don't know what's come over me. Must have been what I had for lunch."

"I understand." Bishop indicated the piles of paperwork. "And I was really looking forward to going through all this stuff. But if you need to postpone—"

"I think that'd be best. I'll just call—" The man

clutched his belly again and ran back to the wash-room.

Berenger stood and Bishop whispered, "Tell Remix to *never* do that again or he'll be fired, and then give him a high five for me, will you?"

Chapter Four

We Are Family
(performed by Sister Sledge)

The team was already assembled in the operations room when Berenger walked in. Remix had put on the latest CD by System of a Down at a very high volume.

"Remix, turn that down or put on something else," Berenger ordered.

"Hey, I thought you liked this prog shit!"

"I don't really consider that prog."

"Sure it is! It's got complex time signatures, weird lyrics, and virtuoso musicianship. All Music Dot Com calls it prog, and they should know!"

Prescott piped in. "But it's loud, raucous, and almost heavy metal."

"What do you call Dream Theater, then?"

"That's progressive metal," she answered.

"What's the diff, babe? These guys are progressive metal, too."

Berenger sat and said, "Remix, you may be right and we may be wrong, but it's still too loud for a team meeting."

"Okay, boss." Remix reached over to the tuner and turned down the volume by a hair.

"A little more, Remix."

"Aw, hell." He shut off the CD. He quickly opened

the player, removed the disk, and popped in a different one. A few seconds later, the new age strains of Enya floated through the room.

"Now I'm gonna puke," Briggs noted.

"Hey, I like Enya," Prescott said. "Good choice, Remix."

"Whatever," Berenger said. "Let's get started."

Bishop rushed in and sat. "Am I late?"

Briggs answered, "For once, you're right on the money, Rudy."

Berenger nodded at Remix. "Okay. What've you got?"

Remix picked up his notes and cleared his throat. "Hear ye, hear ye! Herewith commences the history of the forgotten, neglected, obscure, and underground school of rock music known as Chicagoprog! Lend me your ears! Gather around and—"

"Remix!"

"Sorry, boss. I was just bein' pretentious, like the music." He cleared his throat again. "In the year of our Lord, nineteen sixty-seven, a group of young musicians just out of high school gathered in Chicago, Illinois, and formed a band. They were Stuart Clayton on keyboards and vocals, Joe Nance on guitar and vocals, his younger brother Charles Nance on drums, Harrison Brill on second guitar, and Manny Rodriguez on bass. The band was called The Loop, named after the downtown area in Chicago where all the big buildings are. They kicked around the city for a couple of years, playing clubs and developing a small following. Their music is described as Chicago blues meets the early Moody Blues. It wasn't really what we call progressive rock today. Mind you, Chicago was never a center for prog rock. It's probably why the band never caught on big in this incarnation or the future ones after the 'big split.' "

"I thought Jim Axelrod and Dave Monaco were members of The Loop," Briggs ventured.

"Those guys showed up in nineteen sixty-nine," Remix explained. "Axelrod was a dynamite guitarist and Monaco was an awesome bass player. But as I understand it, these positions were fluid. Brill and Rodriguez still played some shows with the band, and sometimes Axelrod and Monaco played. So, in essence, The Loop had seven members during their four-year stint."

"They never recorded?" Prescott asked.

"Not that we know of. At least nothing released commercially. There are some concert bootlegs floating around and maybe some studio demos."

"I'd like to hear what they sounded like," she commented. "I like Chicago blues. That town is famous for the blues."

"It was pretty much a hybrid of styles," Berenger added. "Not the kind of Chicago blues you're thinking of. Go on, Remix."

"Anyway, due to the age-old excuse 'creative differences,' The Loop split into two separate bands in nineteen seventy. Apparently Stuart Clayton, Jim Axelrod, and Dave Monaco wanted to get out of Chicago and move to Los Angeles, where all the exciting stuff was happening. I also understand that Stuart Clayton and Joe Nance were constantly at each other's throats as to who was the official leader of the band. Clayton was an accomplished songwriter and front man, even though he played keys. And Nance was also a damned fine songwriter and front man. So, there was a rift and a 'big split.' "

"Red Skyez and Windy City Engine," Briggs said.

"Right. Clayton, Axelrod, and Monaco moved to L.A. with a new drummer named Hank Palmer. They formed Red Skyez—spelled S, K, Y, E, Z—how pretentious can you get?—and started doing the kind of stuff we associate with prog rock today. Sort of Moody Blues meets Pink Floyd meets, well, Chicago blues. They recorded two albums between nineteen seventy-one and seventy-three. The first was critically acclaimed but didn't sell too well. The second one was barely noticed, but it kept Red Skyez on the boards."

"And what happened in nineteen seventy-three?" Berenger prompted.

"Stuart Clayton had a heart attack. Or a stroke. We're not too sure. Maybe both. There wasn't a lot of press about it. Red Skyez was not a big name and they had only two records. But *something* happened to Clayton and he dropped out of sight. There was some speculation that he was doing too many drugs, just like all of them nutty rock stars did in those days. But Clayton was especially interested in the psychedelic stuff. LSD, peyote, psilocybin mushrooms, and this weird herb called salvia divinorum."

"What's that?" Bishop asked.

Prescott answered that one. "Salvia divinorum is an herb that, when smoked, produces very intense out-of-body experiences and hallucinations. The effects last only a minute or two but they're heavy-duty. Supposedly it's not dangerous unless you're stupid enough to be driving a car while you do it. It renders you totally helpless and uncoordinated for those two minutes. There are people who use it for meditation purposes. It's not a party drug. It can cause one to be very introspective. It's a 'see God' type of drug. And believe it or not, it's legal in most states."

"Really?" Bishop asked.

"Yeah, you buy it in head shops or online," she replied.

"You sound like you've tried it," Briggs commented.

"I have. I was in India at the time. Early nineties. I was experimenting with all kinds of stuff—Eastern religions, Transcendental Meditation, and, yes, mind-altering drugs. Didn't last long. I didn't like salvia. It wasn't a pleasant experience for me. In fact, it scared the shit out of me. I thought my body had split into a thousand pieces and they were running around the floor with minds of their own. The second time I tried it, I became the chair I was sitting in. Not my idea of fun."

"The point, I think," Berenger noted, "is that Stuart Clayton screwed up his mind and body in a major way. Combining all those different kinds of hallucinogens must have had a detrimental effect on him, even though taken individually those things aren't all that dangerous. He may have had a mental illness to begin with, too. If that were the case—say he had a tendency toward schizophrenia, like Syd Barrett—the drugs could have really messed him up."

"Syd Barrett was that guy in the original Pink Floyd, right?" Bishop asked.

"Yeah. He was one of the founders of the band. He was an early LSD casualty. Dropped out of Pink Floyd after their first album and was in and out of mental hospitals until he died a few years ago. Sad. Brilliant musician. The band's *Wish You Were Here* album was a tribute to him."

"He sort of took his own trip to the dark side of the moon, didn't he?" Briggs muttered.

"Yeah. You have more on Clayton, Remix?"

"Only that no one heard from him much during the rest of the seventies. Then, an independently produced solo album came out in nineteen seventy-nine. The record was called *Trrrrans*. That's four Rs in *Trrrrans*. Sheesh. It wasn't well received and it tanked. The reviews I found said it was very strange. What a surprise! After that, Clayton went to Europe. We don't know where he went. His name didn't pop up in the music press until nineteen ninety-two, when suddenly he was back in Chicago and he put out another solo album. This one was even more obscure and hard to find than the first one. But oddly enough, he has fans. There's a Stuart Clayton fan website that has about twenty people on its message boards."

"What's he done since nineteen ninety-two?"

"Nothing that we know of. Lives in Chicago like a hermit. I don't know how he makes a living, but I know his family had money. Of all these Chicagoprog guys, Clayton's got the most mystique."

"Okay. Go on, Remix."

"Anyway, Red Skyez tried to continue without Clayton. They brought in Lew Krige, a talented songwriter from Chicago who was also in L.A. He played keyboards and was a vocalist, like Clayton. Then, in nineteen seventy-five, Dave Monaco left the band. Lew Krige's wife Sarah was a decent bass player, so she was brought in to replace him. So you had a husband-and-wife team kind of fronting the band with Axelrod and

Palmer still in the group. This lineup recorded one album. Then, in nineteen seventy-six, Jim Axelrod quit the band. And his replacement was none other than . . ."

Remix dramatically made a drum roll with his hands on the tabletop.

". . . Zach Garriott! The wunderkind guitarist from Chicago who was desperately trying to find a foothold in Los Angeles."

"The guy is great," Briggs said.

"I'll say. Anyway, this final lineup of Red Skyez recorded one album, did a tour, and then called it quits in nineteen seventy-eight. Just about everyone moved back to Chicago over the next few years."

Berenger said, "But the Kriges formed their own band."

"Right. It was called—you guessed it—Krige! They kept Hank Palmer on drums and brought in another Chicago guitarist named Paul Trinidad, who had been in a little band in Chicago called South Side. Krige existed and gigged fairly regularly until the midnineties or so."

"Okay, whoa," Berenger said. "Let's back up before you get into that branch of the family tree. Let's hear about Windy City Engine—the other half of The Loop that remained in Chicago when the rest of them moved to L.A."

Remix shuffled pages and continued. "Okay, when The Loop broke up in nineteen seventy, the other half of the band—namely Joe Nance, Charles Nance, Harrison Brill, and Manny Rodriguez—formed Windy City Engine. They stayed in Chicago throughout their long career and were still together until the untimely death of Charles a few days ago. Whether or not they'll stay together remains a question. Over the four decades they've been together, they released a total of ten records and toured a lot. But mostly they stayed close to home and entertained a small but loyal following in Chicago. Joe Nance made a couple of solo albums in the eighties. Brill and Rodriguez did an album together in the eighties as well. Windy City Engine's music could be called folk prog with some blues and country mixed in. Personally, I think it's crap but I know there are *some people here* who like it."

"I always liked Windy City Engine," Berenger admitted. "It's not crap at all. They deserved more success than they got."

Remix turned a page and said, "Now, another branch of the Chicagoprog sound developed in nineteen seventy-two. The band was called Rattlesnake. It consisted of a guy named Bud Callahan on keyboards and vocals, Rick Tittle on drums, and an Italian fellow named Sandro Ponti on bass. You know him, right, Spike?"

"Yeah, he's a good friend. I didn't know him then, though. We met in Italy much later. But keep going."

"Rattlesnake made one album and split up in nineteen seventy-five. Ponti left Chicago and went back to Italy. The other two guys formed a band called South Side. Rounding out the band with Callahan and Tittle were none other than Dave Monaco from Red Skyez on bass, and the aforementioned Paul Trinidad on guitar. Bud Callahan's wife Sharon sometimes contributed vocals. *They* made one album. Then, in nineteen seventy-eight, there was some shuffling. Monaco and Trinidad left, so Sharon picked up the bass—just as Sarah Krige did for Red Skyez—and they hired none other than Zach Garriott on guitar. How they managed to woo him away from Red Skyez is a mystery, because Red Skyez was doing much better out in L.A. Maybe Garriott just wanted to go back home to Chicago, I don't know. Anyway, they changed the name of the band to *North* Side. And *they* made one album."

"This is getting complicated," Prescott said.

"Tell me about it. It's about as bad as that Canterbury thing they have over in England," Briggs said. "You know—Soft Machine, Caravan, Hatfield and the North, and all those guys."

"Don't start knocking them or I'll punch you," Berenger said. "Please continue, Remix."

Remix took a sip of water out of a bottle and read on. "Zach Garriott didn't stay long. He left in nineteen eighty, and he was replaced by a guy named Greg Cross. And believe it or not, North Side still exists today with that lineup—Tittle, Cross, and Bud and Sharon Callahan."

"So Zach Garriott's the only one who really became famous?" Bishop asked.

"Yep. Formed his own band after leaving North Side and never looked back. He occasionally did sessions or played a gig or two with former Chicagoprog members. But mostly he went his own way and developed a sound that couldn't be called prog at all."

"Thanks, Remix," Berenger said. "I think that puts it all in perspective."

"I'm going to need a flowchart to keep all this straight," Prescott commented.

"Here you go," Briggs said. He had been taking

notes during the briefing. He slid a piece of paper across the table. On it he had drawn a family tree that illustrated the various bands, the members, and time-lines.

"Wow, Tommy, this is great!" Prescott marveled.

"I stole the idea from Pete Frame. He's a guy that did a whole book of rock 'n' roll family trees."

"Okay, folks, the big question is who would want to kill off members of these bands?" Berenger asked.

"Is that what's really going on, or are these shootings coincidences?" Briggs asked.

"You tell me, Tommy. We have the Kriges shot and killed in Evanston, which is just a northern suburb of Chicago. Then nineteen days later, Dave Monaco and Hank Palmer are shot coming out of a music club on the North Side of Chicago. Then, nearly a month after that, Charles Nance gets it. According to the newspaper reports, his home isn't very far from the club where Monaco and Palmer bought it. So they're all within a reasonably close distance. I imagine the Evanston case is under a different police jurisdiction since it's technically not Chicago. But the situation is pretty clear to me—within a couple of months, seven members of this rock family tree that Tommy just drew have been killed. Why?"

"Somebody obviously has a grudge," Remix offered.

"But these people weren't big successes. They probably didn't have a lot of money. And is it going to stop with Charles Nance? Or are the rest of them on a checklist?"

"I guess that's what you're going to find out, huh, Spike?" Briggs asked.

He nodded. "Suzanne and I are leaving tomorrow for Chicago."

The room was dark and smelled as if fresh clean sheets, perfume, and air freshener were fighting a losing battle to disguise mold and mildew. Only a single shaded lamp cast a bit of light onto the desk where the killer sat. Someone once said that the place was more like a morgue than a home. That had been amusing.

A piece of paper lay on the desk. A list of names, in no particular order, was scribbled on the paper. Five of the names had lines drawn through them—Lew Krige, Sarah Krige, Dave Monaco, Hank Palmer, and Charles Nance. There were six names left—Stuart Clayton, Joe Nance, Harrison Brill, Manny Rodriguez, Jim Axelrod, and Zach Garriott.

The killer picked up the latest issue of the *Chicago Reader* from the floor and turned to the back, where all the music club listings were printed. Sure enough, the band North Side was playing the very next night.

It was time to cross off another name.

Chapter Five

King of Pain
(performed by The Police)

Berenger was late for his appointment with Linda, his ex-wife, and that wasn't good. One of the problems with their three-and-a-half-year marriage was that he was never on time for things for a number of reasons. He was working. Or he was away. Or he forgot. Once he was with another woman. That was the only excuse he truly regretted.

Linda Steinman was an attractive forty-eight-year-old woman who had not remarried since the divorce in 1987. She had lived on the Upper West Side of Manhattan and taken a healthy chunk of Berenger's salary as alimony, but she also had a high-paying job as a human resources director at a major architectural firm in the city. Berenger maintained a cordial relationship with her because they'd had children together and because he knew he'd always love her.

She had phoned him a week earlier to set up the dinner meeting at Ray's, one of their favorite restaurants in Little Italy. It was not one of the famous New York chain locations of Ray's Pizza, but rather a small family-owned dive that served authentic southern Italian meals. Linda had said there was something she needed to discuss with him. Berenger figured that wasn't a good sign, for she usually called him only to discuss money matters pertaining to their twins. Both Pam and Michael were now in their early twenties and, like most young people, needed help with their finances. Pam was doing graduate work at Albany Law School and Michael had recently left NYU and moved to California to attend the L.A. Music Academy. Both were expensive prospects.

When Berenger arrived at the restaurant, located on Prince Street between Mott and Elizabeth, Linda was already at a table nursing a glass of red wine. He waved at her through the plate-glass window but she didn't return the greeting.

Yep, he was late.

"Sorry," he said as he made his way through the narrow aisle of tables that were already filled with customers. It was a small place and not very accommodating for a guy his size. "I'm going out of town tomorrow and we had to get a lot of stuff ready."

Linda looked at her watch. "Thirty-five minutes isn't too bad. I can remember waiting three or four hours at a restaurant for you."

"I said I'm sorry. Come on. You look great, I'm happy to see you."

She made a face and shook her head. "Whatever. I'm starving. You know what you want?"

"I just got here. Let me look at this for a sec." He scanned the menu for five seconds and then snapped it shut.

"Let me guess," she said. "Lasagna."

He shrugged. "I like lasagna. And they make it good here."

"You're such a creature of habit."

"I know, and you never could change me. Stuck in my ways."

"Forget it. Let's try to have a nice time."

Berenger held out his hands. "I'm having a blast!"

The middle-aged waitress waddled over to the table. "Something to drink, sir?"

He pointed to Linda's glass and asked her, "That's all you want? Care to share a carafe or a bottle?"

"This is good enough for me."

"Bring me a carafe of the red," he told the waitress. "And I think we're ready to order."

He told the woman what they wanted and then they were alone—except for the other customers sitting just a few feet from them on all sides.

"So, what did you want to talk about? Have you heard from the kids?" he asked.

"To answer the second question first, yes, I've heard from them. Pam, anyway. I never hear from Michael. Have you heard from him?"

"Nope. But I'm sure he's fine. When he's *not* fine is when we hear from him. What's Pam have to say?"

"Only that her boyfriend is a jerk but she still loves him and that her midterm finals were really hard."

"She's in law school. What does she expect? And all men are jerks. Didn't you tell her that?"

That brought a smile to Linda's lips. Berenger always thought the sun rose with her smiles. They brought out the warmth and intelligence that otherwise lay dormant behind a composed exterior. Her perfectly round brown eyes also crinkled a bit when she grinned—an endearing feature that he'd never forget. She still wore her dark black hair to her shoulders and Berenger was always amazed that she never had any gray.

Linda was tall, tan, and athletic. She kept in shape by going to the gym regularly and watching her diet. That had been another bone of contention between them during the marriage. Berenger hated to exercise and count calories. Only in the past several years had he taken to working out in the gym at the office.

"You'd think Michael would have the decency to call me on my birthday," she said.

"He didn't call you?"

"Nope."

"I'll murder him."

"Don't bother."

"I'll at least mention it to him. That's just not right."

"He's never remembered my birthday. Ever. When he was young, you always bought the cards for him to sign—or Pam did when they were a little older and still living at home."

"Come to think of it, he doesn't remember my birthday either."

"Children should remember their parents' birthdays. And anniversary. If the parents are still married."

He shrugged at that one. "Yeah. Well."

"So, listen, I wanted to talk to you." That was the way she always began when something serious was coming. "So, listen, I wanted to talk to you." Past tense, as if she'd been contemplating it for days or weeks. Or as if it was his fault that she hadn't gotten the chance to tell him yet.

"Here I am. Let's talk."

Linda took a deep breath and then spit it out. "I'm getting married and moving to California."

For a second, Berenger thought someone had just hit him in the chest with a sledgehammer.

He'd always known that it was a possibility. Linda had been single for twenty-two years and was still an attractive, desirable woman. In many ways, he was surprised that it hadn't happened prior to this. He knew she dated and there was one serious boyfriend that stayed around for nearly ten years in the nineties. But that had fizzled out after the new millennium.

But nothing had prepared him for the shock of hearing those words. He had read somewhere that men always take it harder than women do when their ex-spouse remarries. He didn't know if that was true, but he certainly felt the swell of a jealousy, anger, and pain cocktail. Even after twenty-two years of being away from her.

The waitress brought the carafe and another glass. "Your meal will be out in a few minutes," she said.

Berenger took the carafe without pouring a glass and took a long swig out of it.

"Spike, Jesus!" Linda whispered.

He set down the carafe and exhaled loudly. "That's good wine. Hey, I've always wanted to ask you something. Do you color your hair?"

She blinked. "No. Why?"

"You don't have a single gray thread."

She smiled again. "No, I don't. It's that Mediterranean blood."

"You're really a beautiful woman, Linda. How do you stay looking so young?"

"By practicing habits that you don't. Did you hear what I just told you?"

"Yeah, I heard you." He poured wine into his glass and took a sip. "Is he, uhm, someone I know?"

"You met him once. Richard Noyce. He's an architect at the firm."

Berenger's brow wrinkled. The name sounded familiar but he couldn't place the guy. "Where did I meet him?"

"At my Christmas party a year ago."

"A year ago? Not this past Christmas?"

"Right."

"Describe him."

"Tall. Bald. Mustache. Broad shoulders. Forty-four."

"Bald?" Then he shook his head as if he'd been splashed with liquid. "Forty-four? He's younger than you?"

"By four years."

He thought for a moment. "Okay, I remember him. He's the guy you said had hung mistletoe all over your apartment."

"Yeah."

"Okay." He took another sip of wine. "Okay. Yeah. I remember him. He looks like Mr. Clean with a mustache."

"He's setting up his own firm in California. So we're going to get married and move out there."

"When is this momentous occasion?"

"This fall. Probably September. We haven't set an exact date yet. But he needs to be in Los Angeles by October first."

"Los Angeles? You hate Los Angeles!"

This time it was her turn to shrug. "Not anymore."

"Whenever you were in Los Angeles with me you hated it."

"That was a long time ago."

Berenger's ears were ringing and he felt a headache coming on. He rubbed his eyes and took another sip of wine.

"Do you love this guy?"

"Yes."

"How long have you and he . . . been . . ."

"Seeing each other?"

Berenger rolled his eyes and said, "Well, I was going to say sleeping with each other, but, yeah, that'll do."

"Three years."

"Really? Three years?"

"Uh huh."

"How come I didn't know that?"

"You did know that. I've told you several times. I'd say I was going to such and such with Richard. I was doing this or that with Richard. You didn't put it together?"

"I guess not."

"Well, now you know."

"Do the kids know?"

"Yes."

His mouth dropped. "You told *them* before you told *me*?"

"Yes."

"Now I'm *really* gonna kill Michael for not calling me."

"Leave him alone. I told them not to tell you."

He took another sip of wine and then sat back in his chair. "Wow. I gotta hand it to you, Linda, when you want to talk to me about something, it's usually in the doozy department. And this one's a real doozy."

"I hope you're going to be mature about this."

Berenger snorted and said, "Come on. We're both adults. Of course I will. Linda, we haven't been together in twenty years."

"Twenty-two."

"Whatever. I think I can get used to you living with another man. After all, I've—"

"—been with a number of different women since the divorce."

"But I haven't gotten *married*."

"You would if the right woman came along."

"I don't know."

"Yes, you would."

Yes, he probably would. Berenger hadn't thought about it for many years, though. It was true there had been a few very eligible candidates in his life since the split with Linda, but he had never felt the need to commit to anything more than several months' worth of cohabitation every once in a while.

"Los Angeles, huh?"

"Yes."

"Well, at least you'll be near Michael."

She nodded. "That was a nice incentive as well."

"What does Michael think about that?"

"He doesn't mind. It'll give him a place to go for dinner on the weekends if he wants one."

"Does Mr. Clean have any children from a previous marriage?"

"Yes, two, and don't call him that."

"How old are they?"

"They're grown. Two boys. One lives in Los Angeles as well, and one lives in Washington, D.C."

"What do they do?"

"One's an architect, like his father. He's the one in D.C. The other one . . . is a musician."

Berenger laughed. "Well, that's gratifying. Maybe he and Michael could start their own band."

"Oh. Richard and I are going out of town this weekend. I think we'll be gone a week or so. Just in case you try to get hold of me."

"I said I was going to be away, too. I'm leaving tomorrow."

"Oh, right."

"I'm not sure how long I'll be gone. It's a case."

"Of course. Richard's going to a conference for architects and I'm tagging along."

The food arrived. Berenger took his fork and stuck it into the steaming pasta, but suddenly he wasn't hungry anymore. He set the fork down and took another sip of wine.

"What's the matter?" Linda asked.

"Too hot," he lied.

"So, are you okay with all this?"

"Yeah, it looks delicious!"

"No, I mean the wedding."

"Yeah, yeah, I'm okay with it. If the kids are okay with it and you're okay with it and Yul Brynner is okay with it, then I'm okay with it."

She smiled again. "Okay. And don't call him *that* either."

His two-level apartment in a building at Sixty-eighth Street and Second Avenue—just down the street from the Rockin' Security offices—seemed even more quiet and empty than it usually did when he arrived home.

Berenger locked the door behind him and went directly to the kitchen. He opened the pantry and removed a bottle of Jack Daniel's. He grabbed a glass, filled it with ice from the automatic dispenser on his refrigerator, and poured three inches of forgetfulness. He then took the drink upstairs to the studio where he kept his musical instruments and recording equipment. It wasn't anything as sophisticated as what was at the office, but sometimes in a pinch it would do for laying down a riff or two. Sometimes his best friend, Charlie Potts, would come over and they'd jam for hours. Berenger always digitally recorded those occasions. One never knew when something brilliant would happen.

This wasn't one of those nights.

He took the new, uniquely carved DBZ V out of its case and sat on a stool in the middle of the room. The V was the first guitar released by Dean Zelinsky's new venture, DBZ Guitars, following the designer's departure from Dean Guitars. The instrument had the styling of a red Ferrari, as perfect and exquisite as a woman's body. The flashy logo on the headstock was a large gold Zorro-like *Z* flanked by the initials *D* and *B*. The designer's signature was at the bottom of the *Z* and an eagle was perched atop it. It was a beauty.

Already a little tipsy from the wine, Berenger took a long drink of the whiskey and winced as the lovely fire burned his throat on the way down. He then knew what the night was going to be like. Experience had taught him that before long, the glass would be empty and he'd most likely have another. By then he wouldn't care about his former love remarrying. There'd be hell to pay in the morning and the flight to Chicago would be horrendous—but at least he'd feel better in the here and now.

He plugged into one of the Marshall amps and then took a minute to tune the guitar. He then strummed an E minor chord. From there he went to an A and then back to the E minor. For a moment he messed around with Neil Young's "Down by the River" but then switched to an old Fixers song he had written about his high school sweetheart breaking up with him. Berenger started to sing in the low growl that was his trademark. Howlin' Wolf or Captain Beefheart would've been proud. The Rockin' Security private investigator sang and strummed the guitar as if his guts were on display.

Which they were.

Chapter Six

Hey Joe
(performed by The Jimi Hendrix Experience)

Flights to Chicago had been delayed because of thunderstorms, so they didn't arrive until early evening. As expected, Berenger had a splitting headache and was in a foul mood when he and Prescott arrived at a wet and rainy O'Hare. When Prescott had asked him what was wrong and why he looked like a "strung-out bear," Berenger snapped at her. She didn't speak to him for the remainder of the trip until he apologized.

Zach Garriott had asked them to meet him at a show that featured a new band he was producing. The building actually contained two venues—Reggie's Music Club and Reggie's Music Joint. The Music Club was a large space with a big stage and a balcony for those patrons who might want to sit. The Music Joint was a sports bar that served food and drinks and had a small stage for more intimate acts. In between the two venues, on the second floor, was a CD store called Record Breakers. Reggie's was on South State Street, near the University of Illinois at Chicago. Berenger and Prescott took a taxi from the airport and arrived at the club just as the music was beginning.

The band was a young and talented group called

Chicago Green. Berenger and Prescott had actually seen them before in New York and spent a few minutes standing with the crowd on the floor in front of the stage. Berenger was happy that the group had found someone like Garriott to sponsor them. After a few songs, the couple went upstairs to the balcony and found Garriott subtly disguised in a baseball cap and sunglasses. Garriott gave Berenger a hug, shook hands with Prescott, and then they sat in chairs to watch the rest of the show. Berenger ordered a round of beers for everyone, knowing that the alcohol would go a long way toward relieving his hangover.

Chicago Green played an energetic and impressive set of covers and originals, after which Garriott went backstage for a few minutes with the boys to give them some tips. He then rejoined Berenger and Prescott in the unique sports bar on the other side of the building. Reggie's Music Joint was decorated with all kinds of rock 'n' roll memorabilia and real vinyl record labels were embedded in the clear epoxy-covered tabletops. The menus were made out of classic LP record covers.

As they sat, the club's owner, Robby Glick, came over to give the superstar guitarist VIP attention. Glick was in his forties, had a shaved head, and was dressed in a sports jersey and shorts as if he'd just come from the basketball court. Garriott introduced Berenger and Prescott to him.

"I've heard of you, man," Glick gushed. "You were with The Fixers!"

"You know The Fixers?" Berenger asked, unable to hide his surprise.

"You bet. I have your album, and every once in a while a used one comes in and we sell it in the vinyl section of the shop upstairs. How come you guys didn't make more than one?"

"That's a question I ask myself every day."

"You should try and release it on CD."

"Easier said than done, pal."

Glick turned to Garriott. "How was Chicago Green tonight?"

"Great. They draw a nice crowd here when they play?"

"They do. They're sort of a house band."

"I'll see what I can do for them."

"Nice, kid, nice."

Glick took drink orders for the trio—on the house—and then left them alone.

"Okay, Zach," Berenger said, "tell us what you know."

Garriott nodded and answered, "I'm going to take you to see Joe Nance in a bit. He told us not to show up before eleven. He's still in mourning, naturally, he's drinking a lot, and he's not in the best of spirits. But he can tell you a lot more than I can."

"What *can* you tell us? What's all this about a ghost?"

Garriott became sheepish. "I don't know how to explain it. That's what the other guys all think."

"They believe in *ghosts*?"

"Look. There was this girl named Sylvia. A long time ago. Back when The Loop was together, before they split up into Windy City Engine and Red Skyez. I didn't know her. It was before my time. She was a groupie, I guess. She was also a singer/songwriter. All I really know is that she disappeared in nineteen seventy. Went missing."

"And?"

The guitarist shrugged. "They think it's her that's killing off members of The Loop and the two bands that sprung from it—Red Skyez and Windy City Engine."

"For God's sake, why?"

"I'm not really sure. Maybe Joe can explain it."

"Well, I sure hope so. 'Cause this is just plain nuts."

Prescott interrupted. "Excuse me, but are you saying that this girl, Sylvia, is supposed to be dead?"

"Well, she went missing and was never found. So presumably, yeah, you have to figure she's dead. Met with a bad end."

"How old was she?"

"I'm not sure. Same age as the guys in the band at the time, I think."

"Twenty-one, twenty-two?"

"Yeah."

Berenger asked, "Why would Joe and the others think she's returned from the dead to kill people?"

"Apparently she matches the description that witnesses supplied. She always wore a floppy hat that was hers and hers alone. Had blonde hair. I know, it sounds pretty ridiculous."

"What about the police? What do they think?"

"Joe tried to tell them about her, but you can imagine their reaction. So far they haven't admitted that the shootings are related. The sergeant who's in charge of Charles's case is a dick. Sergeant Doherty."

"He's a detective?"

"I don't know. He's a sergeant."

"All right. So we'll talk to Joe tonight. I'll want to see Harrison Brill and Manny Rodriguez, and also talk to the North Side guys."

"As a matter of fact, North Side is playing here at Reggie's tomorrow night."

"Great. We'll see 'em here, then." Berenger drummed his fingers on the table and said, "Okay, finish your drinks, folks, and let's go talk to Joe."

The rain hadn't let up. Garriott made the comment that they might as well swim to their destination, but no one laughed.

The Nance residence was a town house located on Melrose Street in Wrigleyville, one of the nicer old areas of the city. Just off of Lincoln Avenue, the locale was a hotspot of restaurants, clubs, funky shops, and young people.

"Joe is still married to Lucy," Garriott said as he pulled his SUV into the paved driveway. "Thirty-something years, I think. Their three kids are all grown and live elsewhere but I think they're here for Charles's funeral."

"When is the funeral?"

"What's today, Thursday? There won't be a funeral. The cremation is Sunday, and so is a big memorial party that they've planned. A wake."

They got out of the vehicle and went to the front door. Garriott knocked. The door opened and Joe Nance, looking haggard and disheveled, stood in the light. He was a tall, thin man with a weather-beaten face and silver hair cut short above his ears. The pain and stress of losing his brother was apparent in the man's sad eyes, but Berenger detected something else in Nance's demeanor.

He was afraid.

"Well, lookie here . . . Spike Berenger, hello," he said. "Come in. Hi, Zach."

Nance stood aside as the trio entered the house. Berenger held out his hand and Nance took it.

"Joe, I'm so sorry for your loss."

"Thank you. God, how long has it been?"

"I don't know. Last time I saw you, I was a music manager. That was in the eighties."

"Well, pardon me for saying so, but you look older."

"I guess we all do. Joe, this is my partner, Suzanne Prescott."

"Hi," Prescott said, offering her hand. "I'm sorry for your loss, too."

Nance shook her hand and nodded. "Pleased to meet you. Come into the living room. Can I get you something?"

"We just had drinks, so no thanks," Berenger replied.

They followed the man through a hallway lined with family photographs and into a very narrow living room—as was the case for most town houses in Chicago—and took seats in various comfy chairs. Nance introduced them to his wife Lucy, an attractive redhead who appeared to be in her midfifties. There were bags under her eyes, as it had obviously been a stressful week. As soon as she left the room, Berenger's eyes focused on the handgun that sat on top of the coffee table. It was a Smith & Wesson .38 revolver. He chose to ignore it for the moment and then addressed his host. "Joe, as you know, Zach here has hired us to look into your brother's shooting."

"I appreciate it. The police don't know anything, and if they do, they're not telling me."

"What *have* they told you?"

"Some bullshit about it being a drug transaction gone wrong. Charles had some pot in the house. But you'd think if that were the case, why didn't the killer go inside the house and take the pot? Or anything else?"

"And they don't think it's connected to what happened to Dave Monaco and Hank Palmer?"

Nance rolled his eyes. "I don't know. They won't admit it. I think they believe there's a connection, though. They're just not saying."

Berenger looked at Garriott and raised his eyebrows. Garriott prompted him with a slight nod. "Joe," he said, "I understand you have a theory about who's responsible for this."

"Yeah, I do. You're going to think I'm crazy, though."

"Let's hear it."

"A woman named Sylvia Favero killed Charles. And I think she killed Lew and Sarah Krige, Dave Monaco, and Hank Palmer."

"Who is she?"

Nance laughed a little and bit his fingernails. "She's a ghost, Spike. She's been dead for nearly forty years."

Berenger tried not to show his frustration. "Please explain that, Joe. I want to know everything you know about this woman."

"Right." At that point, Nance stood and went into the kitchen. Berenger noticed Prescott pick something off of the chair she was in. He gave her a questioning look and she shook her head—*I'll tell you later*. Nance returned with a glass full of something—it appeared to be whiskey or bourbon. He had apparently been nursing it before they had arrived. "You sure I can't get you something to drink? I have beer, whiskey, vodka—"

"We're fine, Joe."

Nance sat. "Okay." He took a sip and began the story. "It was back when we were first starting out . . . in the summer of nineteen sixty-seven. We'd just graduated from high school. One of our biggest fans was a girl our age named Sylvia Favero. She was talented. Wrote songs, was a great singer. Hot-looking, too. Hippie chick, you know the type. And a groupie. She went everywhere to see us play. And we became friends. All of us. She'd hang out with the band, do drugs with us, you know . . ."

"Sex?" Prescott asked.

Nance turned red. "Yeah."

"With everyone?"

He paused. "Yeah."

"Okay, go on," Berenger prompted.

"Anyway, in nineteen seventy, she upped and disappeared. Just vanished. No trace. She had no family here. None of us knew where she went. Finally, she became a police statistic. Missing. Possibly kidnapped. Possibly murdered. Who knows? We never heard from her again."

Berenger shifted in his seat and said, "So why do you think her ghost is back and killing members of the band?"

"Because she appeared to me."

Berenger raised his eyebrows. "Oh?"

"It was just before the Kriges were killed. I was leaving a gig at Schuba's . . . that's a club on Southport, not far from my house. Anyway, I was putting my guitar in the trunk of my car and I looked up. There she was. She always wore this same floppy hat. It was unique. It was a real 'hippie' hat, the kind that

60

some chicks wore back in those days. But this one was special. It had flowers and peace signs all over it. She wore sunglasses all the time, too. And there she was, standing in the parking lot. And she told me, 'You'll be the next to last to die. And Stuart Clayton will be the last.' At first I thought I was stoned or something, but I wasn't! The shock of seeing her made me reel for a second. I rubbed my eyes and looked again . . . and she was gone. Vanished. It really freaked me out."

He took a swig from his drink.

"A day later, the Kriges were shot and killed in Evanston. A witness said they saw a blonde woman with a floppy hat. And I knew it was her. Then Dave and Hank were killed and she was seen there, too." Nance leaned forward and picked up the revolver. He held it in his hand and said, "But if she comes for me, I'll be ready for her."

The room was silent for a moment. Berenger didn't want to ask how a handgun would be effective against a ghost. Instead, he said, "I hope you have a permit for that."

"I do."

"Then let's put it back down on the table, okay?"

Nance contemplated the request for a few seconds and then complied.

"Joe, the big question is why would Sylvia want to kill you guys? What's her motive?"

Nance's eyes darted around the room and he shrugged. "I don't know."

He's lying, Berenger thought. There's some kind of guilt in play.

"Are you sure?"

"Yeah. I can't imagine why."

"Did she have a grudge against you guys? Did something happen between her and the band?"

"No. We were all great friends. We loved her. She loved us."

"Then it doesn't make sense."

"I know. It doesn't. But I saw what I saw. Heard what I heard."

"And you told the police this?"

"Yeah."

Berenger looked at Prescott and she made a face that said, This guy is wacko!

"Joe, do Harrison and Manny agree with you?"

"Yeah. I told 'em about seeing Sylvia in the parking lot, and then when the killings started, they believed me."

"Joe, what are you not telling me?"

"What do you mean?"

"You're holding something back. I can see it. I can feel it."

Nance looked away. His feathers were ruffled. "I don't know what you're talking about."

"Joe, I'm a private investigator. I served as a CID investigator in the army. I'm trained to read people. I have to tell you, and please don't be offended, but I think you know something that you're not telling me."

"That's all I know, I swear!"

Berenger and Nance stared at each other for a moment. Finally, the detective slapped his hands on his knees and said, "All right. I'll do what I can. Tomorrow I'll go to the appropriate police precinct and try to find out what they have. The police don't usually talk to PIs, but you never know." He looked at Garriott. "We'll go see North Side tomorrow night, right? I can talk to those guys then. When can I see Manny and Harrison?"

"They're playing a couple of gigs on their own in Michigan this week," Nance said. "They'll be back for the memorial on Sunday."

"And Jim Axelrod? Where's he at these days?"

"Los Angeles. I talked to him this morning. He's flying in for the memorial, too."

"What about Stuart Clayton? Have you talked to him?"

Nance gave Berenger a wry smile. "I haven't talked to Stu in ages. We don't get along." The musician shook his head. "We were so tight in high school and for a couple of years after that. The band tore us apart."

"You started the band in high school, didn't you?" Prescott asked.

"Yeah. He'd say he started it, and I say I started it. I really don't remember how it came about. We were both on the school track-and-field team, so we had to work in band practice between homework and track meets."

"You two were athletes?" Berenger asked.

"We weren't bad. I played football my freshman and sophomore years of high school. My junior year I dropped out and did track. It was more fun. And Stuart was on the team, so we were buds together. I won some medals." Nance shrugged. "It wasn't a big deal."

"Is Clayton in town?"

"As far as I know. The guy fortifies himself in his house. He probably hasn't seen sunlight since the eighties."

"Where does he live?"

Garriott answered that one. "He lives in a dump near Portage Park. A street called Mango."

Suzanne asked, "How's his . . . health?"

Nance answered, "I don't know. He lives like a recluse and doesn't see anyone. I'd say he's totally bonkers."

"Why is that?" Berenger asked.

"Look, we all did a lot of drugs in the sixties and seventies, right? But this guy . . . man, oh man. Stuart was always tripping on something. It was like he wanted to change his brain. I know you can't get addicted to LSD but I'd swear he was. He was tripping every day for a while. That's got to boil your gray matter in the long run."

"But he functions? He lives alone?"

"Yeah. It's hard to believe at one time the guy was rich as a skunk."

"I heard his family was wealthy."

"Damn right! He came from big family money. Clayton owned a yacht at one time. But after his parents died in the late seventies, he sold the family business and squandered all the money. Stuart's one step away from poverty now."

"That's a shame. Well, I'm going to contact him. Hopefully he'll remember me. I met him once."

"When was that?"

"Not long after his first solo album came out. Nineteen seventy-nine, I think. The Fixers were in Chicago and he came to the gig. I met him backstage. To tell you the truth, I was flattered and honored that he came. I used to respect him. He was talented."

Nance nodded. "Yeah. That he was. Then he stepped into the Twilight Zone and decided to stay there."

"Joe, why are you 'next to last to die,' and he's the last?"

Again, Berenger sensed evasiveness. "I don't know," Nance replied. "I don't have a fucking clue."

Berenger sighed and looked at his watch. "Okay, folks. Joe, thanks for seeing us. We'll be in touch. Suzanne and I need to check in to our hotel." He handed the guitarist a business card. "My cell number's on there. Please call me if you think of anything that might be relevant."

"You going to talk to the police tomorrow?" Garriott asked.

"Yeah."

"Good luck."

"Don't worry. My partner Rudy Bishop is friends with your good mayor, but I don't think he'll have to call in any favors. I know police departments don't usually like to share information with private dicks, but I have a buddy on the inside of the Chicago PD who I'm sure will be willing to help out." Berenger winked. "He was a member of The Fixers."

A few minutes later, the two PIs said their goodbyes and left the house. Garriott remained at the front door with Nance as they got into the car. Before Garriott got there, Prescott said, "Look what I found on the chair I was sitting in." She held out her hand with the thumb and index finger together, in an "OK" sign.

Berenger squinted. "I don't see anything."

"It's a hair, Spike. A long, *blonde* hair."

He turned on the car's overhead interior light and saw it. He took the strand from her and held it up. "His wife's a redhead."

"Exactly."

"Are any of his kids blonde?"

"I noted the family photos in the hallway. Two were brunette, one was a red."

"Interesting."

Garriott opened the back door and got in. Berenger looked at him. "Good to go?"

"Sure."

Berenger started the car and pulled away from the house.

Chapter Seven

What To Do
(performed by Status Quo)

"Mike Case, you old bozo!"

Berenger and the plainclothes police officer gave each other bear hugs. Prescott found it amusing to watch two big, barrel-chested men embrace each other.

"How are you, Spike? Damn, it's been, what, twenty-five years?"

"More than that, Mike. God, I don't even want to try counting. It was the seventies, my friend."

Berenger turned to Prescott. "Mike, this is my partner and right hand, Suzanne Prescott. Suzanne, this is Mike Case."

The two shook hands. "Pleased to meet you," Prescott said.

"And extremely pleased to meet you, Suzanne. Damn, Spike, how come you have such a gorgeous partner? My partner is fat, has a mustache, and reeks of Polish sausage."

Berenger laughed. "Just lucky, I guess."

The trio was in a Starbucks not far from the Drake Hotel, where Berenger and Prescott were staying. Mike Case was Berenger's age and weighed perhaps thirty or forty pounds more than he. His hair was cut to a cop's respectable length, but he sported a gold stud in his left earlobe.

"The job lets you get away with that?" Berenger asked, indicating the ear jewelry.

"I'm a Tac guy," Case answered. He looked at Prescott. "Short for Tactical."

She smiled. "I know."

Case raised his eyebrows. "Oh, pretty *and* smart! Better be careful, Spike."

"Believe me, I am. She's knows judo, too."

Case whistled. "Ever think of joining the Chicago PD?" he asked her.

"That thought never crossed my mind, I'm sorry to say," she answered.

"You still play the drums, Mike?"

"Spike, I wouldn't call it 'playing,' but yeah, I bash around on them every now and then. I used to jam with my kids when they were younger. But they grew up and flew the coop."

Berenger turned to Prescott. "Mike left The Fixers when he got married. Moved to Chicago and never looked back." Back to Case. "How is Maggie?"

"I'm sure she's fine, Spike. We got divorced fifteen years ago."

"Really? Gosh, I'm sorry."

"I'm not. Neither is she. Neither are our kids. It was the best thing that could've happened. You know why it's expensive to get a divorce? Because it's worth it! Why should two people torture each other every day just to keep the façade of an archaic and nonsensical institution alive?" He shrugged. "Sorry, I don't know if either of you are married."

"We're not," Prescott answered. "It's okay. I kind of feel the same way."

Berenger mumbled, "Oh, marriage can be okay . . ."

"He's divorced, too," Prescott said to Case.

The unpleasantness of his recent dinner with Linda threatened to rear its ugly head again, so he quickly changed the subject. "This isn't the *Dr. Phil* show. Mike, like I told you on the phone, we're here looking into the shootings of Charles Nance, Dave Monaco, Hank Palmer, and the Kriges. Imagine my surprise when you told me you're on the task force. That's some coincidence."

Case said, "Well, I'm one of the Tac guys assigned to the Fourteenth District, and that's where the latter two shootings took place. But I'm a pretty low man on the totem pole. You're going to want to talk to Sergeant Doherty. He's running the investigation."

"Is he a detective? I thought sergeants assigned and oversaw cases but didn't actually take part in them."

"He was a detective for years. Promoted to sergeant about two years ago. But since these shootings are starting to become heater cases, he's taking a more active role in the investigation. That happens sometimes."

"Heater cases?" Prescott asked.

"That means they're getting media attention. The first two weren't very big news, but after the third one—Nance—the media is starting to connect the dots."

"Joe Nance told me that the police haven't admitted there's a connection between the shootings."

"We haven't. But we know there is. The MO is pretty much the same in all three cases. And then there are the witness sightings of the shooter. We haven't received ballistics results from the Nance shooting, but the first two are identical. The Evanston police are working with us on the Kriges' case. We just don't want to alarm anyone."

"What about the rest of the musicians? They believe someone is bumping off members of Windy City Engine and Red Skyez."

"Man, I haven't thought about Red Skyez since I first moved to Chicago. Good band. I always liked them better than Windy City Engine."

"I preferred Windy City, but I know what you mean. Red Skyez made more of a splash at the time but their flame quickly burned out. At least Windy City Engine has kept going all these years. It's pretty amazing. I don't know many bands that have lasted that long."

Case sighed. "I don't go hear music like I used to. I'm just too busy with the job and then, I don't know, it's just not my scene anymore. The last concert I saw was when The Allman Brothers Band came through Chicago in, what, nineteen ninety-something. The thing is I hate to stand up at a concert. In most of the clubs you have to stand. Even in the big arena venues with reserved seats, everyone ends up standing for the show in front of their hundred-and-fifty-dollar seat. I don't get it. You pay that much money for a seat and then you stand in front of it. I'm too fucking old for that shit."

"I hear you. But if it's a good band and I want to see them, I don't mind standing. For a little while. But back to the case. You think Sergeant Doherty will talk to me?"

"He'll talk to you but he won't tell you shit. He hates private investigators. He thinks they're bottom-dwelling scum. Worse than lawyers, and he *despises* lawyers. He's a stubborn old bull, too. I suggested that we put men in front of the musicians' houses at night, you know, for protection. He won't do it. We don't have the resources or the budget for the OT. Doherty doesn't have a very high regard for rock 'n' roll musicians."

"I think I can understand that. What do you know about the crime scenes?"

"I was off duty when Monaco and Palmer went down. But I was one of the first officers at the scene when Nance was killed. It was a very clean shooting. Two hits in the chest from close range. Nine-millimeter bullets, same as were in Monaco, Palmer, and the Kriges. We recovered shell casings at the Nance scene but not at the others. It was almost like a professional execution. Not Mozambique style, but still an execution."

"So it could be any one of a hundred different types of handguns," Berenger noted.

"Yeah. Nines are pretty damn universal anymore. We're waiting on the ballistics comparison to the Monaco/Palmer/Kriges shootings, but we're betting that they came from the same weapon."

"If that's the case, are the police going to admit that the shootings are related?"

"I would. That's up to ranks higher than Doherty's, though. But Doherty likes to keep as much information as possible close to the vest. But, uhm, there is something I can tell you."

"Oh?"

"This isn't known by very many people. The killer left something at each crime scene."

"What's that?"

"CDs. Two were left near the Kriges' bodies. Two

were left on the sidewalk where Monaco and Palmer were shot, and one was left on Nance's front porch."

"What's on them?"

"Songs, Spike. Each disk contained a different song, sung by a woman. And get this—each disk was marked, 'Track One,' 'Track Two,' and so forth. Nance's was 'Track Five.' "

Berenger and Prescott looked at each other. "What are the songs?" she asked.

Case shrugged. "They're original. I don't think anyone's heard them before."

"So, wait," Berenger said, "you're saying that the killer is leaving recordings of music with each victim? One song for each victim?"

"That's what it looks like."

"Geez." Berenger shook his head. "What's it sound like?"

"I haven't heard the first four but I listened to the one left at Nance's place. I guess if you took it out of context and just played it on the radio or something, it's not a bad piece of music."

"No idea who's singing?"

"Nope. Female with a nice, strong voice."

"What kind of instrumentation?"

"Sounds like a regular combo—guitar, bass, drums, keyboards. There could be other instruments, I'm not sure."

"Does your task force have all the CDs?"

"The Evanston police have the first two originals, but they sent us copies, so, yeah, we have all five."

"Boy, I'd really like to hear them."

"And I'm *positive* Doherty's not going to let you do that. Hell, he hasn't let everyone on the fucking task force hear them. I haven't heard them, except that last one."

"Well, that pretty much cements the idea that the killings are related," Prescott said. "I understand why that information hasn't been leaked to the public."

"Have you already had cranks calling in and accepting responsibility?" Berenger asked.

"Yeah. A couple. And when we ask them what the killer left at the crime scenes, they don't know. So, false alarms there. But there's another reason why Doherty isn't totally convinced the shootings are related. We've had some similar shootings in the city—not of musicians, but of regular people. Armed robberies. We were already up against an alleged serial armed robber before all of this other stuff began. They started a little over a year ago. Same M.O. and witnesses have said that a white female with blonde hair is doing the crimes. There are no floppy hats, but the woman is usually wearing some kind of hat. She approaches people on the street, robs them, and shoots them. There have been eight so far. And we're pretty sure they were all committed by the same offender."

"Unbelievable."

"That sounds pretty unusual for a woman," Prescott said. "It's just not the thing a woman would do. You know?"

"We know. It's a ballsy thing to do—no offense. To just walk up to someone in public and do that . . . no, it's not in the profile for cases like that."

"Are there any suspects for these robberies?" Berenger asked.

"We have a couple, but no arrests have been made and no one has been brought in for questioning.

Doherty hasn't shared that intel with me. My orders are to keep an eye out for suspicious blondes, though."

"What about forensics? Is there anything that connects those armed robberies with the shootings of the musicians?"

"Yeah. Nine-millimeter bullets were used in all of 'em."

"That doesn't mean the same gun fired them all."

"No. But ballistics tests on the recovered bullets have shown that they're very similar. The shell casings match up but we haven't recovered enough of the bullets from the robberies to compare with what we've been able to get from the murders. But it's possible the same gun was used."

Berenger took the last sip of his coffee and said, "Well, that complicates things, doesn't it?"

"Yeah."

"So what about Joe Nance's theory?"

"That a ghost is doing the shooting?" Case laughed. "What do you think?"

"I don't believe in ghosts. But what about this Sylvia Favero? Do you know anything about her?"

"When Nance brought her up, we looked into it. It's a cold case from almost forty years ago, Spike. Twenty-two-year-old girl disappeared one night and was never heard from again. She was declared missing. Back then, you know, we didn't have the resources to find missing people that we do today. And that was the early seventies. Young men and women ran off all the time. And, yeah, there were kidnappings, just like there are today. After about six months, her case was left open but it went into the dead pile. Nobody is still on the job who worked it back then. The notes suggested that she either ran away and changed her identity, or that she was probably dead and buried in a forest preserve or some sicko's backyard."

"Yuck," Prescott said.

"She had no relatives here. Her mother lived in Europe somewhere. I can't remember."

"I'd like to see her file."

"Good luck on that, too."

Sergeant Doherty was not available that day to see them, but an appointment was made for the following day. Berenger then phoned Stuart Clayton.

"Hello?" The voice was quiet and frail.

"Is this Stuart Clayton?"

"Yes. Who is this?"

"Stuart, this is Spike Berenger. Rockin' Security. Remember me?"

"Spike who?"

"Berenger. We met a long time ago when I was in a band called The Fixers."

"Your name sounds familiar. But I don't know . . . when was this?"

"In the late seventies. I run a security service for rock 'n' roll acts and I'm a private investigator. You can look us up on the Web, if you'd like, at www—"

"That's okay, I believe you." There was a pause, then: "What can I do for you?"

"Stuart, my partner and I would like to come by and have a word with you. It's about these shootings of your former band colleagues. I'm sure you've heard about what's happened."

"Yes, I've heard. It's terrible. I've already spoken to the police."

"I'm not the police. Zach Garriott has hired my firm to look into the shootings. I'm talking to everyone who was once a member of Red Skyez or Windy City Engine. Essentially, everyone who was originally with The Loop or the bands that sprung out of it."

Berenger heard the man sigh wearily. "I don't know anything. Jesus."

"I appreciate that, sir, but I'd like to ask you a few questions anyway. More about the past than about today."

There was silence at the other end. For a moment, Berenger thought the man had hung up. "Stuart? Mr. Clayton?"

"I'm here. I'm sorry. I'm . . . I'm not well, you know."

"Do you think we could come by and have a chat? It wouldn't take long."

"Not today. Maybe tomorrow?"

"Tomorrow is good. I have an appointment in the morning, but then I'm wide-open the rest of the day. How about I give you a call after lunch?"

"That's fine. Listen, I don't remember a lot. My mind . . . I just don't remember a whole lot. I'm . . . not well."

"That's quite all right. We'll see how we get along tomorrow, okay? Don't you worry about it. Is there anything we can bring you? Do you need anything?"

"No, thank you. I have a lady that comes twice a week with stuff. And I can go out on my own if I have to. I just don't . . . like to."

Sheesh, the guy sounds like an invalid and a half! Berenger thought.

"All right. Thanks, Stuart. I'll call you tomorrow."

Berenger closed his cell and Prescott asked, "Well? What'd he sound like?"

"He sounds like he could die tomorrow and he wouldn't care. It was like talking to a very old man in a nursing home. It was kind of scary."

"Geez. He must be pretty bad off."

"Well, we'll see tomorrow. You hungry?"

"Famished." She looked at her wristwatch. "But it's a bit early for dinner. Want to walk along Michigan Avenue for a while? We have nothing else to do."

"Sure."

And that's what they did. The private investigator and his assistant walked north past Millennium Park and the Art Institute and up into the Magnificent Mile, Chicago's equivalent of New York's Fifth Avenue. Prescott ooh'd and ah'd at the clothes in store windows while Berenger enjoyed the people-watching. The spring day was cool but pleasant—at least the torrential rains had ceased.

Berenger figured they'd grab a nice meal somewhere and then go back down to Reggie's for the North Side show. He didn't want to tell Prescott that he didn't know where to begin on the case because there was so little to go on. Depending on what Sergeant Doherty would share with him, it was entirely possible that they were spinning their wheels in Chicago.

The key would be to crack Joe Nance's wall of silence. Berenger was certain that the man wasn't revealing everything he knew about the woman named Sylvia Favero.

Chapter Eight

Witchy Woman
(performed by Eagles)

Reggie's was crowded for the North Side show. While the band didn't draw a major venue–size audience, they enjoyed a loyal following that guaranteed ticket sales of a few hundred people. Berenger had arranged for Zach Garriott to meet them in the balcony, but the place was so packed that it was difficult to find the guitarist.

"It's standing room only," Prescott said. "We should've come earlier."

"Sorry, I had no idea. I don't see Zach, do you?"

"He's probably in disguise again. He'll find us, I bet."

Sure enough, the superstar showed up wearing wraparound sunglasses and a cowboy hat. Reggie's manager, Robby Glick, was in tow. Berenger didn't think Garriott's disguise was very good—any serious fan could recognize him.

"Hey, Spike, Suzanne," Garriott said.

"Zach, how you doing?"

"Okay, I guess. No one's tried to kill me yet."

Glick grinned and held out his hand for Berenger to shake. "Welcome back. Glad to see you."

"Thanks, Robby. Say, could you send word backstage to Bud Callahan that I'm here? Suzanne and I want to speak to them when the show's over."

"Sure thing."

After Glick left them, Berenger said, "Zach, I'm afraid the disguise is pretty lame."

Garriott shook his head. "No one's going to recognize me. I'll just stay with you and everything will be cool."

Berenger nodded toward the stage. "I haven't heard North Side in quite a while. They still good?"

"Sure. Do you know them?"

"I've met Bud and Rick. I've never met Sharon or their guitarist."

"Greg Cross is damned good."

"I've heard him, but I didn't think they could ever replace you."

"Aww, shucks, man. I bet you say that to all the guitar gods."

Prescott said, "I'm going downstairs to get a beer. You want anything?"

"Sure, get me one. Zach?"

"I'm fine, thanks."

"You need money?" Berenger asked her.

"What am I, your daughter?" She waved him off and moved toward the stairs.

"That's a fine-looking woman, Spike," Garriott said.

"Tell me about it."

"You sure things are just business between you two?"

"Yep. We dated for about three months a long time ago. Thirteen years or more. Hard to believe it's been that long. Strictly professional relationship now. And we're really good friends, too."

"That's cool."

Three young men, most likely in their early twenties, tentatively approached them. One of them asked, "Are you Zach Garriott?"

"Nope. Sorry," Garriott said.

"Oh. We thought . . . you look like him. Anyone ever tell you that, man?"

"No, can't say they have. But thanks, I guess."

Berenger subtly shook his head and winked at the trio.

"You are Zach Garriott!" one blurted. "Holy shit, man! I just want to shake your hand!"

Completely blown, Garriott smiled and offered his right hand. The three fans eagerly shook it and gushed for a few minutes about the guitarist's latest album and asked when he was going on tour. Garriott humored them for a few minutes and they went away happy.

"That wasn't so bad, was it?" Berenger asked.

"Nah. But I wouldn't want it twenty-four/seven."

"I know what you mean."

"Especially now. You know."

"Yeah, I know."

Garriott eyed Berenger and asked, "Are you carrying?"

"Carrying? What, dope?"

"No, man, a gun! Are you armed?"

Berenger nodded. "Yeah. I have a special PI license. Class C with a piggyback Class G. I have a gun permit for most states. I try to take a weapon with me when I travel. Flying is a bit of a hassle. I have to check it through security and hand it over before getting on the plane, but then I have my own personal firearm when I get to my destination."

"What do you have?"

"I usually use a Smith and Wesson Thirty-eight Special. The Bodyguard AirWeight model. But for traveling I carry a Kahr nine millimeter because it's lighter and easier to carry on trips." He lifted the military flak jacket he was wearing to reveal the Null paddle-type side-belt holster.

"Damn, Spike."

"Don't worry. I know how to use it."

Prescott returned with the beers just as the lights went out. The crowd roared as the band took the stage. Bud Callahan, a tall and heavyset man with a goatee, waved to the crowd before taking his place behind an array of keyboards. Rick Tittle, like many drummers, was thin and wiry. Sharon Callahan strapped on a bass guitar and shouted into the microphone, "Howdy-do!" The guitarist, Greg Cross, had put on some pounds since Berenger had last seen the band. All four musicians were in their mid to late fifties.

The band opened with "Blizzard," one of their better-known tracks from their first self-titled album. Garriott was the original guitarist on the record, and he beamed with pride when Cross perfectly copied the power chord riffs. North Side's music sounded a bit like the electric incarnation of Return to Forever mixed with a complex style of Chicago blues. As with Rattlesnake and South Side, the star of the band was most certainly Callahan and his keys.

Prescott spoke into Berenger's ear. "Do you think any of them are in danger?"

"I don't know," he replied directly into her ear as well. "None of them were originally in The Loop, Red

Skyez, or Windy City Engine. Zach is the only member of North Side that was."

People all around them were dancing in place and rocking to the music. Berenger took the opportunity to scan the crowd in the balcony. Most appeared to be in their midthirties and up, but there were plenty in their twenties.

Then he saw her.

A woman with a floppy hat and long blonde hair stood alone against the back wall of the balcony. She wore dark sunglasses and a trench coat. She had her arms folded across her chest. More interesting was the fact that she wasn't watching the band on stage—it seemed to Berenger that she was looking directly at him and Garriott.

"I'll be right back," he shouted to Prescott. "Keep an eye on Zach!"

Before Prescott could ask where he was going, Berenger turned, pushed his way through the crowd, and headed toward the back of the balcony. But as soon as he started moving, he lost sight of the woman. Berenger frantically looked around the place but didn't spot her. He rushed to the staircase and descended to the ground-floor level. The space was more crowded there—if the woman had preceded him by a few seconds, she'd already be lost in the throng.

Berenger cursed to himself, climbed the stairs, and rejoined his friends.

"What was it?" Prescott asked.

"I thought I saw . . . I don't know. Never mind."

"What?"

"I saw a woman with a floppy hat and blonde hair.

But she was there one minute and gone the next. It's weird."

Prescott raised her eyes. "Was she a ghost, Spike?"

Berenger ignored the comment and looked around the balcony once again. There was no sign of trouble, so he did his best to concentrate on the music.

North Side played a two-hour set without stopping. When it was over, Glick escorted Berenger, Prescott, and Garriott backstage to talk to the band.

"Spike Berenger!" Bud Callahan bellowed. "By God, I think we weigh the same!"

"I hope not, for your sake!" The two men clasped hands.

"Have you met my wife, Sharon?"

"No, I can't say I have."

Introductions were made all around. Glick provided cold beers for everyone as they sat in the dressing room.

"As you all know, some Chicago musicians have been shot and killed recently," the PI began. "I don't want to alarm you. I don't think any of you are in danger. But I need to know if you've heard or seen anything suspicious. Or if you recall seeing a blonde woman with a big floppy hat anywhere."

The band members shook their heads and murmured.

"Did any of you know a woman named Sylvia Favero? She was apparently a groupie that hung around with The Loop back in the sixties."

"I met her a few times," Callahan said. "Rattlesnake hadn't started up yet and The Loop was about to split into Red Skyez and Windy City Engine. I remember her but I never knew her very well. Ran into her at some gigs that the band played."

"What do you recall about her?" Prescott asked.

"She was very friendly with the band. Especially Joe Nance and Stuart Clayton. I think they were both bonking her. That's the impression I got, anyway."

"Do you know what happened to her?" Berenger asked.

"Nope. I remember all the flap about her disappearing. When was it? Nineteen seventy?"

"Yeah."

"Right. She just went missing. It got to where you just expected to see her at the gigs, you know, hanging around after the show. Then one day she wasn't there."

"Did anyone in The Loop say anything about it?"

Callahan scratched his head. "Geez, that was a long time ago. I think I might have asked Joe Nance about her. He just shrugged and said they were all wondering what happened to her."

"Did they seem upset about it?" Prescott asked.

"I don't really remember. I'm sure they were puzzled by it and they were concerned for her safety. I think they were afraid something bad may have happened to her. Since she never turned up again, I guess something did. I have a scrapbook of clippings and stuff at home you can look at."

"That might be useful." Berenger looked at the others. "Anyone else?"

Tittle nodded. "I may have met her but I'm not sure. I do remember the 'missing' posters and some of the talk. I got into the music scene later than Bud."

Sharon Callahan and Greg Cross didn't know her.

"I do remember one thing about Sylvia," Callahan said.

"What's that?"

"She sang like an angel. She wrote her own songs, too. Joe Nance was considering bringing her into the band. He told me so."

"What did the others think of that?"

"I have no idea."

"Did she perform on her own at the time?" Prescott asked.

"Not much. I don't recall her ever having a show of her own. She opened up for The Loop once or twice—just her and a guitar. Sort of a Joni Mitchell act."

"Were you there?"

"I was. I recorded some of their shows back then. Now that I think of it, I might have that show on tape. I'll have to look."

"Did you hear her sing anywhere else?"

"There was a party at Charles Nance's house one night. A lot of people were there. Everyone was high or drunk. She started singing and everyone was mesmerized. I remember thinking, Wow, that chick is talented. I never would have guessed 'cause she was such a *groupie*, you know? Most groupies in those days just wanted to sleep with rock stars."

"Interesting." Berenger slapped his knees. "Okay, folks, I've taken up enough of your time." He handed out business cards. "My cell's on there. Call me if you think of anything—anything at all—that might help."

Everyone stood, shook hands, and said good-bye. As Berenger, Prescott, and Garriott left the dressing room and entered the middle section of the building, the guitarist said, "Hey, I want to look for a CD in the shop upstairs. You want to come with me?"

"Sure," Berenger said.

Prescott said, "I'll meet you guys in the bar."

"Okay. Grab a table and order some more beers."

Prescott went through the door to the sports bar as Garriott and Berenger proceeded to climb the metal stairs to Record Breakers. They reached the first landing, turned to ascend the second flight, and froze.

A woman with blonde hair, a floppy hat, sunglasses, and a trench coat stood at the top of the staircase. She held a pistol in her hand and it was pointed directly at them.

"It's her!" Garriott whispered.

Before Berenger could make a move, the woman's weapon coughed twice. The noise of the gunfire was deafening in the stairwell and at first Berenger was confused by the echo. Had she fired more than twice? Was anyone hit?

Instinct took over. Berenger tackled Garriott and threw him to the landing. At the same moment, he attempted to draw his Kahr. But the woman fired again, and Berenger felt the heat of the round within inches of his head. Then she rushed down the steps and kicked Berenger's arm before he had the gun completely out of its holster. The Kahr flew down the steps as the woman leaped over the two men and descended quickly to the ground floor.

Berenger scrambled to retrieve his weapon and then pointed it at his prey—but she had fled through the front door to the street. He then turned to Garriott.

"Zach! Are you hit?"

Blood was spreading across the guitarist's chest. The man's eyes were wide with fear and pain.

"Oh, God. Take it easy, Zach! I'm calling for help!"

Suddenly the stairwell was full of people. Prescott appeared and rushed up to the landing where Garriott lay.

"Call nine-one-one!" Berenger barked. "I'm going after her!"

Garriott clutched Berenger's sleeve and pulled him close. The PI leaned in to hear what the man had to say.

"Spike . . . she *is* a ghost!" Garriott coughed. "She's supposed to be . . . dead . . . she'll kill us all . . . !"

Berenger lightly slapped his friend's cheek and said, "Hang in there, Zach. Help is on the way."

Then he got up, cut through the crowd at the bottom of the stairs, and hurried out into the night.

Chapter Nine

Jumping Someone Else's Train
(performed by The Cure)

It was raining again.

As it was still fairly early in the evening, South State Street had plenty of traffic on it. But night had fallen and the downpour made visibility a challenge. Berenger peered up and down the sidewalk in front of Reggie's but saw only a small gathering of winos at the corner in front of a liquor shop and convenience store. A few of Reggie's patrons were standing against the building, smoking cigarettes.

"Did you see a woman in a trench coat run out of here?" he asked them.

"Yeah, man." One of them pointed across the street.

Berenger shielded his eyes from the traffic head-lights and saw her. She had crossed State Street and was running like a banshee from hell toward Cermak, an east-west thoroughfare at the end of the block. Berenger took off after her.

When he got to the corner of State and Cermak, she was a good hundred yards ahead of him. Nevertheless, he didn't slow his pace. Eventually she would have to rest, wouldn't she? There was no doubt that the woman was in great shape. She ran like a professional marathon contestant. Berenger, on the other hand, was twenty-five pounds overweight and was already out of breath.

He crossed Clark Street and saw the shooter ascend the stairs to the Cermak/Chinatown El train station. In horror, he scanned the overhead tracks and saw that, sure enough, a train was about to pull in to board passengers. Berenger poured on the steam and ran with all his might. The staircase was tall, but the PI attacked it with ferocity, taking two steps at a time. When he reached the platform, he encountered another obstacle—the turnstile. He had no rail ticket and it didn't take cash. There was certainly no time to stop at the vending machine and buy a ticket, so he did what any action hero would do—he leaped over the turnstile.

"Hey!" shouted a CTA employee who was standing on the platform. Berenger ignored him and ran for the train, the doors of which were about to close. He slid into the last car just as they slammed shut.

He almost collapsed onto the floor as he tried to catch his wind. Passengers looked at him with little pity, for they had seen it all on the CTA bus-and-rail system. Berenger clung to a pole as his heart pounded against his chest. He wanted to catch the homicidal woman, but he didn't care to have a coronary doing so.

The train started to move. Berenger scanned the platform as it swooshed by to make sure she hadn't faked him out and not boarded. Which car did she enter? She must be somewhere up ahead.

Get moving! he commanded himself.

Berenger walked unsteadily to the front of the car. The CTA trains were similar to the subways in New York. One could easily open the door at the end of the car, step out onto a small platform, move to the next car, open that door, and enter. It was against the rules and it wasn't the safest thing in the world to do, but plenty of people did it if one car was particularly crowded. Berenger ignored protocol and slid open the door. Outside, the noise of the rattling train was much louder. It was also on an elevated track, exposed to the rain. He almost slipped on the wet platform, but he grabbed a handlebar to steady himself. Within seconds he was in the next car.

There were maybe ten people in it and the woman with the floppy hat was not one of them. Holding on to an overhead bar, Berenger made his way through, flung open the door, and stepped outside just as the train made a sharp turn and gradually dipped underground toward a subterranean station. He held on for dear life as the darkness of the tunnel enveloped him.

Berenger managed to open the door and get inside the car. This one was more crowded than the others. All the seats were taken and several people were standing and holding the handlebars. Berenger quickly scanned the interior but didn't see the hat. There was a woman with blonde hair, though. She wasn't wearing sunglasses or a trench coat. She probably wasn't the shooter, but Berenger approached her for confirmation. As he moved closer, he saw that she was holding the hand of a small child.

"Look, Mommy, that man has a gun!" the boy exclaimed at the top of his voice.

Damn! Berenger's flak jacket had ridden up his waist, exposing the Null holster and his Kahr. The child's pronouncement caused everyone to perk up and look at him.

"I'm a police officer, folks!" Berenger called out. It

was a lie, but he had been in a similar situation before. It was best to alleviate any fears without having to explain who he really was. He also carried a fake badge inside a wallet in case he ever had to flash it quickly at someone. It was dishonest—and illegal—but Berenger had found that it saved time and trouble. And he'd never been caught doing it.

He addressed the boy's mother. "Ma'am, did you see a woman about your size wearing a big floppy hat?"

Wide-eyed, the mother shook her head.

"That lady with the dark glasses, Mommy! She had a hat in her hand!" the kid announced.

"Oh, right," the woman said. "She went past us just a minute or two ago and went into the next car. He's right, she was carrying a hat."

Berenger was already on the move. He blurted, "Thanks, kid," over his shoulder and rushed to the door at the end. He felt the train slow down as he maneuvered between the cars and burst inside the last carriage. The train pulled in to the Roosevelt station and stopped.

There she is!

The floppy hat moved with the swarm of passengers out of the opening doors. Berenger attempted to push through but there were too many people. By the time he stepped onto the platform, the shooter had disappeared into a passageway leading from the Red rail line to the Orange and Green lines. It was time to run again.

Berenger chased her into the tunnel—and it was a long one. He saw her at the end of the corridor. She looked at him and then quickly jumped on an escalator. The woman climbed it faster than it was moving and vanished. Berenger followed her, reached the next level, and stopped.

She could have exited the station to the street, or she could have continued up another flight to the Orange or Green lines. A CTA employee stood just outside the turnstile, so Berenger couldn't very well go through the gate, take a look outside, and hurdle back inside.

Which way would she go?

Berenger looked up the moving escalator and then back at the exit. Blind intuition told him that he needed to keep moving higher. He turned, boarded the escalator, prayed that his hunch was correct, and ascended the steps two at a time. When he got to the next landing, he found yet another long flight of stairs—and this time the only escalator was going down. He cursed aloud and began the torturous climb.

The next big question was which line would she have boarded? The Green line went north into the Chicago Loop. The Orange line went north but then took a sharp left and headed west so that it could circle around the Loop and head back south toward Midway Airport.

He heard a train screech to a halt at the platform above him. Berenger figured she would board the first train that arrived, so he put forth the extra effort to reach the top of the stairs in time. Once again, he had to hurry and jam his leg into the closing doors so that he could squeeze inside.

It was a Green line elevated train. As it began to move, he saw the floppy hat slip through the door at the far end of the car.

"Stop that woman!" he shouted, but he was so out

of breath that he could barely project his voice. He attempted to chase her but his body rebelled. A severe pain cut through his chest, causing Berenger to collapse to his knees as he held on to an upright pole.

"Are you all right, mister?" an African American woman asked.

His heart felt as if it were playing the drum riff from The Ventures' "Wipe Out" against his rib cage. His head spun. Every breath he took was shallow and inadequate.

Take it easy. You're okay. Just breathe.

He tried counting to ten. He pictured the faces of his children. He thought of Linda.

The train slowed and pulled into the Adams Street station.

Berenger then recalled the voice of his army drill instructor, a man he had simultaneously hated and respected during those horrendous weeks at boot camp in 1975.

"Get your ass up and move, soldier! Where do you think you are, Camp Pussy?"

Berenger almost laughed at the memory. And it worked. He found that he was able to stand, take a solid, deep breath, and recharge.

"Are you all right, mister?" the passenger asked him again.

"Yeah."

The doors opened and this time he was the first person out of the car.

The woman with the floppy hat was already running for the station exit and the stairs leading down to the street. Berenger drew his Kahr, assumed a Weaver stance, and did something crazy. He fired his weapon in the middle of a crowd of innocent bystanders. Everyone screamed and bolted out of his way. Many hit the floor and lay prone, scared to death.

He'd missed. The woman slipped through the turnstile and was already leaping down the stairs, three or four at a time.

"Police officer!" Berenger shouted, hoping it would ease the civilians' fears. He took off after the shooter, burst through the turnstile, and lumbered down the staircase at a much slower rate than his prey.

He hoped that his gunshot would at least attract the attention of the Chicago PD. If he wasn't arrested on the spot for firing his handgun in a crowded El station, perhaps they would help him apprehend the suspect.

Suspect, my ass. She's guilty as hell! I saw the bitch shoot Zach right in front of me!

Berenger reached the ground and spotted the woman running east across Wabash Avenue. Without thinking, he pursued her and ran right in front of an oncoming taxicab. The vehicle's tires shrieked and the driver managed to turn the wheel to avoid a full head-on impact. Nevertheless, the left side of the front bumper hit Berenger's legs. His body flipped up and over the edge of the taxi's hood, and he landed hard on the wet pavement.

At first he didn't know if he could move. Burning pain radiated up the outside of his left leg and into his hips. He cursed through clenched teeth and then rolled away from the taxi.

Get up! Get up! She's getting away!

The angry taxi driver got out of the cab. "What's the matter wif you, man? You tryin' to get us killed?

Did you fuck up my cab? Huh? Did you?" The man examined the front of the car before bothering to see if Berenger was hurt. The PI forced himself to stand and walk away, crossing to the other side of Wabash. "Come back here, man! You put a dent in my cab!"

The shooter had run east on Adams toward Michigan Avenue. If she merged into the herd of human cattle there, he'd lose her for good. Michigan was one of the busiest streets in Chicago.

Berenger held his left leg with one hand—as if that would ease the pain—and limped as fast as he could. He reached the intersection and was immediately surrounded by swarms of people on the sidewalk. He frantically looked up and down the avenue for a sign of the killer but he couldn't see her. He hobbled north as he scanned the tops of heads for that distinctive hat. But the bright headlights on the street blinded him and he had to stop just to shake the noise and confusion out of his brain.

Then he saw her.

She was running on the other side of Michigan, past the Art Institute and toward Millennium Park.

Damn her! How can that bitch run so fast?

He darted into the traffic, waving his arms. Horns blared at him but drivers stopped to let him cross. Berenger made it safely to the other side and continued his limp-run after the killer.

One thing's for sure—she's no goddamned ghost!

He sprinted past the Crown Fountain, which consisted of two fifty-foot glass block towers at each end of a shallow reflecting pool. The towers projected video images from a broad social spectrum of Chicago citizens' faces.

Water flowed through outlets in the screen to give the illusion that it was spouting from their mouths.

Beyond the fountain was the McCormick Tribune Plaza and Ice Rink, backed by the Park Grill restaurant. Parkgoers were dining alfresco under large umbrellas, despite the rain which had thankfully let up. Berenger was pretty certain the woman hadn't dashed through the patio—she must have gone deeper into the park, where it was dark.

Behind the restaurant was Cloud Gate, the silver metal sculpture shaped like a gigantic bean. The 110-ton elliptical monument was forged with a seamless series of highly polished stainless steel plates, which reflected the city's famous skyline and the clouds above. A twelve-foot-high arch provided a "gate" to the concave chamber beneath the sculpture, inviting visitors to touch its mirrorlike surface and see their images reflected back from a variety of perspectives.

The space was surprisingly devoid of parkgoers, the rain having most likely driven them away. Berenger found himself alone, wet, cold, and in pain. And the woman was nowhere in sight. He moved to the impressive metal artwork and put his hand out to lean against it.

The crack of a gunshot split the night air and a bullet hit the sculpture with a resounding *ding*.

Berenger dived for the paved base and lay flat. He then crawled to the shadows beneath the sculpture's arch and pressed his body against the metal.

The shot had come from the darkness, somewhere west of him. There wasn't a whole hell of a lot he could do now. She had the entire park in which to hide. If he emerged from his cover, she could take another potshot at him. He might not be as lucky next time.

He pulled out his cell phone and saw that Prescott had tried to reach him three times. The first thing he did was dial 9-1-1. He then returned his partner's call.

"Spike! Where the hell are you?"

"Millennium Park. I already called nine-one-one. I think I'm just gonna lie here and wait for the cavalry."

"I'm on my way. Where exactly are you?"

"Under that silver bean thing."

"Are you all right?"

He groaned. "I've been better. I lost her. Damn it, Suzanne, I lost her!"

"Spike."

"What?"

He winced, for he knew what she was going to say before she said it.

"We lost Zach, too, Spike. He's dead."

Chapter Ten

Cops and Robbers
(performed by Bo Diddley)

The day after Zach Garriott's death, the Chicago Musician Murders, as the press had dubbed it, had become a heater case. The previous killings had been more or less ignored by the media on a national basis, whereas the death of superstar guitarist Zach Garriott was international news. He may not have been as famous as someone like John Lennon, but the incident was just as notorious as the 2004 onstage slaying of Pantera's "Dimebag" Darrell Abbott.

Berenger was told to attend a meeting at Area Five detective headquarters. Chicago was split into five detective areas; each area contained five districts. The shootings of Charles Nance, Dave Monaco, and Hank Palmer all took place in the Fourteenth District, which was under the jurisdiction of Area Five. Garriott's murder took place in the First District, which was a part of Area Four. Since the Area Five detectives had already begun the investigation—and it was now acknowledged that the incidents were related—the Area Four commander had gladly handed over the case to Area Five.

The building was located on Grand Avenue and Central. It was also the headquarters for the Twenty-fifth District, which wasn't involved in the investigation. Berenger brought Prescott with him, even though she wasn't ordered to attend.

The Rockin' Security team only had three hours of sleep. Once the police had arrived at Millennium Park, Berenger was taken to the First District at Eighteenth Street and South State. He had refused to go to a hospital to be checked out, despite Prescott's badgering that he do so. For four hours, he had told and retold the story. He described the events of what had happened at Reggie's, on the El trains, and in Millennium Park ad nauseam. He provided the best description that he could of the female shooter. At five o'clock in the morning, he and Prescott were released. His Kahr was confiscated temporarily because it was standard operating procedure that all weapons fired illegally be taken. Berenger was promised that he'd get the gun back at the task force meeting. He and Prescott had gone straight to the Drake Hotel and crashed for what little time they had before having to be at Area Five HQ.

An officer escorted Berenger and Prescott to the conference room on the building's second floor. Mike Case was already seated, as were a number of other police officers and detectives. Sergeant D. B. Doherty, the head detective in the investigation, gave them a curt nod. Apparently he hadn't had much sleep either. A female officer pointed at the coffee, which was dispensed from a cafeteria-style pot with a spigot. Berenger pounced on it as if it were the Fountain of Youth.

After pouring a couple of cups, they sat next to Case, who whispered to Berenger, "You look surprisingly awake."

"I feel like one of those potholes you have on State Street."

"I noticed you limping. How's the leg? I heard you were hit by a taxi?"

"Yeah. It wasn't as bad as it sounds. The guy was in the process of braking." He snorted wryly. "Could've been worse."

"Yeah, you could've been shot to death."

"There's that, yeah. Mainly my entire body is one big sore muscle. Don't touch me or I'll yelp like a wounded puppy."

Prescott whispered back, "The fifteen minutes a day of treadmill walking isn't enough to keep you in shape, Spike. I've told you that a hundred times."

"Yes, ma." To Case: "She's pissed off because she didn't get to meditate this morning."

Before Prescott could deliver a retort, Doherty stood and spoke in a hoarse, but commanding, voice. "All right, listen up. Let's get started." He looked at Berenger and said, "First of all, what the *hell* do you think you're doing, *Mr.* Spike Berenger, firing a weapon in a crowded El station?"

Christ, didn't we go over this last night? Berenger thought. The guy just wants to dress me down in front of the Task Force.

Berenger stood, fighting the ache that dribbled down his leg. "I explained all that in my statement, sir. It was a judgment call. If it was the wrong call, then I apologize." Berenger nodded to the rest of the people in the room and then sat.

Doherty hadn't expected such acquiescence. Nevertheless, he couldn't let it go. "You're not one of us, Berenger. You're a goddamned private dick from New York City. You're not a police officer and you falsely identified yourself as one. I should have you arrested and spanked! You just better be damned thankful that your private investigator licenses are in order. Oh, but I'm afraid your handgun is still being processed so I can't let you have it back just yet. After the task force meeting, you'll fill out some paperwork. I know you have a license to carry it in Illinois, but you don't have the superintendent's permission. He's got to okay it from now on. Now, I normally wouldn't allow you to attend a meeting like this, but since you're the only one in the room that's actually *seen* our offender, and since you are unfortunately already heavily involved in this case, then we welcome you with goddamned open arms."

"Thank you, sir." Berenger grinned and fluttered his eyelids.

"Are you giving me shit?"

"Sir?"

"You were giving me shit!"

"I said 'thank you, sir.' Sir."

Prescott nudged him with her knee—*Cut it out!*

"You made funny eyes at me."

"Sir?"

"Are you deaf, Berenger? You made a stupid face."

"I didn't mean to, sir. I'm in a lot of pain this morning."

Doherty chose to end the confrontation. He glared at Berenger and then turned to a whiteboard.

Bastard, Berenger thought. And I don't need the damned superintendent's permission to carry my weapon. That's bullshit and Doherty knows it.

He wanted it now, damn it. He felt incomplete.

"All right, everyone," Doherty began. "Mr. Berenger did provide us with a description of the woman, although he didn't see her face. She's a white female, slim, around five feet, seven inches tall. Blonde hair to her shoulders. Pale complexion. Athletic and in shape. Age undeterminable. Now, thanks to our friends in the Evanston police force, and thanks to our colleagues in Area Four, we've amassed a collection of case files on all of the shootings of these musicians. I know we were reluctant to admit that the crimes were related, but it looks now as if they are. The Garriott murder busted the case wide-open and now the whole world is looking at us. I don't like heater cases, but we've got one and we have to work with it."

Doherty spent the next thirty minutes going over details from the four crime scenes that were similar—things Berenger already knew. Ballistics tests from the rounds recovered from the bodies of the Kriges, Monaco, Palmer, and Nance proved that they were fired from the same weapon. However, because they were nine-millimeter bullets, they could have come from a variety of handguns. "I suspect that rounds recovered from Mr. Garriott will be the same," Doherty said.

Aren't you smart? Berenger thought to himself. He raised his hand.

Doherty shot eye-daggers at the PI for interrupting him. No one did that, especially civilians who had no right to be in a Chicago PD task force meeting. He finally acknowledged the upraised arm. "Yes, Mr. Berenger?"

"What about the CDs found at the crime scenes?"

Doherty blinked. "Excuse me?"

"The compact disks. I know there were CDs with songs recorded on them found at each of the crime scenes. Except the one last night, of course. The shooter didn't have time to leave one, unless it was already hidden before the shooting and no one has found it."

"How do you know about the CDs, Berenger?"

The PI shrugged. "I just do."

Doherty scanned the room for any sign that one of his team members was the guilty party who divulged classified information. Luckily, Case made an impenetrable poker face.

"Berenger, you are indeed well informed. Yes, there were CDs left at the crime scenes, and no, there was not one left at Reggie's Music Joint."

"I'd like to hear them, sir."

"Why?"

"They could contain valuable clues as to who the killer is."

"I've listened to them and some of our other detectives have listened to them. We don't think there are any clues on the CDs."

"With all due respect, sir, how much do you know about rock 'n' roll?"

"I beg your pardon?"

"I'm an expert on rock 'n' roll. I might be able to hear something you didn't."

"Only select members of the task force will be allowed to listen to the CDs, Berenger. Last time I looked, you were not a member of the Chicago Police Department. You're a guest in this meeting."

"Does that mean you're not going to share the disks with me?"

"That's right, Berenger. I'm going to ask you to leave the crime-fighting to us. I can't force you to leave our fair city and butt out of the investigation, but I do believe that the party who hired you to come to Chicago is now dead. The City of Chicago is certainly not going to pay Rockin' Security for you to continue your investigation. So I suggest you and your pretty partner go home."

Berenger felt Prescott bristle beside him.

Doherty didn't wait for a response. He turned back to the group and continued. "You each have a folder containing some mug shots. We've put together a group of suspects. You'll all be assigned to track these people down and bring them in for questioning. To be honest, I don't put a lot of stock in most of them—they appear to be long shots. However, there is one suspect at the top of the list and I want us to take a good long look at him."

Him? Berenger wasn't sure he'd heard correctly.

Doherty held up a mug shot of a man in his forties. He wore makeup—eyeliner, eyeshade, and lipstick— but it had smeared during his arrest process. "This is Felix Bushnell. He's an ex-con and he has a history as a cross-dresser. He was pinched in the eighties for Peeping Tom activity and indecent exposure. Got probation. He was arrested in nineteen ninety-two and served six years in the state pen for armed robbery. His M.O. was dressing up as a woman and robbing people on the street. Very similar to what we have now—the only difference is that he didn't kill anyone back then. It's possible his crimes have escalated. Another consideration is that the robberies he committed were all after rock concerts. He targeted kids and young adults leaving various Chicago venues—you know, they were high or drunk after a show, making them easier victims. Currently lives in the Belmont and Clark area in an apartment above a sex shop."

Berenger took Case's copy of the mug shot and looked at it. Felix Bushnell was terribly ugly. The PI tried to imagine what the guy might look like wearing a blonde wig. He supposed it was possible Bushnell was the "woman" he had chased. The question was why would Bushnell want to start killing off rock musicians—and not rob them?

The meeting went on for another twenty minutes and Berenger tuned Doherty out. He and Prescott had an appointment with Stuart Clayton sometime that day, and Berenger didn't want to miss it. He needed to call the musician and set the time.

Finally, Doherty dismissed everyone and left the room. Mike Case rolled his eyes at Berenger and said, "Thanks for not giving me up on those CDs."

"I'm not a rat, Mike. Your secret is safe with me. Just see if you can get copies so I can hear them. I've got to call Stuart Clayton. Suzanne and I are supposed to go see him."

Prescott raised her eyebrows. "We're staying?"

"What do you mean?"

"We're continuing with the case? Without Zach?"

"For now, yeah. Is that a problem?"

She shook her head. "No, boss."

A young police officer approached Berenger and said, "Sergeant Doherty asked me to take you to fill out some paperwork on your handgun."

Berenger looked at Case. "Do I really have to do this?"

Case sighed. "I'm afraid so. Sorry. It shouldn't take more than an hour or two."

Berenger groaned and went with the officer.

* * *

It was after sunset when Berenger and Prescott finally pulled up in front of Clayton's house, which was located on Mango Avenue, just north of Irving Park Road. The paperwork Berenger had to fill out at the police station was ridiculous and time-consuming, and he knew Doherty had ordered it just to make the PI angry. There was an implication that if Berenger promised to get out of town, the return of his handgun could possibly be expedited. It was late afternoon by the time he finally phoned Clayton and made the appointment for that evening.

The neighborhood was middle-class but Clayton's house might have belonged in the ghetto. Even in the dark it was an eyesore. The yard and flower beds were overgrown with weeds, the place was in serious need of a paint job, and most of the shingles had long disappeared from the roof. No outdoor lights were on but dim illumination could be seen through drapes behind a front window.

"Joe Nance was right about Clayton living in a dump," Prescott said. "I bet his neighbors hate him."

"The poor guy's an invalid, you know."

"What, he can't hire a lawn service?"

"Maybe he doesn't have a lot of money, Suzanne. What's the guy live on? Surely not his record sales."

"Sorry. You're right."

"Let's go knock on the door."

They got out of their rented Subaru and approached the door. Prescott found a bell and pushed the button. They didn't hear anything, so Berenger knocked loudly. Nothing happened for thirty seconds, so he knocked again. Finally, there was the sound of shuffling feet behind the door.

"Who is it?" The voice was high, as if the speaker were frightened of whoever might be calling.

"Mr. Clayton? It's Spike Berenger and Suzanne Prescott from Rockin' Security. We spoke on the phone earlier today, remember? We had an appointment?"

Nothing happened for a moment. Berenger looked at Prescott and made a face—*What do we do now?*

But the lock rattled and the door creaked open.

The hallway was dark, so they saw only a silhouette of the man standing in front of them. He was of medium height and very thin. He supported himself on a cane, which he held in his left hand.

"Stuart Clayton?" Berenger asked.

"That's me. Come inside."

Distinct odors assaulted them as they stepped through the door. The stronger ones were of mildew and neglect, another being burned toast. Clayton closed and locked the door behind them, and then led them through the hallway and into a kitchen. The man walked slowly and with a limp, although not as pronounced as Berenger's.

The kitchen was filthy. Dirty dishes were stacked in the sink and appeared as if they'd been there for days, maybe weeks. Empty cans of food lay on their side and on the floor. A table that might have come from an abandoned diner was covered in stains. The refrigerator was old—probably from the sixties—and its motor made a gurgling, grinding noise.

"Sorry if the place is untidy," Clayton said. "Have a seat."

There were exactly three chairs around the table. They, too, appeared to be filched from a diner. The vinyl covering on all three was split in several places.

Clayton lowered himself slowly into one of the chairs and hooked the handle of his cane on the edge of the table. Berenger and Prescott took the other seats.

Now that the man was in the light, Berenger thought that Stuart Clayton looked pretty much the same as he had when the PI first met him in 1979. Sure, he was older, gaunter, and most of his short, dirty brown hair had turned gray. The man's skin was pasty white and creamy, as if he used moisturizer on a daily basis. Clayton's sad, haunted eyes told the whole story—he was a man who was not well.

"Do you remember me now, Mr. Clayton?" Berenger asked.

"You do look familiar, but I'm afraid I don't. Sorry. My memory isn't what it used to be. Please call me Stuart." He turned to Prescott. "And if I'd known you'd have such a lovely sister, I would have told you to come sooner!"

Prescott smiled. "Thank you. I'm Spike's partner, not his sister."

"Oh, I beg your pardon. I must have misheard you. That happens a lot, too."

Clayton had a voice high in timbre, but it was shaky and fragile—much the way he sounded on early Red Skyez records or his own solo albums. It was a singing voice that was an acquired taste for most listeners, but Berenger had always found it plaintive and poignant.

"Can I get you something to drink? I don't have much to offer. Maybe some fruit juice?" He had addressed this to Prescott.

"No, thanks."

"Thanks, Stuart, but we just had dinner," Berenger

said. "We'll ask some quick questions and then get out of your hair."

"All right."

Berenger then noticed that the lower left quadrant of the man's face was paralyzed. The left corner of his mouth refused to part when he spoke. A remnant of the man's stroke, perhaps?

"I'm sure you've heard what has happened to your old musical colleagues?"

"Yes. It's terrible. To tell you the truth, I'm afraid for my life. I told the police that when they came to see me but they don't seem to want to protect me."

"I understand they don't have the budget to put extra men on protection duty, Stuart. I know it sucks, but there's not a lot that can be done about it. Don't you have someone to come to the house and help you out? You told me on the phone that you have a maid or nurse or someone?"

"I told you that? No, no. I *used* to have a nurse who'd look in on me twice a week. I think she got fed up with me. I can be a cranky old fart. She gave notice . . . let's see . . . two weeks ago. I need to hire someone new."

"Are you able to get the things you need? Food? Supplies? Medicine?" Prescott asked.

"Oh, sure. I can drive my old car that's in the garage. I try not to, though. I still have a license but my reflexes are not what they should be. I drive pretty slow. Other drivers get mad at me and honk their horns. I only go out when I absolutely have to."

"If you don't mind my asking, how do you support yourself?"

"Oh. I have some money from a trust that my family set up when I became disabled in the seventies. It's not much, but I can live on it if I'm careful and don't spend too much each month."

"Do you still have family that help out?"

"No, they're all gone now."

Berenger nodded. "I see. Okay, then. Stuart, do you have any idea why someone is killing Chicagoprog musicians?"

Clayton made a face. "I hate that term. Chicagoprog. It doesn't make any sense. I don't know who coined it. We sure didn't. Probably some fool music journalist."

"But do you have an idea why this is happening?"

Clayton spoke slowly and hesitantly as if he had to think about what he wanted to say before he said it. "Well, sure. It's Sylvia. She's come back from the dead to kill us. It's that simple."

Berenger and Prescott shared a glance. "Tell us about Sylvia."

Clayton sighed and closed his eyes. "She was a young, beautiful girl. Very talented. She wrote wonderful songs and sang beautifully. I thought she could be the next Judy Collins. I wanted to take her under my wing, so to speak." He opened his eyes. The images he had conjured in his mind were gone.

"When did you first meet her?"

"She started coming to some of our early gigs. Nineteen sixty-seven, I guess. She wasn't shy about being a groupie."

"I understand the entire band became very friendly with her," Prescott said.

"That's right. She dated Joe Nance, I'm pretty sure.

I dated her. I use the word 'date' loosely, if you know what I mean. We all discovered drugs in sixty-seven and she was one of our suppliers. And don't ask me where she got them. I don't know and never asked. If I did know, I've forgotten."

"What do you think happened to her?"

"That first time she left town, she said she went to Europe to see her mother. The second time, well, I think she was abducted or something."

Berenger frowned. "Wait. You said 'first time.' What do you mean?"

"Oh. She left Chicago for several months in . . . I *think* it was late sixty-eight, early sixty-nine. We didn't see her for a long time and then she pops up again. Said she was in Europe."

"Where in Europe?"

"I don't remember."

"Okay, go on."

"So, she was back with us and things were just like they were before she left . . . and then one day she was gone again. We didn't think about it at first. Figured she was kind of flighty, you know? But after a few weeks we got nervous. I went to the police and filed a missing-person report. They didn't do much. And I never saw her alive again."

There was a short moment of uncomfortable silence.

"So, Stuart, if Sylvia is a ghost and she's really come back, why would she want to kill you all? I thought she was your friend."

"Oh, she's come back, all right. I've seen her!"

Berenger raised his eyebrows. "Tell us about that."

"It was right here in the house. I was in bed. I woke

111

up and there she was, standing at the foot of the bed. She was wearing that floppy hat she always wore. And sunglasses. It happened twice."

"And you're sure you weren't dreaming?"

"I wasn't dreaming, Mr. Berenger. I was wide-awake. And scared out of my wits."

"Did she say anything?"

"Yes. She told me that I would be the last to die."

Chapter Eleven

Photographs and Memories
(performed by Jim Croce)

Berenger and Prescott stayed longer at Clayton's house than they had planned. After talking for a while, Clayton mentioned that he hadn't eaten. Berenger offered to send out for a pizza and Clayton accepted. While they were waiting, Clayton suggested that he show them his home studio.

Unlike the kitchen and what they had seen of the house so far, the studio was clean and neat. It consisted of an extremely small soundproofed room containing a Yamaha baby grand piano, three different electronic keyboards, drum machines, amps, and microphones. All of the equipment was jammed tightly together and Berenger wondered how anyone could manage in there without becoming claustrophobic. The recording booth was big enough for two people to sit at a mixing board. Clayton explained that he usually did all of his own producing and mixing. He had to painstakingly walk back and forth from the booth to the studio as he set levels before actually sitting down to lay tracks.

"I never got along with outside producers," he explained.

Berenger noticed a door next to the studio and reached out to open it, but it was locked.

"Oh, that's just a storeroom," Clayton said. "I keep master tapes in there. Recordings of shows we did back in the sixties. That kind of stuff."

"You have recordings of any Loop gigs?" Prescott asked.

"Yes, I do. A few. Most of them are terrible quality. There are a handful of good ones."

"I'd love to hear one."

Clayton seemed to take pleasure in her request. "I don't normally dig those things out for people . . . but for you, my dear, I will."

The man hobbled to the door, reached into his pocket, and removed a ring containing several keys. He fumbled with them until he found the right one, and then unlocked the door. As Clayton went inside, Berenger got a glimpse of the interior. The storeroom was as big as the studio and mixing booth combined. It appeared to contain nothing but shelves filled with cartons of all shapes and old reel-to-reel tape boxes. Clayton grabbed one of the latter, emerged from the storeroom, and locked it behind him.

"I'll put it on in the studio, but you'll be able to hear it in my living room."

Unfortunately, the "living room" was as dusty and messy as the kitchen. Berenger found it strange that Clayton kept the music side of his residence sparkling, and yet the personal areas were pigsties.

Prescott sat on a couch after brushing off a layer of dust. She sneezed and pulled a tissue out of her handbag. "I'm not sure I can stay in here very long," she whispered. "Allergies."

"I know what you mean."

The music drifted through speakers that were attached to the upper corners of the room. The source was definitely an old tape of bootleg quality, but considering the time frame and primitive equipment upon which the concert was likely recorded, it sounded remarkably good. After an announcer introduced the band to scattered applause, The Loop launched into some old-fashioned Chicago blues but with decidedly up-tempo and technically proficient musicianship. Blues with a progressive slant—the cradle of what became known as Chicagoprog—and it was fabulous. Berenger felt as if he were listening to a piece of musical history that few people would ever experience.

Clayton entered the room, leaning heavily on his cane. "Is it too loud?" he asked.

"No, it's great," Berenger said.

"This sounds really good!" Prescott remarked.

"It does, Stuart. You should release this stuff. It's amazing!"

"Thank you. No, no, I don't think I can release it. It's too painful, really. I find I can't listen to it for very long. But we did play some pretty good music back then, I must say."

Berenger, who was still standing, wandered over to a fireplace that was full of age-old ash and debris. Above it was a mantle upon which dusty framed photographs sat. Berenger picked up one that caught his attention. It was a picture of The Loop onstage, probably circa the same time as the performance they were hearing. Clayton stepped over to join him.

"Ah, yes. That's us. I think that photo is from nineteen sixty-nine. Maybe."

Berenger pointed to the various members. "That's you on keys, of course, and there's Joe Nance. Charles is on the drums. Let's see, is that Harrison Brill and Manny Rodriguez?"

"Yes. That was taken before Dave Monaco or Jim Axelrod were part of the band."

A portion of the audience could be seen in the photo. A woman with a floppy hat and sunglasses stood against the edge of the stage, staring up at the band.

Berenger indicated her. "Is that . . . ?"

"Sylvia? Yes, that's her. I think I have another picture . . ." He went to another side of the room and picked up a frame from a cluttered desk. Berenger joined him and saw that it was a later photo . . . this time with Monaco and Axelrod instead of Brill and Rodriguez. The band, dressed in swimwear, was on the deck of a boat. They were holding up beer bottles and smiling at the camera. Everyone looked as if they were having a good time. Three women were also in the picture—including Sylvia. She still wore the hat and sunglasses, but this time with a one-piece bathing suit.

Sylvia Favero was model material.

"That's a nice picture," Berenger said.

"I wanted to use it for the cover of our album, but it turned out that The Loop never made one. That picture was in . . . late nineteen sixty-nine, maybe early nineteen seventy . . . just before Sylvia went missing."

"Where was it taken?"

"Lake Michigan. That was my boat. I had a nineteen sixty-eight luxury yacht, sixty-two footer. It was a . . . uhm . . ." Clayton snapped his fingers. "My brain can't remember things anymore. Pos . . . Posillipo! It was a Posillipo."

"Looks nice."

"I had to sell it when I . . . became ill." He put the photo back and then eased himself into a cushy chair. Berenger continued to stand as he examined the other photos and listened to the music. After a while, there was a loud knock at the door.

"Must be the pizza," Prescott said. "I'll get it." She got up and left the room.

Clayton struggled to stand. Berenger offered his hand but the man wouldn't take it. He relied upon his cane and stubbornly did it himself. "Let's go back to the kitchen to eat. You can still hear the music in there."

The three sat around the table with the food and glasses of fruit juice, and ate as they talked about mundane things such as the price of gasoline. When they were nearly done with the pizza, Berenger said, "Stuart, you never answered my question."

"Which one was that?"

"Why would Sylvia want to kill you all? She was your friend."

Clayton took a long time to answer. "I think perhaps we hurt her in some way."

"What do you mean?"

"She wanted to make a record of her songs. She wanted me or Joe to produce it. She wanted the band to play on it. We kept putting her off and putting her off. She was upset about it. One night, we were all pretty drunk and stoned. We were that way a lot, I'm afraid. She got mad at something. I can't remember what it was. It's all very foggy. She threatened us with violence if we didn't help her. She cursed us. I'm pretty sure that was the last time we saw her before she disappeared. That's one reason why I personally felt so bad about it. I didn't get a chance to make it up to her.

I was . . . well, I can say this, I suppose . . . I loved her." Clayton gave a wry smile—as much as he could with a corner of his mouth paralyzed. "So did Joe. I think Sylvia was one of the reasons Joe and I didn't get along too well there toward the end. Don't get me wrong—we each wanted different things with the band. He wanted to be the leader. I didn't mind that, but I wanted to leave Chicago and go to Los Angeles. He didn't. There were a number of problems, too. So, in nineteen seventy, The Loop split into two bands."

Berenger thought of the CDs in the possession of the police and asked, "Did Sylvia ever make *any* recordings?"

"I recorded her a few times. Demos. Very early on after we'd met. I don't have them anymore."

"You don't?"

Clayton shook his head. "I abandoned many things in the seventies. After I . . . was ill, I guess you could say I made a lot of changes in my life. I only kept the things that were most dear to me—and there weren't a lot. I lived in Europe for most of the eighties and got rid of even more trappings. By necessity I had to live simpler, and I've continued to do so since coming back to the States."

"Where did you live in Europe?" Prescott asked

Clayton took a sip of juice and said, "Oh, I . . . traveled . . . here and there."

Clayton looked down at his plate and didn't move for a while. Berenger and Prescott exchanged glances—*What now?*

"Perhaps we should leave you alone, Stuart," Prescott said. She reached out and touched his hand. Clayton slowly nodded, but he placed his hand on top of hers and held it tightly. "That might be a good idea. I think I need to turn off the music now."

Prescott gently pulled her hand away as she and Berenger stood. The PI reached into his pocket and removed one of his business cards. "My number's on there, Stuart." He put it on the kitchen table. "Call me if there's anything you need. Or if you remember anything that might help us solve these crimes."

Clayton nodded again. He appeared that he might be about to cry.

"Good-bye, Stuart," Prescott said.

"We'll show ourselves out," Berenger said. Together, they went to the front door, unlocked it from the inside, and left the house.

Once they were inside the rental car, Prescott said, "That was pretty uncomfortable."

"Strange guy. I feel sorry for him."

"Me, too. It's like he could break apart any minute."

"Yeah." Berenger started the car. "I think he liked you, though."

"I do, too."

"You probably gave him a little touch of something he hadn't felt in a long time."

Prescott laughed lightly. "Yeah, I have that effect on men."

Berenger pulled away from the house and headed back to the Drake Hotel. "You know what, though?"

"What?"

"I think he's hiding something, too. Just like Joe Nance."

"Really?"

"Yeah. Just a feeling. Those guys are not telling us everything about Sylvia Favero."

119

* * *

The killer sat naked on the bed, slipped on silk panties and a bra, and then pulled on the panty hose, one leg at a time. She then sat at her desk, dressed only in the underclothes. This made her feel something close to erotic.

Funny term, that. *Erotic.*

It had been a long time since she had experienced anything remotely sexual. There were times when the music made her feel young again. Sometimes putting on makeup and the feminine underthings did the trick.

But never mind that. She had given up sex long ago. On to more pressing matters . . .

She took her hit list and scratched a line through Zach Garriott's name. All that remained were those of Jim Axelrod, Harrison Brill, Manny Rodriguez, Joe Nance, and Stuart Clayton.

She sighed as she pondered the last one . . . *Stuart Clayton.* He would be the toughest to murder. But it couldn't be helped. He had known all these years that there would come a reckoning. As much as Clayton meant to her, the man would have to die.

And then she could finally lay to rest.

But what of her album? It had to be released, come hell or high water! She was entitled to it! And she needed the right person to see that it was done, too.

She leaned over and rummaged through the stack of periodicals and newspapers in the rack beside the desk. She found an old copy of *Rolling Stone,* turned to the page that was dog-eared, and opened it to a feature all about the firm in New York called Rockin' Security, Inc. There was a picture of the man who had been with Zach Garriott in the stairwell at Reggie's when she'd shot the guitarist.

Spike Berenger.

He had connections in the music business. He had clout. He was respected.

The killer smiled.

Chapter Twelve

Old Time Rock & Roll
(performed by Bob Seger
& the Silver Bullet Band)

Charles Nance was cremated on Sunday with no formal funeral. However, a memorial party was scheduled for that afternoon. Berenger and Prescott showed up at Schuba's, a music club that the remaining members of Windy City Engine and the guys in North Side rented out for the afternoon. It was located at Belmont and Southport in what was the Chicago PD's Area Three, Nineteenth District. Schuba's was also the club outside of which Joe Nance had allegedly seen the ghost of Sylvia Favero.

When the PI and his partner arrived, there were approximately a hundred people in the space. The bar was open in the next room and the guests were treating the event as a rock 'n' roll wake—plenty of booze and loud music. This suited Berenger fine. The last few days had been stressful. He was still sore from chasing the shooter the other night and he needed to unwind. The fact that it was the middle of the afternoon was not a deterrent.

"You're not going to get wasted, are you?" Prescott asked him as he made his way to the bar.

"Isn't that what you're supposed to do at a wake?" He ordered a beer and asked her what she wanted.

She rolled her eyes and shook her head. "Orange juice."

With drinks in hand, they joined the party. Joe Nance was already inebriated and holding court at a table near the stage. His wife sat next to him and Berenger thought he recognized their grown kids mingling nearby. Bud and Sharon Callahan sat at another table and it appeared that Bud and Nance were discussing the fine points of Internet CD promotion—very loudly. Rick Tittle and Greg Cross were clinking beers with two guys Berenger recognized as Harrison Brill and Jim Axelrod. Manny Rodriguez was laughing with a group of young women at a different table. There were other attendees from the music world on hand, the most famous being Bill Bruford, the prog and jazz drummer who had played with such bands as Yes, King Crimson, and UK, and now had his own outfit called Earthworks. Berenger thought he spotted a few members from younger Chicago acts like Umphrey's McGee, Fluid Time, The Buffalo Grease Band, Travel, Art Ensemble of Chicago, Tortoise, and Mr. Blotto. Chicago's XRT radio station DJs Terri Hemmert, Lin Brehmer, Marty "The Regular Guy" Lennartz, and Doug Levy also blended with the musicians. The rest of the crowd was made up of friends and family.

"I feel like an interloper," Prescott said.

"Come on, let's mingle." Berenger headed straight for Brill and Axelrod.

"Whoa, it's Spike Berenger!" Brill exclaimed. He firmly grasped the PI's hand. "I heard you wuz in town. How've you been?"

"Okay, Harrison. Good to see you. It's been a long

time." Berenger introduced Prescott to them and reminded Axelrod that they'd met many years ago.

"Sorry we have to see each other under these circumstances," the PI said.

"Yeah. How's the investigation going?" Brill asked.

"Too slow. In fact, with Zach gone, we have to de-
cide what we're going to do. Prescott and I can't stay
in Chicago indefinitely."

"I understand. Let me talk to Joe and Manny. Maybe
we can scrounge up enough cash to pay you for some
more time."

Manny Rodriguez and his entourage of women
came over and joined them. More handshakes and introductions.

"I'm glad I have the three of you together," Berenger
said. "You're the last guys I haven't talked to about all
this."

"Yeah, sorry. Manny and I were in Michigan," Brill
explained.

"I just flew in from L.A. last night," Axelrod offered.

Rodriguez shooed his female friends away and then
asked; "What do you think, Spike? Are we in danger?"

"Difficult to say. But if I can make a recommenda-
tion, you should travel around with a group when
you're in public. The killer's M.O. has been catching
her victims when they're alone or with one other person."

"Yeah, I heard about what happened to Zach. You
were there, weren't you?" Brill asked.

"I was there. We were in a stairwell with no one
watching. That's the thing. Stay with a group."

"So, do you have any suspects?" Rodriguez asked.

"Well, Joe thinks it's this girl you used to know

back in the sixties. Someone who went missing and was never heard from again."

Berenger noted that the three musicians shared glances.

"Sylvia Favero? You knew her, right?"

After a pause, Brill answered. "Yeah. We knew her."

"Joe's being a little nuts about that," Rodriguez said under his breath.

"So none of you have had any 'visions' of Sylvia?"

They answered negatively.

Prescott asked, "What do you remember about her?"

There was another hesitation, as if the men didn't want to talk about the woman. Then Rodriguez answered, "She was a party girl. A groupie. She hung out with us, smoked dope, drank, and had sex. And she liked all of those things."

"Gee, I understand she was a musician, too," Prescott said, not without sarcasm.

"Yeah, she was that. I guess she was pretty good. Joe thought she was. Stuart Clayton really liked her. He got her to open for us at least once."

Brill said, "I happen to think she had genuine talent. But she was wild and unpredictable. She lived alone and you never knew how to contact her. She didn't have a phone, if I remember correctly."

"That's right," Axelrod added. "I remember one night Stuart was trying to get hold of her for drugs and he was pissed off that he couldn't call her."

"So she did supply the band with drugs?"

"Yeah. Mostly pot and acid."

Berenger continued. "Clayton said that she might have been angry at the band for not backing her with the recording of her own album. Any truth to that?"

Rodriguez scratched his head and looked at the other two. "I don't remember that. Do you?"

Brill shook his head, but Axelrod said, "Yeah, I kind of remember something about it. She was after Stuart and Joe to produce it, I think. She wanted The Loop to be her backup band. I'm pretty sure there was a feeling among the band that we didn't want to do it."

"You mean besides Clayton and Nance?"

"Yeah. They were the ones bonkin' her the most," Rodriguez said.

"What about the rest of you?" Prescott asked with a little too much of what Berenger thought was an accusatory tone.

The three of them exchanged looks again. Rodriguez answered, "We all partied with Sylvia. But Stuart and Joe were her main squeezes."

"At the same time?"

Axelrod rolled his eyes. "I don't know. I never could figure out that relationship." The other two agreed.

Berenger said, "Look, guys, is there something about this girl you're not telling me? 'Cause I get the feeling that you, and Joe, and Stuart are all hiding something."

Before the men could answer, the clinking of a utensil on a glass interrupted them. The music was turned down and all eyes turned to Joe Nance, who was standing on the small stage.

"Can I have everyone's attention?" he shouted. Eventually the room quieted enough for him to speak. "Uhm, hi everyone. Thanks for coming. I'm sure Charles would have appreciated it. I'm not going to stand up here and say some maudlin speech or anything. I just wanted to say that you should have yourself some drinks—it's an open bar until five o'clock. If each of you has a drink for Charles, then that'll amount to what he usually drank each day."

People laughed.

"Uhm, I've talked to my buddies at Park West, and they've agreed to let us do a big blowout benefit concert this coming Friday night. It'll be to help out Zach Garriott's family and set up a musicians' scholarship fund in Charles's name at DePaul, where he went for, uhm, a semester. Windy City Engine—what's left of it—will headline. I've asked Jim Axelrod to participate, and I'm going to call Stuart Clayton tomorrow. Maybe we can coax that hermit out of his cave."

More laughs—skeptical ones.

"I'm sending out the word to some other Chicago bands to help us out. So, anyway, I hope everyone will cancel whatever plans you might have that night and come to the Park West for a historic gig."

Applause and cheers. Nance held up his hands to silence everyone again.

"Charles and I . . . well, we grew up together, you know. He was my kid brother. We were playing music together since we were old enough to pick up a guitar and bash on a drum. All my life I've played with Charles and I just can't imagine playing music without him. So I just want to say, well, I'm gonna retire now. As far as I'm concerned, Windy City Engine is no more as of Friday's show. Sorry Harrison, Manny. You guys can do what you want. If you want to keep the band's name, go ahead. I don't care."

"Shit," Rodriguez whispered. "Did you know that was coming, Harrison?"

"No."

Nance continued. "Anyway, that's my decision. But enough of me talking. Go on. Have a good time. Charles would have wanted a big blowout like this, so I don't want anyone walking out of here sober!"

The crowd applauded once more and Nance stepped down. He rejoined his wife at the table and took a big swig of beer.

"I guess we're not regularly employed anymore," Brill said.

"Fuck it," Rodriguez answered. "Windy City Engine should've hung it out to dry a long time ago. We'll do okay without it. We had a good turnout for the two of us in Detroit."

"I guess."

"It's the end of an era," Axelrod muttered.

Berenger wanted to continue pressing the men about Sylvia Favero, but he noticed Mike Case come into the room. "Excuse me fellas. There's someone I need to talk to."

Prescott broke away as well and went to speak with some of the other Chicago musicians. Berenger sided up to Case and asked, "What's up?"

The plainclothes officer handed Berenger a large envelope. "Those are copies of all the case files. The Kriges, Monaco and Palmer, Nance, and Garriott."

"Wow. Thanks, Mike."

"Still no luck with the damned CDs, though."

"Oh, geez. There's got to be something important on those disks."

"I think Doherty knows it was me who told you about them. He's been giving me more shit than usual. He figured out we were friends from way back."

"Sorry, man."

"It's nothing I can't handle." He looked at his watch. "I'm on third watch today and have to go on duty at three. I've got fifteen minutes to get to the station."

"Okay, Mike. I'll talk to you later. Thanks again."

Case left the party and Berenger rejoined Prescott, who was talking to a group of musicians in their fifties. Rodriguez, Brill, and Axelrod had separated and drifted away. Berenger figured he'd catch them another time in a more conducive environment.

"These guys are The Buffalo Grease Band," Prescott said, introducing her new friends to Berenger.

"Are you a musician?" one of them asked.

"Yeah, but that's not my day job," Berenger answered. "I was in a band called The Fixers, once. Ever hear of them?"

The four men shook their heads.

"Figures." He looked at Prescott. "I'm getting another drink. You want anything?"

"No, thanks."

Bud Callahan intercepted Berenger on the way out of the room.

"Hey, Spike."

"Hello, Bud."

"Listen, remember I told you I have a whole mess of newspaper clippings and articles all about the Chicago-prog scene? They go back to The Loop days. I have stuff on Sylvia Favero's disappearance, too. You might want to take a look at it. Could be helpful, I don't know."

"Where are they?"

"At my house."

"Thanks, Bud. Maybe I'll send Suzanne over to have a look. Is tomorrow okay?"

"Can't see why not." He gave Berenger his card. "My number's on there. Just call first."

"Will do."

Berenger stuck the card in his pocket and went to the bar. As he ordered another beer, he noticed an elderly African American man standing next to him, reading the *Chicago Sun-Times*. The paper was spread on the bar, open to an article about Zach Garriott's killing and the Chicago Musician Murders. The man, who appeared to be about seventy-five, tapped the paper and said, "This kind of thing didn't happen when I was playin' music."

"You a musician?" Berenger asked.

"I was. Until the arthritis got s'bad I couldn't play no more."

"What's your name?"

"Sonny Drake."

The bartender nodded at the man and explained. "Sonny's one of Chicago's great blues guitarists. He's a legend."

"I've heard of you," Berenger said. He held out his hand. "It's an honor to meet you, sir." The old man shook his hand.

"Back in my day, we didn't have to worry about assassins. It was dope that was killin' us off. Horse. Heroin."

"I hear you."

Drake jerked his head toward the party. "You wit' that crowd?"

"Yeah."

"I heard some of their music. Some years back. Can't say I liked it much. They took the blues and twisted it. Squeezed the soul right out of it."

Berenger shrugged. "It was a different take on it, I guess."

"I s'pose. Rock 'n' roll ain't what it used to be, that's for sho'. Back in the day it was all about what came from the heart. It was simple and to the point. Gimme some of that old-time rock 'n' roll. That's where it's at."

Berenger took a long sip of his beer and sighed. "Maybe you're right, pal. Maybe you're right."

The 1998 Chevrolet Malibu that sat in a legal space on Southport was positioned so that one could look out the back window—or in the rearview mirror—and see the front of Schuba's, approximately two hundred yards away. The car appeared empty to anyone who might have given it a glance. Even if someone had looked in the passenger window and seen the circa-1960s floppy hat on the seat, it was doubtful that there would be much concern.

Nevertheless, the owner was inside of the car. It was possible to place long objects in the trunk by folding the backseat inward. The excess portions of the items could extend into the car, lying across the seat. Thus, the killer found it easy to lie inside the trunk with a high-powered Heckler & Koch PSG1 sniper rifle. She had stolen the idea from the notorious Beltway shootings that occurred in the Washington, D.C., and Maryland area in 2002. By drilling a hole in the rear bumper large enough for the barrel to protrude, a sniper could shoot at a target without being seen.

From her vantage point, she had a perfect shot at Schuba's front doors.

Chapter Thirteen

Assassin
(performed by Motörhead)

At five o'clock, a hundred intoxicated party guests began to file out of Schuba's front doors. Prescott collected Berenger at the bar and helped him off the stool. He had been drinking steadily since he had struck up a conversation with Sonny Drake and was feeling, in his words, "comfortably numb."

"Come on, you big bozo," she said. "Let's go back to the hotel."

"Aww, Suzanne. You ain't mad, are you?"

"No. I had a good time in there talking to everyone. I could care less if you were out here wallowing in beer. But you better hand me the keys to the car."

"You're not drunk?"

"I've only had fruit juice, remember?"

"Oh, yeah." Berenger belched.

"Nice, Spike. Nice."

"Excuse me. Maybe it was that Polish sausage I had earlier."

She grimaced and waved her hand in front of her face. "Ugh! I think it was. Come on, let's get some fresh air."

Jim Axelrod stepped out of the main space just as

they reached the front door. He grinned widely when he saw them. "Spike! Suzanne!" The Red Skyez guitarist was also comfortably numb.

"Hello, Jim," Berenger said. "You've met my partner, Suzanne?"

"Sure have! You introduced us when you came in."

"Oh, yeah."

"She does TM, too!"

"TM?"

"Transcendental Meditation!"

"Oh, right. You're into that, Jim?"

"Uh huh. Twice a day for twenty minutes keeps the doctor away." He hiccupped.

"Spike," Prescott said. "Out. Now."

She opened the door for them and the two men stepped outside. Berenger lifted his arms and stretched. The sun was shining and it felt good after the rainy days.

"Hey, it's like spring!" Berenger bellowed.

"It *is* spring, Spike," Prescott said. "Come on, give me the car keys."

Axelrod stood next to them and peered at the sky as the PI dug into his trouser pocket.

The guitarist pointed. "Does that cloud look like a Fender Hot Rod Stratocaster or am I nuts?"

Berenger handed Prescott the keys, put a hand to his brow and looked up. "Damn, Jim! That *is* a Fender Hot Rod Stratocaster!"

"The Great Fender Hot Rod Stratocaster in the sky!"

They both laughed.

Berenger and Prescott heard the first *zip* but didn't associate it with what sounded like a car backfiring some distance away on Southport. But Axelrod inhaled loudly and violently, as if he'd suddenly had the wind punched out of him.

When they heard the second *crack*, the Rockin' Security team knew something was wrong. Axelrod stumbled backward and fell into the arms of Manny Rodriguez, who was just stepping out the door.

"Jim!" Berenger shouted.

Two crimson stains began to spread rapidly across Axelrod's chest. Rodriguez registered what was happening and, in fright, dropped the guitarist. Axelrod fell on his back in the doorway, still trying to catch his breath. He clutched his rib cage and writhed as Prescott pushed the crowd back into the club.

"Get back inside! Someone call nine-one-one! Now! Get back inside!"

Berenger dropped to a squat and went to draw his Kahr, but it wasn't there. The handgun was still at Area Five. He cursed aloud and stood straight, not caring if he was in the shooter's sights or not. He continued to look up and down both Southport and Belmont, but he didn't see any sign of the sniper.

"Spike, get inside!" Prescott shouted. She and Rodriguez dragged Axelrod back into Schuba's, but Berenger remained on the sidewalk. He was determined to find the perpetrator. The fog of alcohol had vanished in an instant. A massive dose of adrenaline had taken over and he was as sober as his partner.

"Spike!"

"I don't see anyone, do you?"

"Get inside!"

He slowly backed up, but his eyes darted in every direction, searching for any movement that might betray the sniper's position. Traffic continued to move on both streets and there were a few pedestrians, oblivious to what was happening.

"I'm gonna get you!" Berenger yelled as loud as he could. "I'm gonna find you, you hear me?"

Both Rodriguez and Harrison Brill pulled the PI inside and shut the door.

She waited until the ambulance and police cars arrived. As soon as there was a beehive of activity in front of the club, she left the rifle in the trunk, crawled out backward, pushed the backseat into a locked position, and maneuvered into the driver's seat without having to leave the vehicle. She started the car, carefully pulled out of the parking space, and drove away unnoticed.

It had worked. She had known Jim Axelrod lived in Los Angeles and today was probably her best opportunity to strike him off the list. The sniper rifle from her collection of firearms finally came in handy.

Surely it wouldn't take long for the police to find the plastic bag attached to the parking meter. It contained one compact disk and a song for the Garriott shooting, which she was unable to leave at Reggie's the other night, and a second CD and song for Axelrod.

Tracks six and seven. The album was nearly finished.

Chapter Fourteen

Would I Lie to You?
(performed by Eurythmics)

At midmorning on Monday, Berenger walked into the Area Five headquarters and asked to see Mike Case. He'd spent another several hours there the previous night, making a statement and going over it a hundred times. The station was the last place he wanted to be that morning except that Case asked him to come in. As Berenger waited in the reception area, he could feel the other police officers and support staff looking at him and whispering. *The star witness in the Chicago Musician Shootings is a dreaded private investigator and—even worse—from New York. The guy looks like an aging pothead. Sergeant Doherty wants to kick his butt back to the East Coast but the PI is connected with the mayor. Twice now he was standing next to a victim that was shot. Could he be involved? What's his story? Why is he here? And who's the good-looking woman who's always with him?*

Fine, Berenger thought. Let 'em talk. He didn't care.

Case eventually appeared and sat next to him on a bench. "Hey, Spike."

"Mike."

"Where's Suzanne?"

"I sent her over to Bud Callahan's place. He's got a

bunch of old clippings about the various bands. Who knows, maybe she'll find something everyone's missed. She's good at that kind of thing. How's Jim?"

Case shook his head. "Doesn't look good. He was in surgery most of the night. Still in ICU."

Berenger sighed heavily. "What'd you want to see me about?"

"The suspect, Felix Bushnell, is coming in for questioning. I thought maybe you'd want to get a look at him."

"You bet I do. But what about Doherty?"

"He doesn't want you around at all, but your friend the mayor must have said something to the superintendent, who said something to the commander. Doherty's supposed to cooperate with you. Not only that, you can pick up your handgun today."

"That's really fab, but the mayor's not my friend. I've never met him. Did Rudy get involved? Rudy knows him."

"Rudy's your boss?"

"He's my partner. We co-own Rockin' Security."

"That must be what happened."

Berenger smiled. "Good old Rudy. I knew I liked that guy for some reason. So, can we go upstairs?"

"Yeah. Come on. I was told to escort you and make sure you don't roam around by yourself."

They got up, were buzzed through the door, and climbed the stairs to the second floor.

"Doherty doesn't still think these shootings are armed robberies, does he?"

"I don't know what he thinks. But we had to lay it on pretty thick to get Bushnell to come in this morning. Threatened to put on a big show on his street with patrol cars, flashing lights, the whole shebang. I understand he's lawyered up, too."

"He's already here?"

"Yeah. His lawyer made sure he was brought in the back way. No publicity."

"I didn't see any press outside."

Case shrugged. "It's what Bushnell wanted."

Case led Berenger through a series of doors to an interrogation viewing room, where Doherty and several other detectives were watching. There was a one-way glass through which law enforcement officials could observe the questioning without being seen or heard by the suspect.

"You again?" Doherty grumbled. "Don't you ever go away?"

Berenger smiled and answered, "I've grown accustomed to your face, Doherty. I've decided to spend all my waking hours in your picturesque station. Gee, I left last night at two in the morning and I couldn't sleep because I just *had* to get back over here and see all my friends in uniform again."

"You're really annoying, you know that?" the sergeant fumed. He nodded at the window. "There you go, Berenger. Felix Bushnell. Ain't he pretty?"

The interview was already in progress. In the next room, two detectives sat at a table across from a man and his lawyer and their voices could be heard through a speaker above the glass.

Felix Bushnell looked like Iggy Pop during the glam heyday of makeup, androgyny, and glitter rock. He resembled the mug shot Berenger had seen, but in the flesh the guy appeared much more effeminate. He was a drag queen with a man's haircut. The makeup was pristine, complete with lipstick, eyeliner and shadow, and dangling earrings. His fingernails were polished red and he wore a black turtleneck pullover and black trousers. It was a very bizarre getup. Berenger wondered why the guy wasn't wearing a wig—it would have made the ensemble a bit more palatable.

"I *told* you where I was that night," Bushnell was saying in a voice that channeled Joan Crawford. "Would I lie to you?"

"Yeah, you said your alibi is airtight," the detective answered.

"Just like my anus. Can I leave now?"

Doherty groaned, looked down, and shook his head. "Un-fucking-believable." Others in the viewing room laughed.

One of the detectives said. "What'd you expect, Sarge?"

"Shut up, everyone," the sergeant said. "Berenger, the guy works as a drag performer in a club frequented by a—how do I say? An alternate lifestyle clientele. When he's working he does the whole female impersonation bit. By day he . . . looks like this."

Berenger didn't care about the suspect's lifestyle. He was more interested in the man's build and demeanor. Bushnell was in his early to midforties and was the right size. The suspect was thin and appeared to be in good health. Like many gay men, he apparently took good care of his body. With the right wig and sunglasses, it was entirely possible that Bushnell would resemble the shooter.

"Does he own any firearms?" Berenger asked.

"It's a condition of his parole that he can't own firearms," Doherty answered. "But he has a handgun in his apartment. He volunteered that information. It's registered to his brother, who lives in Rockford. And guess what—it's a nine-millimeter Browning."

"What about a sniper rifle? Whoever shot Jim Axelrod knew what he—or she—was doing. Does Bushnell have military or law enforcement experience?"

"No. But that doesn't mean he's not our guy. Or girl."

Berenger continued listening to the interview.

Detective: "Do you have a grudge against rock musicians?"

Bushnell: "Of course not. I love rock musicians. They throw great parties."

Detective: "Where were you yesterday afternoon at five o'clock?"

Bushnell: "I *told* you already. I was walking my dog in my neighborhood. You can ask Cinderella and Aurora's mom."

Detective: "Cinderella and Aurora?"

Bushnell: "Those are the pugs that live on my block. They're my dog's girlfriends. Named after the Disney princesses. I don't know their mom's name, but they saw me walking Butch."

Detective: "Your dog is named Butch?"

Bushnell: "That's right. Appropriate, wouldn't you say?"

Detective: "Why do you have a handgun, Felix? You know you're not supposed to."

The lawyer leaned over and whispered something to his client.

Bushnell: "I told you already. That's not my handgun. It's my brother's. He left it at my house the last time he was visiting. Look, would I lie to you?"

Detective: "We can get a search warrant to take it, you know. Run some tests on it. We can determine if certain bullets were fired from it."

Bushnell: "I know that. I watch television. Go ahead. Be my guest."

Berenger turned to Doherty and said, "Have you tried putting a wig on him?"

Doherty grimaced. "What the hell for?"

"I'd like to see him with a blonde wig on. Remember—I saw the shooter."

"But you didn't see his face. Or her face. If you had, we wouldn't let you watch this interview. If this ever went to trial and the defense knew you'd witnessed an interview, you couldn't testify for the prosecution."

"I understand that. I'm just trying to get a better idea of what this guy looks like with a blonde wig on."

The sergeant rubbed his eyes and said, "We don't have a blonde wig at the station, Berenger. This isn't a costume house. And the suspect didn't bring one with him, all right?"

Berenger nodded toward the window. "You say that's how he dresses when he goes out in public?"

"Yeah."

"So he's not really a cross-dresser."

"He puts on women's makeup and jewelry."

"But he wears men's clothes when he's not working."

Doherty shrugged. "So?"

"So, the man is gay and he's eccentric. He dresses up as a woman when he works. But unless he actually wears women's clothing when he's off duty, then he wouldn't be a cross-dresser."

"What the hell difference does it make? You think you're pretty smart, don't you, Berenger? When he was

142

arrested for armed robbery in ninety-two, he was dressed as a woman. We're waiting on a search warrant for his house, which we'll get this afternoon. Among other things, we'll be looking for a blonde wig, sunglasses, and a sniper rifle. Satisfied?"

"I guess so."

One of the other detectives in the room cleared his throat and asked, "Sarge, you gonna let the commander call in the feds?"

"Fuck no. We don't need no goddamned FBI. We're going to solve this case ourselves."

Doherty looked at Berenger and asked, "You think you could talk Joe Nance and the others into not having that benefit concert this Friday night?"

"Why would I do that?"

The sergeant held out his hands. "Gee, I dunno . . . maybe because they might get *shot* or something?"

"Look, Doherty, I'm just as concerned for their safety as you are. But if they want to put on a show to benefit their friends' and loved ones' families, I'm not going to stop them. I would, however, like to call in Rockin' Security's resources and work the concert. We're experts at that sort of thing and I believe we can protect them."

"You mean, you think you can protect them better than we can?"

"I think you should consider it."

"And who's going to pay Rockin' Security? Is Zach Garriott's family going to do that? Come to think of it, who's paying your bill now? The City of Chicago sure ain't. Are you working for free?"

"Maybe I am. I haven't thought about it."

"Well, you can forget about providing security for

the concert. We can handle it. The venue has its own security teams and we'll beef it up with a few men and work the street outside."

"What about the CDs?"

"What CDs?"

"The compact disks left at the crime scenes. I understand the shooter left two more yesterday. One for Axelrod, and one to make up for not leaving one when she killed Zach."

"No, Berenger. Forget it."

"I can help you, damn it!"

Doherty addressed Case. "That's it. Get him out of here. He's seen enough. I don't care if your buddy in New York did call the mayor. I can cooperate as much as I see fit. I'm lead investigator. I call the shots. Go on. Scram."

Everyone in the room except Case looked at Berenger with contempt. Case was simply embarrassed.

The PI sighed and said, "Okay. I hope you guys know what you're doing. I'm going to pick up my weapon. Thanks for keeping it *safe* for me."

He turned to leave just as Bushnell answered a question with, "Yes, I shave my legs. Would I lie to you?"

Chapter Fifteen

Long Time Gone
(performed by Crosby, Stills & Nash)

Prescott sat in front of a table cluttered with newspaper clippings, envelopes, music posters, ticket stubs, and other artifacts of memorabilia associated with Chicagoprog's long and tortured history. It was a bit overwhelming, but Bud and Sharon Callahan were hospitable and friendly by providing her with plenty of coffee and refreshments. Neither of them worked day jobs, so they were available all day to answer questions.

"I can't believe how well organized this is," Prescott told Bud. "It's all in chronological order and everything."

"That's 'cause I'm anal. And a Virgo," he remarked. "I haven't looked at this stuff in years. Let me know if you find my orthodontic retainer. I lost it years ago."

A centerpiece of the collection was a scrapbook that Sharon had put together during the seventies but eventually allowed to let slip. Nevertheless, it was fairly complete up to the midseventies. Beyond that, the clippings were loose and not archived. Prescott spent most of the morning going through the book, reading the articles and examining candid photographs taken at gigs and backstage.

"How well did you know The Loop when it was active?" she asked.

"I knew all those guys pretty well. I was a couple of years behind them in high school, so they were like gods to me. After I graduated in sixty-nine, I tried going to college and doing the sensible thing. But after two years, I was fed up with school. I followed my calling, which was music. So in seventy-one, I formed Rattlesnake. Rick Tittle, the drummer, and I were already good friends and he knew this bass player from Italy who was interested in being in a band. So by seventy-two we were gigging and recording our first and only album."

"The guy from Italy was Sandro Ponti?"

"That's right. You're well-informed."

"Spike knows him. What happened to the band?"

"Success was slow and pretty much nonexistent. Sandro went back to Italy in seventy-five. So Rick and I formed another band and we called it South Side. By then Red Skyez was in Los Angeles and doing fairly well, but there were personnel changes going on. Dave Monaco came back to Chicago and joined us. We enlisted a young guitarist named Paul Trinidad and the new band was complete."

"And then South Side became North Side?"

"Yeah, when Dave and Paul left, we replaced them with Zach Garriott on guitar and Sharon took up the bass. That's when things really started happening for us."

Prescott touched some photos in the scrapbook. "Okay. Let's go back to The Loop for a minute. When were these pictures taken?"

Callahan leaned over her shoulder. The photos depicted a young band on stage and in a dressing room.

"Oh, yeah. That's from nineteen sixty-nine. The Loop was playing at the old Kinetic Playground, which isn't there anymore. I was at that show. I took the pictures."

Prescott pointed to a girl hanging on to Stuart Clayton in the dressing room. "Is this . . . ?"

"Yeah. That's Sylvia."

Other photos from the same set also showed the young woman clinging to the arm of Joe Nance.

"She seems to be pretty friendly."

"That she was."

"Was there any jealousy going on within the band?"

"Over Sylvia?"

"Yeah."

"If there was, it was only between Stuart and Joe. Charles, Harrison, and Manny weren't that interested, although I'm sure they had their way with her a few times. And later on, Jim and Dave probably had their turns, too, but there wasn't any rivalry that I know of."

A couple of photographs featured Sylvia on stage, singing into a microphone. She was wearing the trademark floppy hippie hat and sunglasses, along with flower-child clothing.

"Her outfit is very 'summer of love,'" Prescott remarked. "Isn't sixty-nine a little late for that?"

"Yeah, Sylvia always dressed that way, before *and* after it was fashionable. She was in tune with what was going on in England and Europe long before that stuff came over here. She was kind of locked into that peace-and-love spirit, if you know what I mean.

Hey, remember I mentioned that I think I have a recording from that show? I found it."

"Really?"

"Hold on, let me go get it."

Callahan left the room and Prescott continued to study the scrapbook. Eventually she found a small news item from August 1970, reporting a missing woman. The article stated that Sylvia Favero, age twenty-two, was reported missing and hadn't been seen in two months. She was described as an aspiring musician and poet. Her only known family was an American mother in Italy.

"Italy," Prescott murmured.

A second clipping, dated two weeks later, featured a poor photo of the woman. The detective in charge of the case was quoted as saying, "Young people run away every day without telling anyone. Until we have evidence of anything otherwise, that's how we're treating this. But we're not discounting theories that Ms. Favero ran into foul play."

A few minutes later, Callahan returned with a portable reel-to-reel tape recorder and a tape. "Found it. Let me plug it in."

The recording was primitive. The microphone was obviously in the audience, so it picked up more chatter and noise than it did of the music. Nevertheless, Prescott could get a sense of The Loop's performance and repertoire. It was very similar to what she and Berenger had heard at Clayton's house, only not as well recorded.

"Hold on a sec," Callahan said. He fast-forwarded the tape a bit and then switched it back on. The setting was different. People were talking and laughing.

"This was recorded in their dressing room during the intermission," Callahan said. "I brought the recorder back there with me and got all this on tape."

The band members were recounting how the first set had gone, describing who was in the audience, and what they were going to do after the show. Prescott recognized the voices of Joe Nance, Stuart Clayton, and Manny Rodriguez. She assumed the other ones belonged to Harrison Brill and Charles Nance. Women also occasionally laughed or said something.

"Who are they?" Prescott asked.

"One of them is Sylvia. I couldn't tell you who the other two are. Girlfriends at the time, I suppose. Or other groupies. I don't know."

Prescott listened carefully.

JOE: "<GARBLED> . . . FOR ANOTHER SHORT SET. YOU UP FOR IT?"

SYLVIA: "SURE."

STUART: "WANT ME TO PLAY PIANO?"

SYLVIA: "<GARBLED> . . . NOT NECESSARY . . . <GARBLED> THE FUN OF IT!" (LAUGHS.)

CHARLES: "YOU CAN SAY THAT AGAIN!" (MORE LAUGHS.)

SYLVIA: "<GARBLED> . . . TONIGHT AFTER THE SHOW!"

SEVERAL MEN: "WOO HOO! ALL RIGHT!"

STUART: "NO WAY, GUYS! SHE'S ALL MINE!"

JOE: "SCREW YOU, MAN. SHE KNOWS WHO'S GOT <GARBLED> . . ." (LAUGHTER.)

STUART: "HEY, BUD, GET THAT OUT OF HERE! GO ON . . . <GARBLED>"

The recording switched again. This time Sylvia was performing alone with a guitar. She had a strong soprano voice that carried the melodies in a wistful, ethereal style. The audience was talking more than before, not paying much attention.

"I remember she opened up both sets, which was unusual," Callahan said.

"She sounds like Judy Collins," Prescott noted. "Or maybe Joni Mitchell, a little. And this was sixty-nine?"

"Yeah. I thought she was pretty talented. Unfortunately the audience didn't give her a fair shake."

"Is this her material?"

"She always performed her own material."

"It's pretty good. Do you have more of her?"

"Nope. I'm pretty sure that was the only time she opened for them. There *may* have been another time later, like early nineteen seventy, but I wasn't there."

Prescott went back to the scrapbook. There were no more clippings about Sylvia after the last one she'd seen.

"So that's it?" she asked. "No more news on Sylvia? The police just wrote it off?"

"I guess so. There was never any closure to the case. We all just went on with our lives and, well, forgot about it, I'm sorry to say. Like I told you before, I never really knew her. The only guys who really knew her well were in The Loop."

"Zach Garriott didn't know her well. The Kriges probably didn't know her well."

"But they were in a band that sprung from The Loop. They were in later incarnations of Red Skyez."

"Yeah, that seems to be the killer's thing. She's targeting anyone who was connected to The Loop. You never played with them?"

"No, I was just a friend. I never played with them, or Red Skyez, or Windy City Engine."

"Then maybe you're lucky."

"Maybe I am."

Prescott's cell phone rang. She dug it out of her purse, noted that it was her partner, and answered it. "Hey, Spike. What's up?" She listened for a few seconds and then her face dropped. "Oh, no. Yeah. Okay. I'll meet you at the hotel. I'm just about finished here. Yeah. Bye."

She hung up and sighed.

"What is it?" Callahan asked. Sharon entered from the kitchen to join him.

"Jim Axelrod just died. The killer can now claim seven victims."

Chapter Sixteen

Taken by Surprise
(performed by The Outfield)

Prescott met Berenger in the Coq d'Or Lounge at the Drake Hotel. It was an elegant, dark-wood martini bar with comfortable red leather chairs where guests could order drinks, refreshments, and breakfast all day long. The Drake was a classic establishment that opened during the height of Prohibition and the era of the legendary Chicago gangsters. Berenger was impressed that Frank "the Enforcer" Nitti kept an office in the hotel in the thirties and forties. Sitting in the Coq d'Or made him feel as if he'd stepped through a time tunnel and was holding court with Al Capone and his cronies— even though the only other people in the bar were a few Japanese businessmen, a group of elderly women, and Prescott.

He had Case's files with him and was going through them when his partner joined him. They both ordered bar snacks and Virgin Mary's. The previous day's binge hadn't sat well with Berenger, so he had vowed to lay off the alcohol for the next day or two.

"There's nothing in these files we don't already know," he said. "Nothing that gives us any clue as to the identity of our shooter. I tell you, Suzanne, I'm not sure what to do next."

"Should we go home?"

Berenger looked at her. She had a point. They were no longer being paid for the job. Nance and the rest of the band had not come back with an offer to keep them on. It didn't appear that the City of Chicago wanted them around either. And yet Berenger felt an obligation to stay and figure the thing out.

"I'll give Rudy a call. But in a minute. Tell me what you learned at Bud's."

Prescott quickly ran through what she had discovered, including the fact that Sylvia Favero's mother lived in Italy. She told him about the concert tape and hearing Sylvia's speaking voice and songwriting talent.

Berenger opened his cell and dialed New York.

Melanie Starkey's pleasantly sexy New Jersey voice answered the ring. "Rockin' Security."

"Ringo, it's Spike."

"Hi, Spike. Howzit goin'?"

"Okay. Let me talk to Rudy, will you?"

"Hold on."

After a few seconds, Bishop answered. "Hey, Spike."

"Rudy, we need to talk."

"Okay."

"Suzanne and I are sitting here wondering what we should do about this case. As you know, Zach is not with us anymore and no one is paying the bill."

"Yeah, and that concerns me. How close are you to solving the damned thing?"

"Well, to be honest, I'm not very close at all. In fact, I'm kind of stumped."

"Then maybe we should get out now, Spike. The firm does pretty well, but it doesn't pay for vacations in Chicago."

"I know. It's just that . . . I just need some more time and I think maybe something's going to break. I feel it."

Bishop sighed heavily. "I appreciate your sixth sense about these things, Spike, that's why you're good at what you do. But I don't know. We have some other cases pending. I could use you back in New York."

"I know. Listen . . . this has become a little personal for me. After all, I was shot at. Twice! The assassin's bullets could have missed their targets and hit me instead."

"But they didn't. She's obviously a pretty good shot."

"Whatever. Okay, how about this? Friday night there's a benefit concert for Zach and some of the others. Windy City Engine is playing. How about I stick around through Friday? If I haven't picked up something solid to go on by then, we'll come home this weekend."

"I don't know . . ."

"That's only four days. We'll fly back on Saturday morning."

"Spike, you're the other half of this organization. You can do what you want. But if you're looking for my blessing, all right. Go ahead. But how about you let me know by Thursday how the progress is going."

"Will do. Now transfer me to Tommy."

"Okay. See you."

Another few seconds of dead air, and then—

"Briggs."

"Tommy, how are things?"

"Spike! Okay."

"Remix staying out of trouble?"

"No. Are you kidding?"

154

"Well, it's good to know nothing changes when I'm gone. Listen, I need you to use all of your connections to do extensive background checks on some people. By that, I mean I want to know their movements—in and out of the country—and at home. For the last thirty years."

"Jesus, Spike. We have a special on building pyramids. I think we can get that done faster."

"And I need it by Thursday."

Berenger knew that Briggs was wincing. "Who are they?"

"The first is Sylvia Favero. We know a little about her, right? We need to know everything. Who are her parents? Where are they? We have some information that her mother may have lived in Italy—or maybe still does. Find out. Also, what kinds of attempts did law enforcement make in trying to find her when she went missing? Where did she go in nineteen sixty-eight when she was gone for a few months? And what conclusions did the police make regarding her disappearance?"

"Okay."

"The next two are Joe Nance and Stuart Clayton."

"Really?"

"I'm afraid so. They're hiding something. They *all* are, but I have a feeling that whatever is happening is because of something involving these three people."

"I'll do what I can."

"Thanks. Talk to you soon." He hung up and then concentrated on finishing his snack.

"What do you want to do the rest of the day?" Prescott asked him.

"I'd like to see Clayton again. I'd like to see Nance

and the other guys again. I'd like to hear those damned CDs that Doherty's hogging like gold. And I'd like—"

Berenger's jaw dropped as he stared toward the lounge entrance. Prescott followed his gaze and was just as surprised.

"Oh my God . . . Did you know she was going to be here?" she asked.

Berenger simply shook his head.

His ex-wife, Linda, had just walked into the Coq d'Or with a tall, bald man. The mustache gave his identity away as her fiancé, Richard Noyce. The look of surprise on her face when she saw Berenger was just as individualistic as his own.

"I don't believe this," Berenger whispered.

"That's the guy she's marrying?"

"Uh huh."

"He looks like Yul Brynner."

"I know. I keep wanting to ask him to 'let my people go.' Oh, hell, they're coming this way."

Linda and her fiancé approached the table. Berenger immediately put on his best smiling face and stood.

"Linda! Well, I'll be. What are you doing in Chicago?"

"I was going to ask you the same thing," Linda said, smiling but obviously not pleased. "Hello, Suzanne."

"Hi, Linda. How are you?"

"Fine."

Both Berenger and Linda seemed at a loss as to what to do next. Finally, Berenger blurted, "Suzanne, this is Mr. Cl—"

He had almost said "Clean" but stopped himself in

time. The man finished the introduction for him. "Noyce. Richard." They shook hands.

Linda put a hand to her face and turned red. "I'm sorry, I wasn't thinking. Richard, this is Spike—you've met him before. Suzanne Prescott."

Berenger stood there nodding his head like a fool and then Prescott said, "Why don't you two sit down and have a drink with us?"

The PI concurred through his teeth while still grinning, but he wanted to strangle his partner.

Linda looked at Noyce inquisitively, and he said, "Sure. We have time."

It was a booth—Prescott had been sitting across from Berenger, so Noyce sat next to her. Linda was forced to sit in the vacant space beside her ex-husband. Berenger reclaimed his spot, the smile frozen onto his face.

"So what are you doing in Chicago, Spike?" Linda asked.

"I told you I was coming here. We have a case, remember?"

"You said you were going out of town, but you didn't say it was Chicago."

"I didn't?"

"No. Otherwise I would have said, 'Gee, what a coincidence, Richard and I are going to Chicago, too.'"

"I do remember you saying you guys were going to a conference somewhere. You didn't say Chicago?"

"I guess not," Linda said, shrugging.

Noyce spoke up. "I'm attending the annual AIA national convention. It's in Chicago this year."

"AIA?" Berenger asked.

157

"American Institute of Architects."

"Oh, right. You're an architect. Suzanne, Richard's an architect."

"I think I got that, thanks," Prescott said.

A waitress appeared and took their order. Linda and Noyce each ordered a glass of white wine. Prescott ordered fruit juice. Berenger ordered a double vodka martini.

So much for laying off the alcohol for a couple of days! he thought. As soon as it arrived, he consumed several sips very quickly.

"Chicago's nice this time of year," Linda said.

"It's been raining a lot since we've been here," Prescott remarked. "The sun just came out in the last couple of days."

"Yeah, we've been here since Friday," Noyce said.

"Where are y'all staying?" Berenger asked. That was one of the remaining traits from his Texan upbringing. He had managed to get rid of a Texas accent, but he still couldn't help saying the word "y'all."

"Here, in the Drake," Linda answered.

"Here? The Drake Hotel?"

"That's right."

"We're in the Drake Hotel, too."

"Really?"

"You've been here since Friday?"

"Yes."

"And we haven't seen you before now?"

Prescott snickered. "It's a big hotel, Spike."

Berenger took a big sip of his martini.

"I love it," Noyce said. "The design is fabulous. Chicago has some of the best architecture in any American city. Have you done the architectural boat tour?"

Berenger shook his head. "Can't say that I have. There's an architectural boat tour?"

"Yes, sir. It goes along the Chicago River and they point out all the interesting landmarks."

"Sounds . . . great!"

"I've done it, Spike," Prescott said. "It really is cool."

"When did you do it?"

"I don't know. Years ago."

"So," Noyce said, "I understand you're in the rock 'n' roll business?"

"That's right."

"Linda's told me a little about it. You're not a musician, right?"

"Well, I am a musician. Just not a working one."

"Oh, that's right. You run a security operation. You're one of those guys that frisks kids when they go to a concert?"

Berenger wasn't sure if the guy was insulting him or just stupid. "No, I don't do that myself, but sometimes I hire firms that employ guys that do that."

"Spike's a private investigator in the music business," Linda explained. "I've told you that."

"Oh, that's right, I forgot," Noyce said. "That sounds pretty interesting. Do you get to meet a lot of famous rock stars?"

Berenger shrugged. "Sometimes." He had a sip of martini.

"Who have you met?"

Berenger didn't know where to begin. "Oh, I don't know. Just about everyone, I guess."

"Bruce Springsteen?"

"Sure."

"Wow, you've met The Boss? That's incredible! I love Springsteen. How about Billy Joel?"

"Billy Joel?"

"Yeah, have you met him?"

Berenger slapped the table. "Damn. You got me there. I haven't met Billy Joel. The score is one to one. Name someone else."

Noyce was getting into it. "Paul McCartney?"

"Yes."

"Eddie Vedder?"

"Yes."

"Miles Davis?"

Berenger frowned. "He's not a rock star. He's a jazz star." As he finished the martini, both Linda and Prescott eyed each other—they both knew what could happen if he drank too much too quickly.

"So? He's in the music business."

"Who?"

"Miles Davis."

"He was in the music business. But, no, I never had a chance to meet him."

"Then the score is three to two."

"Are you guys *nuts*?" Linda spouted.

Noyce laughed. "I'm just having fun. What kind of music do you like, Spike?"

"Please, don't get him started," Linda groaned.

"You want to talk music?" Berenger asked.

"Sure. Everyone likes music, don't they?" Noyce nodded at the two women for approval.

"Richard, really, I—" Linda said with a little more apprehensiveness.

"Let's see," Berenger began, "I like early rock 'n' roll, I like The Beatles, I like rhythm 'n' blues, I like jazz, I like jazz-fusion, I like film music, I like TV music, I like hard rock, punk rock, heavy metal, psychedelia, new wave, alternative, I like novelty music, pop rock, soft rock, folk rock, country rock, space rock, jam bands, glam and glitter rock, Krautrock, Zeuhl, world music, reggae, new age, rap, hip-hop, a lot of classical stuff, experimental and avant-garde—"

"Spike, Jesus!" Prescott snapped.

"—but mostly I'm into prog," he finished, and then looked around for the waitress. "How about another round?"

Prescott cleared her throat. "Uhm, Spike, you probably shouldn't have another. We have some work to do—"

Berenger caught the waitress's attention and summoned her over.

"What's prog?" Noyce asked.

"Richard, no!" Linda shuddered.

Berenger asked for another martini and then turned back to Noyce. "Progressive rock. You know, the stuff that draws from not only rock 'n' roll, but from classical music. It's more complex and the musicianship is of virtuoso level. I'm sure you'd know it when you hear it."

"Name some bands I'd know."

"Well, the biggest prog bands were Pink Floyd, Yes, Genesis—the early stuff with Gabriel, not what they did later—a few years in the career of Jethro Tull, Emerson Lake and Palmer, The Moody Blues, King Crimson, some Frank Zappa. Hell, The Who did a rock opera and that's prog—"

"Oh, sure, I know what you mean now. I like that stuff okay."

"But that's just the most well-known . . . the true believers like more esoteric stuff, you know, like Gentle Giant, Gong, Soft Machine, Marillion, Porcupine Tree—"

"I haven't heard of those," Noyce admitted.

"Hatfield and the North?"

"No."

"Ozric Tentacles?"

"Nope."

"Samla Mammas Manna?"

"What?"

"Spike! Enough!" Linda said. "Come on, Richard, finish your drink and let's go, otherwise we won't have a lot of time in Old Town."

Noyce nodded. "We're going to Old Town this afternoon."

"I thought you were at an architects' conference."

"That was over the weekend. Linda and I had planned to stay a few days in Chicago and see some sights."

Before Berenger could react to that, his cell phone rang.

"Excuse me." He whipped it out and answered the call. "Spike Berenger."

"Mr. Berenger?"

It was a woman's voice. Low in pitch. Friendly. Almost sensual.

"Yes?"

"Is it a good time to talk?"

"Who is this?"

There was a pause before the woman answered, "My name is Sylvia Favero."

Chapter Seventeen

Living Dead Girl
(performed by Rob Zombie)

Berenger put his hand over the mouthpiece and announced to the group, "I have to take this call." He then quickly stood, moved out of the booth, and walked toward the front of the bar, where he couldn't be heard.

"How do I know it's you?" Berenger asked. "And how did you get my number?"

"Your number was easy to get. And you'll know it's really me after I ask you a question."

"What's that?"

"Have the police allowed you to listen to my CDs yet?"

Berenger felt a cold chill run up his spine. Only the Chicago PD knew about the compact disks. And the killer.

"No, they haven't. I'd like to hear them."

"Well, Mr. Berenger, I want you to hear them. In fact, I'd like to interest you in a little business deal."

Berenger's heart was pounding. He didn't know if he should tell her that he never made deals with murderers, or if he should play along and perhaps get her to reveal more about herself.

"What do you have in mind?" he asked.

"You have connections in the music industry, right?"

"I suppose."

"You could help get a record made. With your influence. You know some people. You've probably done favors that need repaying. If you had to—or *wanted* to—you could get a record made. Am I correct?"

Berenger knew where this was going. "I could probably do that, yes. But getting it distributed is another thing altogether."

She was persistent. "But you have connections. To major labels. To distribution."

"Okay, let's say I do."

"I want to turn over my album to you. You're going to produce it and see that it gets distributed. I'll give you fifteen percent of all sales, just like an agent or manager."

Berenger almost laughed at the absurdity of it. "You want me to produce your album?"

"That's right."

He needed to keep her talking. Learn more about her.

"Why are you killing these musicians, Sylvia?"

"They know why, Mr. Berenger."

"You can call me Spike. What do they know?"

"They know why I'm doing this. Every one of them. And I can't let any of them continue the sickness."

"The sickness?"

"The plague that began in nineteen sixty-seven, when I first met them. The pestilence that ended in nineteen seventy, when I died."

Berenger rubbed his eyes. The woman was out of her mind. "Are you telling me that you're dead?"

"Look, if I get you the CDs, will you agree to the deal?"

"You know I can't guarantee I can get an album produced and distributed. I can try but I can't guarantee it!"

"Once you hear it, you won't just try, you'll *want* to do it."

"Maybe that's true. How do I get the CDs?"

"I'll get back to you. Don't tell the police I've called you, or you won't hear from me again."

She disconnected the call. Berenger immediately tried to redial the number but it was busy. According to his Calls Received list, it was a Chicago number. He quickly punched in Rockin' Security's number and told Melanie to transfer him to Tommy Briggs.

"Tommy, I need you to get the records for a mobile phone number. Fast! Grab a pencil."

"Go ahead, Spike."

Berenger gave him the number. "Get back to me as soon as you can."

He hung up and went back to the table. "Who was that?" Prescott asked.

"I'll tell you later." He addressed Linda and Noyce. "Listen, guys, it was really, really awesome to see you here, but Suzanne and I have to run."

"Oh, sorry to hear that," Noyce answered. "I was just getting interested in the music talk."

"You check out some of those bands I mentioned." He shook hands with the man.

"Uhm, I will!"

Berenger then clumsily leaned over and kissed Linda on the cheek. "See you later, babe."

Surprised, Linda gasped slightly and said, "Goodbye, Spike." She rubbed her hand across her cheek and tried her best to smile. Berenger helped Suzanne up and rushed her out of the bar.

"What's going on, Spike?"

"Sylvia Favero just called me."

"What?"

"You heard me."

"Jesus! Where are we going?"

"I don't know. I had to get away from those two. I couldn't think."

They stood in the expansive hotel lobby. "You mean you don't have a plan?"

"I have to wait for her to call me back. She's going to give me the CDs." He told her about the killer's proposition.

"Spike, you can't agree to do that."

"Why not?"

"That woman has been killing friends of yours!"

"I know. But maybe this will get us closer to her."

"Are you going to tell Mike Case about it?"

Berenger rubbed his chin. "Not yet. I want to see how this plays out. I want to be absolutely sure I'm not being taken for a ride."

"So what do we do while we wait for her to call you back?"

"Let's try to see Stuart Clayton again. Then we'll go talk to Joe Nance."

Berenger tried to redial Sylvia's number one more time but it was still busy. "Let me use your phone to call Clayton. I want to keep my line open."

Prescott handed her cell to him and he dialed Clayton's number.

"Hello?"

"Stuart, it's Spike Berenger. How are you?"

"Who?"

"Spike Berenger. Suzanne Prescott and I were over at your house a couple of days ago. From Rockin' Security."

"Oh, yes. Hello."

"Listen, Stuart, I've thought of some more things I'd like to talk to you about. Would it be convenient if we stopped over again today?"

"Stopped over?"

Clayton sounded disoriented. He'd either been asleep or was drugged.

"For a little while. I have a few questions I'd like to ask you about Sylvia."

There was silence at the other end.

"Stuart? You there?"

"Mr. Berenger, I have nothing more to say to you. I've already told you everything I know. I've told the police the same things. All this stuff brings back painful memories and I have enough problems. Please leave me alone and don't call again."

Berenger tried a different tact. "Stuart, I heard from Sylvia. She called me."

There was some shuffling on the line and then Clayton said, "Perhaps you'll believe me now. I told you I'd seen her."

"So let's get together and talk about her."

"No, I don't think so. I said I didn't want to discuss her anymore. Good-bye, Mr. Berenger. I hope you catch her."

Clayton hung up and Berenger cursed.

"No luck?" Prescott asked.

"No. Let's try again tomorrow and you ask him. He liked you better than me."

167

"Okay."

"Let's go drop in on Joe. Screw this calling people and warning them beforehand. Let's surprise him."

And they strode out of the hotel to the parking lot.

There were visitors at the Nance house, for two other vehicles were parked out front. Lucy Nance opened the door and didn't seem surprised to see him.

"Come in. Joe and the others are in the music room." Lucy held open the door for them.

"Thanks. Who's here?"

"Manny and Harrison."

"Just the people I need to see, all in one place."

"Well, I warn you. They're a little drunk . . . and Joe is *really* drunk." She led them to a room in which Berenger and Prescott had never been. It contained a grand piano and other musical instruments, chairs, and some recording equipment for laying down home demos. It was a comfortable space for music-making, not a soundproofed studio.

The Windy City Engine members sat in chairs around a coffee table. The smell of marijuana was strong and the floor was littered with several empty beer cans.

"Spike! What are you doing here?" Nance asked. He didn't stand.

"Hello, boys. How are things? You remember my partner, Suzanne?"

"We were in the middle of a band meeting, Spike," Nance said. "Did we have an appointment or something I forgot about?"

"No, I just decided to drop by. Sorry to interrupt your meeting, but I have some more questions for you guys." He sat on the piano bench and straddled it. "You mind?"

The three musicians looked at each other. Nance shrugged. "Have a seat, Spike. You, too, Suzanne."

Prescott sat on a stool near Berenger.

"Okay, I'll get right to the point. I believe you're all hiding something. It's about Sylvia Favero. What is it? Why is this woman going around killing off Chicago-prog musicians and saying she's the ghost of Sylvia Favero? There's a rational explanation to this and I think you guys know what it is."

Nance's already pink cheeks turned red. "What the fuck? How dare you come in here with an accusation like that!"

Suzanne said, under her breath, "That was tactful, Spike."

"It's true, isn't it, Joe? Why are you so defensive about it?"

"It isn't true!" Nance spat. "We don't know a thing about her or what happened to her!" He turned to Brill and Rodriguez. "Isn't that right?"

They nodded and murmured in agreement.

"Come on," Berenger said. "I know bullshit when I smell it. And frankly, I think I stepped in it coming in here."

Prescott said, "Hold on, you guys . . . Spike had a couple of martinis before coming over here, and it looks like you've been dr—"

Nance threw a half-full beer can across the room. It struck the wall and sprayed a foamy mess all over it and the carpet below. Then Nance stood, ready for a fight.

"Who the fuck do you think you are, coming in here

and talking that way to me? I've just lost my brother, for Christ's sake! What's the matter with you?"

Berenger stood to face him. "I'm sorry for your loss, Joe, but *I'm trying to save your life!*"

"Goddamn it, I've told you everything I know! We all have!"

"What is it, Joe? Did you and Stuart come to blows over her? You wanted her for yourself? He wanted her for himself? Whose girlfriend was she? Or maybe you didn't like it that she was *everyone's* girlfriend!"

Nance couldn't maintain control. He threw his weight at Berenger and they both tumbled over the piano bench, fell hard onto the floor, and began to pummel each other.

"Spike! Joe!" Prescott shouted.

Fists flew as the two grown men wrestled like animals until Rodriguez and Brill jumped up and intervened. It took both of them to pull Nance off of Berenger and throw him onto the sofa. They held him down as he struggled.

"Get him out of here!" Nance shouted. "Get out of my house!"

Prescott helped Berenger stand. There didn't seem to be any harm done aside from bruised egos.

"I want you off the case, Berenger!" Nance said. "Zach isn't around to pay you. We don't need you sticking your nose into our lives anymore. Either the police will catch this woman or ghost or whatever the hell she is—or they won't! Now get out!"

Brill said, "Better do as he says, Spike. I'm sorry."

"Me, too," Rodriguez added.

"Don't apologize to that fuck!" Nance yelled.

Lucy Nance entered and took in the sight of the two

band members restraining her husband. "Joe? What's going on?"

"We're leaving," Berenger said to her. "I'm sorry for the trouble. Come on, Suzanne."

Prescott whispered to the woman that she was sorry as well and followed her partner out the door. Berenger stormed outside, got into the rental car, started it, and waited for Prescott to join him.

"That certainly went well," Prescott mumbled as she got into the passenger seat.

"What?"

"Nothing."

Berenger pulled the car out into the street and sped away.

Chapter Eighteen

Angel of Death
(performed by Thin Lizzy)

On Tuesday, Berenger and Prescott met for breakfast in the hotel and the first thing out of his mouth was, "Didn't Sylvia Favero have any other friends when she lived here? *Someone* had to have known her."

Prescott told him about the other girls in the photos she'd seen at Callahan's house but that he couldn't remember who they were.

"Probably the only guys who'd know aren't talking to us. Clayton is brain fried and Nance is just an asshole," Berenger said.

"What about Manny and Harrison? Will they talk to you if you get them away from Joe?"

"Maybe." He pulled out his mobile, scanned his address book, and dialed Rodriguez's number. After it went to voice mail, Berenger hung up and reported, "Manny didn't answer. I'll try Harrison."

Brill picked up on the third ring. "Hello?" The man sounded sleepy.

"Harrison, it's Spike Berenger. I hope I didn't wake you."

Brill groaned. "You did."

"Sorry, man. Listen, I'm also sorry for last night. I'd

had a few drinks and I was a little frustrated with the way Joe was acting."

"What do you want?"

"I was hoping you'd talk to me. I'm trying to find out more about Sylvia Favero. Do you know where she lived? Did she have other friends? Where did she go when she wasn't hanging out with the band? How did she support herself? You know, things like that. There's got to be *some* history other than the fact that her mother lives—or lived—in Italy."

Brill grumbled for a moment and then answered, "Spike, I'd love to help you but I don't know jack shit. As far as I know, Sylvia made a living selling drugs. She may have had another job, but I just don't know."

"Would she have turned tricks or anything like that?"

"No, I don't think so. She may have been wild and she was a party girl, but she was into *free* love, if you know what I mean. Taking money for it would have been reprehensible to her, I think."

"What about girlfriends? Didn't she come to concerts with any friends?"

"Yeah, but I don't remember who they were!"

A woman's voice behind Berenger spoke. "I was one of her friends."

Both Berenger and Prescott whirled around. Lucy Nance stood alone, dressed in blue jeans and a sweatshirt. She appeared as if she had just rolled out of bed, thrown something on, and come to the hotel. Her hair appeared to be redder than usual.

"Harrison, I'll get back to you," Berenger said and hung up. "Hello, Lucy." He stood and offered his

173

hand. Hers felt cold and fragile. "Would you like to sit down?" She nodded and took one of the chairs as Berenger reclaimed his own seat. "Can I get you something? Coffee? Breakfast?"

"Coffee would be nice."

Prescott waved for the waitress and told her what they wanted.

"I don't know why I'm here," Lucy said. "Joe would kill me if he knew."

"I'm glad you came, Lucy," Berenger said. "You say you knew Sylvia?"

She nodded. "We went to high school together. We were friends. We were both into music. We both discovered The Loop at the same time."

The waitress came by and poured coffee in all three cups. After she left the table, Berenger said, "What can you remember? Please tell us . . . anything."

Lucy took a deep breath and sipped her coffee. "Sylvia had an Italian father and an American mother. While Sylvia was in high school, they lived in Wrigleyville, not far from where I grew up. As soon as she graduated, her parents moved to Italy. Her father had some kind of merchandise sales business. Sylvia didn't want to go. She wanted to pursue her music, maybe go to college . . . she just didn't want to leave Chicago. Her parents, of course, wanted her to come to Italy—so she moved out of the house. She was eighteen by then and could do what she wanted. Sylvia was definitely a free and independent spirit. So her mom and dad finally accepted her decision and they left the country without her."

"Where did she live once she moved out?" Prescott asked.

"She lived in a communal house with several other individuals of like-minded lifestyles. I guess you'd call them hippies. It was a real 'peace-and-love' type of environment. Lots of drugs, of course."

"And she was still your friend?"

"We weren't as close as we were in high school. It's funny how that changed almost overnight. As soon as she adopted the hippie lifestyle, things changed between us. Mind you, I was no prude. I was into that stuff, too, but I still lived at home."

"Did you already know Joe?"

"I knew who he was. I liked the band. I discovered them early on, too. But I didn't start seeing Joe until much later . . . maybe ten years later. In the mid-seventies. I actually got married in seventy-one, but that didn't last. After my divorce in seventy-six, I went to see a Windy City Engine concert and Joe remembered me. We started talking and then he asked to see me socially. And that's how it started with us."

"I see. So tell me more about Sylvia. Do you have any idea why Joe and the others think it's her that has a vendetta against the band?"

"Something happened. Something bad. I don't know what it was. But the band members do. Joe never talks about it but over the years I've gotten a tiny piece here, a little kernel there. Whatever it was that happened caused Sylvia to leave in nineteen seventy. She left and never came back."

"Do you think she's still alive?"

Lucy sighed. "I'd like to think so. I do believe that she was the type of person who, once she'd decided to make a change and leave a past life behind, she'd burn her bridges and never look back."

"Interesting. Do you think she went to Europe? Italy, perhaps?"

"She did go to Italy in sixty-eight for about ten months."

Berenger nodded. "We know she left for a period of time that year. You say she went to Italy? To visit her folks?"

"That . . . and to have a child."

Berenger and Prescott shared a glance.

"A child?"

"She was pregnant. She went to Italy to have the baby. I know this because we ran into each other a couple of weeks before she left. We hadn't seen each other in nearly a year and we did some catching up. You know, it was just like high school for just a few hours. Suddenly I was her confidante and best friend all over again. So she told me. She was pregnant and she was going to have her mother take care of the baby. I don't know how many weeks or months she was, but she wasn't showing yet. She left and didn't tell anyone else where she was going. Maybe she gave the baby up for adoption. I really don't know. But after about ten or eleven months, Sylvia came back to Chicago and resumed her former life as a hippie, Joni Mitchell wannabe, and number-one groupie for The Loop. We lost touch after that."

"That's astonishing," Berenger said. "I'm beginning to get a clearer picture of who this woman is . . . or was. Thank you."

"You're welcome."

"Do you happen to know who the father was?"

"Sylvia's father?"

"No, the father of the child."

"Oh." Lucy pursed her lips. "Sylvia told me it was either Joe or Stuart Clayton. She didn't know which. But she also said it could have been any of the other members of the band!"

"Jesus," Prescott said quietly.

"But she was pretty certain it was one of those two. She spent equal time in both of their beds."

Berenger's cell phone rang. He didn't recognize the number but he answered it anyway. "Berenger."

"Hello, Spike," Sylvia said.

"Oh, hi!" He whispered, "Excuse me a second," to Lucy, stood, and walked away from the two women. "Uhm, how are you?"

"I'm great. How are you?"

"Okay. Just sitting here with my partner Suzanne and Joe Nance's wife, Lucy. You remember Lucy?"

"Of course I do. I doubt, though, considering the circumstances, that she would care to hear from me. So don't tell her I'm on the line."

"All right."

"Have you thought about what I asked you, Spike? Are you ready for those CDs?"

"I have and I am. I'll do my best to get the CDs heard by the right people and do everything in my power to see that the album gets distributed."

"That's what I wanted to hear."

"So how do I get the CDs?"

"Meet me here at midnight tonight." She gave him an address that he didn't recognize. "Enter the building alone. Don't tell the cops about this call or everything is off. And bring a flashlight."

The call switched off. Berenger pulled a small notepad from his pocket and jotted down the address. He then tried to redial Sylvia's new number but got a busy signal. Then, he did the same thing he did the previous day—he called Tommy Briggs in New York, gave him the number, and asked him to get the records.

"How's the research going?" Berenger asked him.

"Slowly. But I've found a couple of things I'll go over with you as soon as I get some confirmation on some details."

Berenger told him what he'd learned about Sylvia Favero.

"I'd like to find out who her child is, if he or she is still alive, that sort of thing. If Sylvia had the baby in nineteen sixty-eight, then the kid would be an adult now."

"I'll see what I can find out, boss."

Berenger hung up and went back to the table, only to discover that Lucy Nance had left.

"Where'd she go?"

Prescott answered, "She said she had no more to say. She hoped the information was useful. But she wanted to get home before Joe woke up. She asked that you keep her visit confidential, especially to Joe."

Berenger sat down to finish his breakfast. "I don't have a problem with that."

The address Sylvia Favero gave Berenger was that of an abandoned building south of Cermak Road, on the edge of Chinatown and near the I-55 overpass. Not a residential area, the street was a relic of Chicago's past. Long-closed Chinese storefronts marred by graffiti lined the short block and there was not a soul in sight. A complete absence of street lighting only served to make the place even more uninviting.

At 11:55 P.M., Berenger parked the rented Subaru across from the building and turned it off. Prescott said, "This is creepy, Spike."

"A little."

"You're not really going in there, are you?"

"I'm not even sure I can get in. The place looks locked and forgotten for decades."

"How do you know she's in there?"

"I don't."

"What if it's a trap?"

"It probably is."

Berenger checked his Kahr to make sure it was fully loaded, and then shoved it back into its holster. He reached across Prescott's lap, opened the glove box, and removed two sets of in-ear devices. These not only worked well for musicians to monitor themselves while performing onstage, but when used in combination with hands-free microphones they were also great communication tools for a security team.

"Here you go," he said, handing her one and placing the other in his own ear. After testing the signal and volume, he was good to go.

"Hand me the flashlight, will you?"

She reached into the glove box and gave him the heavy-duty model they'd purchased earlier. Berenger flicked it on and off to make sure it worked.

"Okay, Suzanne, you stay here in the car. If you see anything weird, let me know. If I see anything weird, I'll let you know. If I get into any trouble, you come running."

"I'm not armed, you know."

"Oh, yeah. Okay, if I get into trouble . . . call the cops."

179

He opened the door and got out. He quickly scanned the street and saw no sign that a human being had been in the vicinity since the end of the twentieth century. Prescott gave him the thumbs-up and he nodded. Berenger walked across the street to the front of the building and examined the door. Faded Chinese characters identified the place, but he had no idea what they were.

A padlock had been split open, most likely with a bolt cutter. Someone had recently been inside.

Berenger carefully lifted the broken lock off the door latch and set it on the ground. He then slowly opened the door—which was rusty and squeaky—and peered inside.

Pitch-black.

He flipped on the flashlight.

The front room of the building was completely empty of furnishings. It was just a vacant, old space with a rickety wooden floor and millions of cobwebs. Berenger stepped inside and let the door close behind him. He was shut off from the outside with only the flashlight beam to keep him company.

"Hello?" he called.

Silence. He thought he might have heard the scuttling of a mouse—or a rat.

"Anyone here?"

He took a few steps forward. The floor creaked as his weight moved across the boards. An archway led to the rest of the building. Berenger figured the place was once a business of some kind. The front room was a reception area. Beyond that was a short hallway leading to a closed door. Two rooms that may have served as offices were connected to the hallway. Berenger cast the light around both spaces; one room was empty and the other contained a very old desk. He moved slowly into the office and examined the furniture. The top was thick with dust and cobwebs stretched from the sides to the floor. No one had touched the thing in ages, so he didn't bother looking in the drawers. Berenger turned and went back to the hallway.

"Suzanne, can you hear me?"

"Loud and clear."

"You're right. This place is creepy."

"What's in there?"

"Nothing so far. It's just me and the spiders and rats."

"Ewww."

"There's a door at the end of this hallway. I bet I'm supposed to go through it."

"If it's any help, the storefront right next to where you are was a dentist office. The Chinese sign says, 'Painless Dentist.'"

"There was some Chinese writing on the outside of the door but you're too far away to read it. I don't think it matters. The place has been gutted and left to rot. It smells as if it's a hundred years old."

"These buildings look to me more like nineteen forties."

Berenger reached the door, examined it in the light, and saw no identifying markings. The only thing to do was open it.

He entered a very large square space that was just as dark and musty as the rest of the building. Four wooden columns stood from floor to ceiling; if one were looking down from above, the room would appear as the number four on a die. Berenger swept the light across the space and saw a couple of old tables, a few broken chairs, and piles of debris.

"This was a storeroom or a workroom of some kind," Berenger announced.

"What's in there?"

"Junk. But I'm going to take a closer look at everything."

His light beam focused on a double door at the far end of the room. Probably the way out to the back of the building and the alley.

He stepped farther into the space and then directed the flashlight on the floor in front of him.

There were dozens of footprints in the dust. They pointed in no particular direction; instead they gave the impression that someone had been moving back and forth in the room, performing a task of some kind.

"Hello?" Berenger called again. "Anyone here?"

"What do you see, Spike?"

"Someone's been in here. Today, too."

"Shit, be careful, Spike."

He moved to one of the tables. Something smelled odd as he approached it. It was a scent he knew and it brought back the nightmares of his three-year stint as a criminal investigations special agent during his military service. His military occupational specialty was 95D—ninety-five Delta—which made him responsible for supervising or conducting investigations of incidents and offenses or allegations of criminality that affected army or defense personnel, property, facilities, or activities. Sometimes that included homicides. Usually wherever there was a homicide, there was the stench of blood.

Berenger smelled blood on the table.

He aimed the light at the top and noted the large puddle of congealing red goo. Some of it had dripped onto the floor.

"Christ," he whispered.

"What?"

He wanted to say that the Angel of Death had been there but he didn't speak. Instead, Berenger backed away, turned the light toward the rest of the room, and quickly made sure he was still alone. Then he noticed something on the floor beside one of the columns. He didn't see it when he first came into the room, for the object lay on the opposite side of the pillar.

"Spike, did you say something?"

"Shhh."

He stepped slowly toward the column, noting the footprint patterns—and blood splatter—on the floor between it and the bloody table. It seemed to take forever for him to walk across the room. With each step, Berenger felt a cold, sick fear develop and grow in his bowels.

He was close enough to shine the light on the object. From ten feet away it appeared to be the head of a mop. Or something with fur or hair. Was it a wig?

Berenger moved closer. Then he saw blood on the floor.

Lots of it.

He had to step around puddles in order to get to the other side of the column.

There, propped neatly on the floor at the base of the pillar, was one of the grisliest things Berenger had ever seen. He gasped, quickly averted his eyes, and held a hand over his mouth to keep from losing his dinner. In doing so, he inadvertently focused on yet another object, duct-taped to the side of the column: a plastic baggie containing several compact disks.

His hand trembling, Berenger reached out and pulled off the baggie, tape and all. He wouldn't want the police to know it had been there. As for the other horrible thing that lay at his feet, he had no choice but to alert the cops. How he was going to explain his presence in the building would take some thinking but he had a few minutes before the patrol cars arrived.

Berenger stepped back, making sure he hadn't left his own footprints in the puddles of crimson. He then forced himself to shine the light beam back on the ugly abomination and confirm his identification of it.

No doubt about it. It was Manny Rodriguez's severed head.

Chapter Nineteen

The Voice
(performed by Ultravox)

The proverbial shit hit the fan with regard to Sergeant Doherty, the Chicago PD, and Spike Berenger's involvement in the Chicago Musician Murders case. Berenger and Prescott were at Area Five headquarters all night making statements and were still there when the sun rose.

Berenger could think of nothing better than to tell the truth. The one thing he withheld was that he had received copies of the compact disks. He told the police that the killer phoned him, saying that she wanted to meet with him and "give him something." When he arrived at the designated address, he discovered Manny Rodriguez's head and nothing else.

He hadn't known that the rest of the musician's body was lying in the alley behind the abandoned building. This detail was revealed to him during the interview at the station. By the middle of the night, enough physical evidence had been accumulated to form a clear picture of what had happened. How the killer managed to overcome Rodriguez, behead him, and transport the body to the location was a mystery. The amount of blood on the table in the building's storeroom suggested that the actual deed was done there. It was

185

conjecture that Rodriguez had been lured to the site in much the same way that Berenger had, but the victim's cell phone was not on his body. Perhaps the killer took it. The police made a request for Rodriguez's phone records to see what calls he had received that day.

At eight o'clock, Berenger asked Doherty if Suzanne could leave. "She was just following my orders as an employee of my company," he told him.

"I tell you what, Berenger," Doherty said. "I'm cutting both of you loose. But I'm also telling you to get out of town. Yeah, that's right. The party's over. I don't want to see your face again. If I hear you're still working the case after lunchtime today, I'll haul you in. Believe me, there are plenty of charges we can dream up. Interfering with a police investigation is one off the top of my head."

"Doherty, you can't make me leave town. I haven't done anything wrong and you know it."

"The hell you haven't! You should have called the police as soon as you heard from that murderous bitch. You should have brought professionals in at that point."

"Sergeant, how many times do I have to tell you? She told me not to call the cops or she wouldn't go through with the meeting. I honestly thought I was going to get close to her and *help you guys out!* I'm on your side, Doherty. My intentions were honorable and in your best interest. And I *am* a professional, goddamit!"

Doherty chewed on that for a moment, but said, "I still think it best that you and your partner leave Chicago." With that, he departed from the interrogation room where Berenger and Prescott had been sitting for hours. After a moment, a police officer came in, gave Berenger his weapon, and told them they were free to go.

On the way out of the building, they saw Mike Case at a desk doing paperwork.

"Good morning, Mike," Berenger said.

Case barely looked up. "Spike, I'm not supposed to be seen talking to you. I have some rather strict orders."

"I see. Sorry, man."

"It's okay. We'll stay in touch. There're no hard feelings. Now get out of here before Doherty catches us."

"So long, Mike. Take care."

"Nice meeting you," Prescott said.

"Same here."

They got to the street and realized that the rental car was still parked in front of the murder-scene building. Berenger hailed a taxi that took them where they needed to go, and then the couple headed back toward their hotel. But instead of turning toward the Drake, Berenger kept going.

"What are you doing?" Prescott asked.

"I'm going to the first audio component store I can find."

"What for?"

"We have some CDs to listen to, remember? I didn't bring my damned computer or my Walkman. Have to buy one." He dug the baggie out of his flak jacket pocket. "Good thing they didn't frisk me."

"Spike, I have my laptop at the hotel. We can use that."

"Geez, why didn't I think of that? I must be more tired than I thought. Suzanne! Did I ever tell you I love you?" He made the next turn and headed back toward the hotel.

"Are we going back to New York, or not?"

"Hell, no. We're getting close, now! I'm going to catch that crazy woman if it's the last thing I do. I'm going to hand her to Doherty on a silver platter. I'll make that son of a bitch eat his words."

"Spike, this isn't about—"

"It's about doing the right thing, Suzanne. I don't care if we're not getting paid. I took this job on as a favor to Zach Garriott. Zach is dead as a result of *this case*. I have to see it through to the end, don't you see?"

She nodded and allowed herself to smile. "Yeah. I see."

"Both phone numbers were bought with prepaid minute plans from two different phone companies," Briggs told Berenger when he called New York. "Registered under the name S. Favero. The accounts have been terminated, so I bet she threw away the phones after she used all the minutes. The lady is smart."

"So there's no way in hell we can trace them back to her. She's probably got a couple more phones and numbers, too."

"Probably so."

"What else you got, Tommy?"

"Remix has been helping me on the immigration records. It's a big job, Spike. We're talking about three to four decades that my contact at Immigration and Customs has to go through. It's taking time. But I do know this. Sylvia's father was Emilio Favero and her mother was Caroline Kimball. Favero ran an import/export business from Italy. Turns out he was mob connected and was wanted for tax evasion both in this country and in Italy. He was arrested in nineteen sixty-nine and went to prison. Naturally, his company went belly-up and is no longer around. Favero died in prison in nineteen seventy-two. We're having a harder time tracking down the mother. We don't know if she's still alive, if she remarried and lives under a different name, or what. But we're working on it."

"Finding the mother is the key to finding the baby," Berenger said and hung up. "Boot up the laptop, Suzanne. Let's listen to these mothers."

Within minutes, she had the disk marked Track One in the CD-ROM drive. As soon as it began playing, they were both surprised by how good the music was. The woman had a strong, soprano voice and the songwriting was complex and inventive. While she had a folk-rock quality much like a Joni Mitchell or Judy Collins, there was an element of Kate Bush's experimental sensibility as well. Berenger liked it a lot. There was also something very familiar about it, but he couldn't place what it was.

"I've heard this song before," Prescott said. "Over at Bud Callahan's house. The tape he played of that concert from sixty-nine! Spike, this is really her!"

"You know, I feel like I've heard her before, too, but I don't know where."

"This is one of the songs she sang at that concert— only this is fully produced in a studio."

"The question is—is it newly recorded, or was it made in the sixties?"

They finished listening to track one and then popped the second disk into the laptop. Once again, they were impressed with the contents.

"I don't know this one," Prescott commented. "She performed only three numbers on that concert recording."

By the time they had listened to track six, something clicked with Berenger.

"Oh, man! I know where I've heard her! In fact, I've heard *this song* before!" He immediately picked up his cell, dialed New York, and had Melanie transfer the call to Remix.

"Yo Spikers, howzit hangin', my man?"

"Remix, I need you to do something for me."

"Whassat, o wise master?"

"You know where I park my Altima?"

"Uhhh, on the street?"

"No, in the parking garage beneath the building where I live. Just up the street."

"Okay."

"I need you to grab the keys out of my desk drawer— get Rudy to unlock it for you—and go get something out of the car."

"What's that?"

"I have a pile of CDs in the accessory compartment in the dash. Grab 'em all. But there's one that's a CD-R that was made by my friend Sandro. It's labeled 'Italian Sampler' or something like that. I need you to upload all the music from that CD onto our server, and then I'll access it from here."

"Okay, boss. It's not some of that prog shit you listen to, is it?"

"Never mind what it is!"

"What if it ain't there?"

"Remix, it's there. It's where I left it. Call me once you've got it uploaded, all right?"

"You betcha. Anything else?"

Berenger thought for a moment. "Yeah. See if you can get hold of all of the albums by Red Skyez and Windy City Engine. I know I have maybe three Red Skyez albums on vinyl, and a few Windy City CDs in the gym. Figure out what we're missing and then scour the used music stores in the city and see if you can pick them up."

"What about eBay?"

"That'll take too long. But if any Internet shops have them and can ship them overnight, that would help, too."

"You forget I'm a techno geek, boss. There are other ways to find those records. I can maybe find them on a usenet peer-to-peer network like BitTorrent or eMule."

"Whatever."

"But even if I find 'em there, it can still take a long time to download the things."

"Whatever, Remix!"

"And I suppose you want me to upload all these albums on our server, too?"

"You got it. And while you're at it, pick up the solo albums by Stuart Clayton and Joe Nance."

"Shit, man, now you're really gettin' esoteric! Last time I looked, Clayton's first album was sellin' for nearly a hundred bucks!"

"I think the firm can afford it, Remix."

"Then how come my expense report for the third week of January wasn't approved? It was only seventy-eight dollars and ninety-nine cents!"

"Remix, if I remember correctly, you submitted your movies-on-demand bill as your expenses for the week."

"But they wuz all *music* movies, man! *Woodstock*,

Monterey Pop, The Song Remains the Same, Stop Making Sense . . ."

"Wasn't *Hardcore Gangstas* on that list, too?"

"Uh . . . yeah. Okay, never mind."

Berenger hung up and they finished listening to all the disks—tracks one through eight.

"Three more tracks and she's got herself a full album," Prescott noted.

"Yeah. Brill, Nance, and Clayton. One song for each."

"We have to get them some protection."

"The police won't listen to me, Suzanne, you know that. And you know what'll happen if I try to warn Nance. Clayton won't speak to me. Why don't you try calling him? Here . . ." Berenger read off his number from his cell phone. She dialed it from her own mobile and got voice mail.

"Mr. Clayton, it's Suzanne Prescott calling. Please call me back as soon as you get this." She gave him her number. "It's important. Spike and I think you might be in danger."

Berenger decided to leave messages with Brill and Nance as well. It wouldn't hurt to warn them, but neither of them picked up. He left a similar message on both voice mail systems.

An hour later, Remix called back and said the Italian sampler was on the server. Prescott accessed it on her laptop and Berenger went directly to the song performed by Julia Faerie, the woman he had been impressed with.

It was identical to the song marked Track Six that Sylvia Favero had left for him.

Chapter Twenty

Walk on the Wild Side
(performed by Lou Reed)

Berenger got up early on Wednesday morning so that he could check his voice mail. He had already left a message for Sandro Ponti in Italy but that was several hours earlier and the time difference would have meant the middle of the night for the Italian musician. Luckily, Ponti received Berenger's missive and left a text message for the PI to call at seven A.M., central time.

"*Pronto?*"

"Sandro?"

"Spike! How are you?" The jovial bass player spoke with a thick accent and somewhat broken English that reminded Berenger of Chico Marx.

"Okay, Sandro. You doing all right?"

"Yes, yes. I am fine. It is so good to hear from you. Did you get the sampler I sent you?"

"I did, and in fact that's what I'm calling about."

"Ah, you want more good Italian progressive rock music?"

"Sure, that'd be nice, but what I need to talk to you about concerns one of the musicians on the sampler. Julia Faerie."

"Oh, yes! Wonderful singer, no? She is very talented."

"Wait . . . do you *know* her?"

"Yes, I do! I help to get her music produced."

Berenger was astonished. Were they talking about the same woman? "Sandro. How old is she?"

"Let's see . . . about forty, I think. But she looks much younger."

"When's the last time you saw her?"

"Uhm . . . maybe three months ago. We lay down tracks in the studio in Rome."

Berenger felt his pulse quicken.

"How well do you know her? What can you tell me about her?"

"Spike, what is this about?"

"Sandro, have you heard about what has happened in Chicago over the past two or three months?"

"No, I do not listen to American news. I do not like it."

"Sandro, many members from Red Skyez and Windy City Engine have been murdered. One by one, someone has been killing them."

"What? Oh my God!"

Berenger did his best to bring Ponti up to date on the tragic events. The Italian seemed to be genuinely upset.

"Charles? Manny? Dave Monaco? I can't believe it!"

"You were friends with all these guys, right?"

"Sure, I knew them all when I was in Chicago. When I was in Rattlesnake, I met them. Bud Callahan was tight with them, so I knew them through him."

"Did you ever know a woman named Sylvia Favero?"

"Sylvia Favero . . . no, who is she?"

"She was a friend of the band . . . well, when the band was The Loop. Remember The Loop?"

"I was not in Chicago then, but I heard of them, of course. That's what Windy City Engine was before they changed their name, right?"

"The Loop split into two bands—Windy City Engine and Red Skyez."

"Oh, right."

"Sylvia Favero was a groupie, for lack of a better word. She also performed, sang her own songs. She disappeared in nineteen seventy."

"No, I do not know about her, Spike."

Berenger explained a little about the CDs that the killer had left for him, and that one of the tracks was identical to Julia Faerie's cut on the sampler.

"But . . . how can that be?" Ponti asked.

"I don't know! That's what I need to find out. Tell me about Julia."

"She has been . . . how you say? 'Kicking around' the music scene in Italy for twenty years or more. She was with popular choral group that sang religious music for a number of years. When she was in her thirties she became solo act. She is not well-known . . . yet. I met her about six years ago. I heard some of her original songs and thought they were fantastic. I encourage her to make a record. So, slowly, she has been recording demos. The track on the sampler was a demo. Hopefully we make album soon."

"I need to talk to her. Does she speak English?"

"Of course! Her mother was American."

Bingo, Berenger thought. There's the connection.

Berenger didn't tell Ponti that he suspected Julia Faerie might be Sylvia Favero's long-lost child. He didn't want to believe it himself until he learned more and talked to the singer. Nevertheless, Ponti said he would find Julia and get back to him. The Italian was afraid she might be away from Rome but he would search for her. Berenger informed him of the benefit concert on Friday night, and Ponti said he would like to be there and might actually try to come.

That afternoon, Berenger and Prescott left the rental car at the hotel and took a walk through Old Town, a quaint and affluent area of trendy shops, restaurants, and clubs. Berenger had other things on his mind but felt he was at a loss. He didn't know what to do next since his investigation depended on others getting back to him. So when Prescott suggested that they get outside into the fresh air, he didn't mind. It would clear his head.

While Prescott window-shopped, Berenger noted the diversity of people that populated the area. Young people dominated Old Town and there was definitely a bohemian vibe that reminded him of West Greenwich Village. He was surprised by the number of couples—boy/girl, boy/boy, girl/girl—as if everyone in Chicago had a significant other. He knew it wasn't so, but it was the impression that the beautiful spring day brought. Perhaps the cessation of the rains had brought out the lovers.

A guitar shop on Clark Street caught Berenger's eye, so he stopped and admired the goods in the window. He stood slavering over a vintage circa 1950s Les Paul Goldtop when he saw the moving reflection of a familiar figure in the window. Berenger turned and confirmed that Felix Bushnell was walking north with a purpose. The man was dressed as he had been at the police station—in a black turtleneck, tight black pants, and the dangling earrings, which were what caught the PI's attention. Without a second thought, Berenger followed the suspect. Although he had serious doubts that Bushnell had anything to do with the musician murders, the guy was definitely a strange bird. Given the man's history with armed robberies while dressed in drag, Berenger supposed it was possible that he could be wrong. After all, if Julia Faerie was the woman singing on the tapes that Sylvia Favero had given him, then Favero couldn't be the performer. And if the real Sylvia Favero was dead, then someone was impersonating her. Could it be Julia Faerie? Or what about Nance's wife, Lucy? Was it a coincidence that she had blonde hair and suddenly dyed it red? Or could it be Felix Bushnell—a man with a record and questionable lifestyle?

Berenger was an expert in tailing someone on foot. He knew when to stop, when to move, when to blend in with a group of pedestrians, when to cross streets, and when to wait. It helped that Bushnell never slowed. The man didn't look back or bother with the shop windows or restaurants.

The PI's cell phone rang when he crossed Armitage Street. It was Prescott.

"Where are you?"

"I'm following Felix Bushnell. Sorry. I didn't have a chance to tell you."

"Gee whiz, I go into a shoe shop and you disappear!"

"I'm walking north on Clark. Looks like I'm crossing Dickens now. It's only been about ten minutes if you want to try and catch up."

"Why are you following him?"

"I don't know. I got a funny feeling about him."

"He's not your type, Spike."

"Ha ha. I'm hanging up now."

"If you don't mind, I'm going to continue shopping. After all, we're not on the payroll now, right?"

"As you wish." Berenger hung up and kept his pace with the suspect.

The PI tailed the man for a good distance. They crossed Fullerton and Diversey streets and eventually came to Belmont. Bushnell headed west at this point. Berenger remembered Sergeant Doherty saying that the suspect lived in an apartment in the Belmont and Clark area. Bushnell was most likely headed for home.

The neighborhood had more trendy shops but they were decidedly more fringe in nature. Head shops, sex shops, and tattoo parlors were the norm. If Clark Street had been more like West Greenwich Village farther south, then this part was more akin to East Greenwich Village.

Sure enough, Bushnell entered a door next to a store that sold erotic novelties. The PI took a look at the call button buzzer—the name "Bushnell" was next to the number three. The suspect probably lived on the third floor of the building.

Berenger wondered what the hell he was going to do now. There was no telling if Bushnell was in for the day, which was doubtful, or how long he would be. He used his cell to phone Prescott.

" 'Sup?" he asked when she answered.

"Nothing. Where are you?"

"Belmont and Clark. I followed Bushnell to his building. Now I don't know what I'm supposed to do."

"Some private investigator you are."

"I know. What are you doing?"

"I was about to head back to the hotel. You want me to come up there?"

Berenger heard a beeping. "Hold on a sec. There's another call."

"Okay."

He switched over. "Berenger."

"Hi there."

Sylvia.

"Hi."

"What are you doing?"

"Nothing at the moment. What about you?"

"You sure you aren't following someone?"

Shit.

Berenger scanned the street. There was nothing suspicious.

"What makes you say that?"

"Looked like you were following someone."

"Are you watching me?"

"Could be."

"Where are you? Why don't we meet? Have a chat?"

"I don't think so, although it might not be a bad thing. You seem like an honorable man."

"I am. What do you say?"

"What did you think of my music?"

"Sylvia, I have to be honest. After all, I'm an honorable man."

"You didn't like it?"

"I didn't say that."

"Then what?"

"It's pretty damned good, Sylvia. You have real talent. I don't think there's going to be a problem selling your album."

"Really?" There was an excitement in her voice that he hadn't heard before.

"Yeah. There's just one thing."

"What?"

"Are you sure you're the one who's making this music?"

"What do you mean?"

"Sounds an awful lot like an Italian singer I've heard before."

There was a pause. "I don't know what you mean."

"Ever hear of Julia Faerie?"

More silence.

"Sylvia?" He waited a few moments. "Are you still there?"

"Yes."

"What happened to your daughter, Sylvia?"

He could sense that he had surprised her.

"Is Julia your daughter?"

The woman didn't answer.

"Who is Julia's father?"

The call ended. Berenger cursed and immediately tried to redial the incoming number.

"Hello?" A woman's voice.

"Sylvia?"

"No, it's Suzanne!"

"Suzanne! Shit, I was trying to call Sylvia back. I don't know what happened—"

"You had me on hold, remember?"

"Hang up!" He ended the call and tried to redial again. Busy signal. "Damn!" He called Prescott back and told her what had just occurred.

"She's playing with you, Spike."

"How the hell did she know I was following Bushnell? Unless . . ."

"Unless he made you and called you from his apartment—as Sylvia."

Berenger rubbed his chin and looked up at the third-floor windows. "I think I'm going to hang around here a bit. You can go back to the hotel if you want or whatever."

"Gee, thanks. I love being so useful."

"Okay, then come up here." He looked at his watch. "Meet me at the corner of Belmont and Clark in fifteen minutes." He hung up, walked back to the corner, and noticed a head shop with a sign in the window that read: SALVIA DIVINORUM—R.I.P. Curious, Berenger went inside. He was greeted by a tattooed, long-haired old man who looked as if he had just walked out of the original 1969 Woodstock festival.

"How's it going, my man?"

"Fine," Berenger answered. "I saw the sign in the window. About salvia?"

"Oh, yeah. What about it?"

"What does it mean?"

"It's illegal now. In this state, anyway. In a lot of states now. It used to be legal. We sold it up until January first, two thousand and eight."

"Yeah? You sell a lot of it?"

The man shrugged. "It sold pretty well. It was a legal high so some people were attracted to it. I didn't care for the stuff myself."

"Why not?"

"Too weird. You ever try it?"

"No."

"It's not a party drug by any means. I found it pretty unpleasant. But there are some folks who were regular customers. They loved the shit. They liked leaving their bodies and trying to figure out if they were still a human being."

"I hear it's pretty intense."

"Depending on the strength of the extract, it can be. We sold packages of five-X, ten-X, fifteen-X, twenty-X, all the way up to thirty-X concentrations."

"Ten-X as in 'ten times'?"

"Yeah. Five being the lowest strength."

"So what happened to all of your stock when it became illegal?"

"Some blonde chick came in sometime in December of '07 and bought everything we had."

"A blonde chick? Do you remember her?"

"She was one of our best customers for the stuff."

"Do you remember her name?"

"Nah. She always paid cash. Never used a credit card. But there was something odd about her."

"What do you mean?"

The old man winked at Berenger. "I think she was really a guy."

Berenger nodded. "Okay. Thanks."

"Can I help you with something else? Need any rolling papers? We make our own pipes."

"No, thanks, I'm good. See you later."

"Have a nice day!"

Berenger walked out of the shop in time to see Prescott stepping out of a taxicab.

"Hold the cab!" he called.

She looked at him in confusion.

"Come on, we're getting out of here," he said as he

got in. She made a noise of exasperation and got into the seat beside him.

"Where are we going? I thought you were shadowing Bushnell?"

"I changed my mind. I want you to keep trying to call Stuart Clayton and see if you can see him. And I want to have another talk with Joe Nance."

Chapter Twenty-one

Voyage 34
(performed by Porcupine Tree)

Prescott stayed at the hotel while Berenger took the rental car to Nance's house. It was late afternoon, so he hoped the musician would be in a better frame of mind than he had been during their last encounter. Berenger parked in front of the house, got out, and knocked on the door. No one answered, but the PI could hear the television. He tried knocking louder but there was still no response.

What the hell . . .

He tried the door and found it unlocked. Berenger stepped inside and called out, "Hello? Joe? Lucy?"

He felt a sudden trepidation and hoped to God he wasn't about to discover another severed head. Berenger drew his Kahr and slowly walked through the hallway toward the sound of the television. He stopped and listened for any sign of human movement but there wasn't any. Another few steps and he was standing in the archway that led to the living room. The TV was blaring and Joe Nance lay on the sofa, his mouth open and eyes closed.

"Joe?"

The man didn't move.

Berenger eyed the rest of the room and determined

they were alone. He holstered the gun and crossed to the sofa.

"Joe?"

Nance started violently out of a deep sleep and sat up, scaring Berenger out of his wits. They both shouted at the same time.

"Fuck, Joe!"

"Wha—what?"

"You scared the shit out of me! I thought you were dead!"

"Spike! What the hell?"

"You all right?"

Nance had that look of confusion and surprise when one wakes from a bad dream. "Man. Oh, man. I must've been . . . I was asleep!" He also reeked of liquor. Joe Nance was even drunker than he was the other night, if that was possible.

"Sorry, Joe. The door was open. I knocked and knocked, but no one answered. I heard the TV, so I just came in. Sorry."

"Where's Lucy?"

"I don't know. She's not here."

"Oh, yeah." Nance rubbed his head and put his feet on the floor. "She left. Last night."

"You two had a fight?"

"I guess. I need a drink." He reached for a bottle of Jack Daniel's that was on the coffee table, but Berenger grabbed it first and moved it out of the man's reach.

"Haven't you had enough for now, buddy?"

"Don't 'buddy' me. Gimme the bottle."

"I need to talk to you. I don't care if you are wasted. You're going to give me some answers."

"Fuck you, Berenger."

"Thank you very much, and fuck you, too. Joe, I'm your friend. I'm on your side. I'm trying to get to the bottom of all this. Why won't you help me out?"

Nance rubbed his face again and then tried to stand. "I have to take a piss." Berenger helped him up and then the man staggered out of the living room to the hallway. Berenger picked up the bottle and empty glasses and took them into the kitchen. Sitting on the counter was an empty box for red hair color. Berenger picked it up and noted that it was the same shade that Lucy Nance was sporting when she appeared at the hotel. He set down the box, found a clean glass, poured water from the tap, and looked in the pantry for coffee. He found none, so he returned to the living room with the water and waited for Nance. It wasn't long before he heard continuous, repulsive retching coming from the hallway bathroom. Eventually the toilet was flushed and Nance walked unsteadily back into the room. He flopped onto the sofa and groaned.

"I brought you a glass of water," Berenger said, handing it to him.

"Thanks." The man emptied it but held on to the glass.

Berenger sat in a comfy chair next to the sofa and asked, "Does Lucy color her hair?"

Nance belched and winced. "Yeah. Why?"

"Just wondering. What's her natural hair color?"

He gave a short laugh. "She changes it so much I forget. It's been red for . . . I don't know. A few days."

"What was it before that?"

"Uh . . . blonde. Why?"

"No reason. Okay, Joe. Can you talk about it, now? It's important."

"Talk about what?"

"You know. Sylvia. The past. Whatever's eating you."

"I have nothing to say."

"Look, someone is killing your friends and colleagues because of something that happened a long time ago. I need to know what it was!"

"Nothing happened!"

"Yes it did!"

"No it didn't!" Nance threw the empty glass at Berenger. Luckily, the man's aim was off due to his condition. The glass shattered on the wall behind Berenger.

"Goddammit, Joe!" Berenger stood, grabbed Nance by the shirt, and pulled him to his feet. Nance swung wildly and managed to land a blow squarely on Berenger's left cheek. The PI had no choice but to punch the musician hard in the nose. Nance yelped and fell back onto the sofa, clutching his face.

Berenger stood there breathing heavily for a moment and then leaned over to examine the man's injury. "Joe . . . I'm sorry. Damn it! Let me see."

Nance waved him away. "Leave me alone!"

"It's not broke, is it?"

"Screw you!"

Berenger gave up and reclaimed his seat. Better to let the guy recover with dignity. He watched Nance fiddle with his nose, wipe the snot off his face, and wince. "I don't think it's broken," he mumbled. "Is it bleeding?"

"No. I'm kind of surprised it isn't."

"Damn you."

"Sorry, Joe. You threw a glass at me and you slugged me. I got pissed off."

And then the unexpected happened—Joe Nance

began to sob. He buried his face in his hands and cried as if he'd just learned his soul had been condemned to hell.

"Jesus, Joe, I didn't hit you that hard, did I?" Berenger asked, but after a few moments he realized that what he was witnessing was not due to the fight. Whatever Nance had been hiding for years was about to come out, and it wasn't pretty. Berenger stood, went to the kitchen, failed to find a box of tissues, and returned with a handful of paper towels. He handed them to Nance, who used them to blow his nose and weep into.

"It was . . . an accident," he finally said. "But we didn't think so . . . at the time."

"What, Joe?" Berenger tried to be as gentle as possible. "Tell me. It'll do you good."

Nance took a few more minutes to get hold of himself, and then he told the story.

June 1970

Stuart Clayton, Joe Nance, Charles Nance, Dave Monaco, and Jim Axelrod poured themselves into the greenroom backstage of the Kinetic Playground after a grueling three-hour show and collapsed into chairs. Harrison Brill and Manny Rodriguez were already there, waiting with a cooler full of beer. They could hear the crowd calling for a third encore but the band wasn't going to have any part of it. Enough was enough.

"You guys blew their minds tonight!" Brill said. "Wish I'd been up there!"

"Sorry, man," Monaco replied. "You and Manny said you didn't want to play this gig. And when you step out, Jim and I step in."

"Hand me one of those," Joe Nance said, indicating

the beer. "Stuart, you fucked up the chords during my solo again."

"No, I didn't," Clayton countered. "You weren't listening to the changes."

"That's bullshit and you know it!"

"You want to go back out there and do it again? You'd just fuck it up a second time."

Nance stood, ready to pummel his band mate, but Charles held him back. "Cool it, Joe. Be cool."

Nance pointed at Clayton. "I'm sick and tired of you acting like you own this band. You are not the leader, Stuart!"

"Who is, Joe?" Clayton calmly asked. "It isn't you. I'm the one that brought us all together."

"That don't make you the leader."

"Guys!" Axelrod shouted. "Stop it! You're acting like middle-school kids. Shut the fuck up and drink some beer. We have a party to go to, remember?"

Joe Nance took a bottle and grabbed his gig bag. "I'll meet you at the boat." He walked out of the room.

"Joe, wait up!" his brother called. The drummer jumped up and ran after him.

Rodriguez turned to Clayton and said, "Hey, Stuart, you gotta cut that shit out. When you and Joe are at each other's throats, it makes it real uncomfortable for the rest of us."

Clayton shrugged. "If we could get out of this sinkhole and be on the West Coast, things would be different."

"Hear, hear!" Axelrod chimed in.

Brill said, "Let's not talk about it tonight, okay? I'm looking forward to getting totally *out of my head*. Where's Sylvia, Stuart?"

"She's meeting us at the boat."

An hour later, all parties concerned had made their way to Burnham Harbor, where Clayton's sixty-two-foot Posillipo yacht was moored. He had bought it brand-new in 1968 and everyone agreed that it was a beauty. It was an ideal party boat and Clayton was a more than competent captain. The Loop had spent many nights and weekends on it, as it was purchased primarily to entertain the boys in the band and any female friends that happened to tag along. Clayton didn't like to flaunt his wealth and usually pretended that he was as poor as the rest of the band members. The boat was the one way he made up for it, although the others wondered why he didn't put more money into promotion for the group.

It was a warm, beautiful night. The moon was full and the sky was clear. The lake emanated an ominous, yet inviting glow. Manny Rodriguez commented that the pond was already tripping. He always called Lake Michigan "the pond."

The seven members of the band sat aboard the yacht, drinking beer, smoking joints, and waiting for the arrival of the woman with the goodie bag.

"Where is she, Stuart?" Charles Nance asked after they'd been there for an hour.

"She'll show," the captain replied, although he wasn't totally sure about it. Sylvia Favero was unpredictable and they all knew it.

"I'm already so high it don't matter if she does show up," Monaco said with a smile on his face. He was lying on his back on the deck, looking up at the stars. "Will you look at that universe? Man . . ."

"How much beer we have left?" Joe Nance asked.

"Plenty," Rodriguez answered. "Enough to last two days if need be."

"Anyone hungry?"

"Oh, man, don't ask me that!"

"There're hot dogs inside. We can cook 'em later."

"Hey, look, someone's coming."

Everyone focused their attention on the figure walking toward them on the pier. Even in the dark, the floppy hat gave her away.

"Hooray!" the boys shouted.

"The goddess cometh!"

"Hello, fellas!" she announced. "Are you ready to change your lives tonight?"

She was a little unsteady on her feet, so Joe Nance helped her aboard. Clayton started up the engine. Charles jumped onto the pier, untied the moorings, and leaped back on as the boat slowly pulled away. More cheers.

Sylvia was dressed in a flowery sundress, the hat, and the sunglasses. She lit a cigarette, indicated a large handbag she was carrying, and said, "Okay, boys, come and get it." She sashayed into the cabin, where she dropped the bag onto the kitchen table. Everyone except Clayton piled inside after her.

She emptied the contents. There was an ounce of weed, a bag of white powder, two pipes, rolling papers, and another baggie containing a sheet of blotter paper. She held up the latter and giggled. "You're not going to believe this shit. It's total. It's so pure." She took off her sunglasses and the men could see that her pupils were dilated, as large as saucers.

"Are you already high?" Joe asked.

"I dropped two hours ago. Man, I'm *flying*! I don't

know how I even got here." She carefully tore off squares of the paper and handed a couple to each band member.

"Two?" Brill asked.

"Uh huh," she said. "This night is going to be special." She tore off another one for herself and tossed it into her mouth. She then tore off two more hits and said, "I'll take these to Stuart."

"Uh oh, he'll become someone else!"

"He won't be captain no more!"

Laughter.

"Clayton says he always stops being Stuart Clayton when he does acid!"

"It'd be an improvement!"

More laughter.

The boat sailed several miles out on the vast ocean that was Lake Michigan. Clayton eventually dropped anchor so that he wouldn't have to concentrate on piloting. The next two hours flew by quickly as their trips took shape, intensified, and soared toward a peak none of them had ever experienced before. By the third hour, the travelers were no longer on a boat on the lake. It had become an interplanetary shuttle caught in a galaxy of sea. The hot dogs were forgotten, but the beer, marijuana, and cocaine wasn't. By the fourth hour, anything and everything was possible.

"Will you look at that universe?" someone asked.

At some point, Joe Nance kissed Sylvia in front of the others. No one was sure how long that lasted, but it seemed as if she was on Stuart Clayton's lap and kissing him a mere second later. Then it was as if time reversed itself and she was with Nance again. Or was it Dave Monaco? No, she was kissing Charles Nance.

Wait, she was sitting in Manny Rodriguez's lap and had her mouth locked with his. Where had the sundress gone? Sylvia said it had been cast away and offered as a gift to the alien beings in the new galaxy, which made the boys laugh.

"Will you look at that universe?" someone asked.

The glow from the moon and the lake continued to penetrate their retinas and time finally came to a dead stop. Everyone's clothing had been shed. During the fifth hour, they were singing songs and dancing in the nude, laughing and crying and holding each other in fear and awe. By the sixth hour, dawn was beginning to creep across the ceiling of stars overhead . . . and Sylvia Favero had given her body to all seven men—to some of them more than once. The party was out of control. A couple of the guys got sick, probably from too much beer and not enough food. One of them became too wired from the cocaine, but later no one remembered who it had been.

"Will you look at that universe?" someone asked.

During the seventh hour, as the sun rose and turned their surroundings into a bright orange blaze of color and warmth, someone noted that all the LSD was gone. They must have each taken more hits during the night. It was no wonder that they couldn't land the spacecraft. One of the guys became afraid and had to be coaxed out of the latrine. Sylvia sang and cried and laughed and danced in the nude. Someone poured beer all over himself to wash off the parasites that had grown out of the spaceship's deck.

"Will you look at that universe?" someone asked. Or was it just a broken record? Someone had said it. No one could remember who. Everyone said it. No one could remember who. They forgot what it was to forget. Someone thought that was a profound statement. No one could remember who.

Time passed, even though it was standing still.

The clock advanced, even though it didn't.

The boat floated in the heat of the day. The eight humans lay on the deck, broiling in the oven like lobsters on the aliens' dinner plates. Someone laughed at that notion but no one else did. Most of them were very quiet.

The beer was completely gone as the sun dropped closer to the horizon. Someone said that the lake was perpendicular to the universe. No one knew what that meant exactly, but it was heavy. Somebody wrote it down so they could remember it, but a few minutes later he lost the piece of paper.

By nightfall, the boat was no longer a spaceship. The lake was no longer perpendicular to the universe—it was just a flat body of water on which they were floating. Bodies stirred. Stomachs ached. Throats were parched. Skin was sunburned.

When the moon was shining above them once again, the men had found their clothes and put them on. Sylvia lay asleep on deck, still nude. Someone threw a blanket over her. They couldn't find the sundress, although it was Rodriguez who remembered it had been donated to the aliens. Only the floppy hat was left on board. Everyone laughed.

"What time is it?" Monaco asked.

"Fuck that. What *day* is it?" Brill answered.

More laughter

"It's not day, it's night!"

"Should I head back to shore, guys?" Clayton asked.

"I guess."

"Why not?"

"I'm hungry."

"I'm thirsty."

"Will you look at that universe?"

Laughter. "Shut up with that already!"

"Sylvia, wake up. What do you want to do?"

"Hey, Sylvia!"

Someone shook her. She didn't move.

"Sylvia! O Goddess of Interplanetary Travel, wake up, wake up!" they sang.

She still didn't move.

Joe Nance was the first one to become concerned. "Shit, guys. I don't think she's breathing."

"What the hell?"

"Wait, sit her up."

"Throw water on her."

"I'm serious! She's not breathing!"

Suddenly the boat was a beehive of anxiety and pandemonium. Clayton tried to give her mouth-to-mouth resuscitation. Then Joe Nance attempted it. Nothing worked.

It took them twenty minutes before someone had the guts to say, "I think she's dead."

Tears. Fear. Paranoia.

"What are we going to do?"

"We gotta go back. Hurry."

"Wait, guys, wait a second!" It was Clayton. "We can't do that."

"What do you mean, we can't do that?"

"Do you realize how much trouble we'll get into? Seven guys and one woman?"

"What are you getting at?"

"Fuck, they'll do an autopsy and figure out we *all* had sex with her! They'll find all kinds of drugs in her blood."

"We don't know why she died. It's not our fault."

"Tell that to the cops!"

"Was it an overdose?"

"Could have been the heat."

"It was an accident."

"The cops won't see it that way."

"Damn, damn, damn!"

"What do we do?"

"Shut up, let me think!"

"Oh, God!"

The seven men discussed and argued about the situation for the next hour. Because they had not eaten in twenty-four hours, were dehydrated, and were coming off of the most intense psychedelic experience they'd ever had, their judgment was not the best it could have been.

"She has no family here."

"No one will miss her."

"She went away a year ago and no one knew where she was, remember?"

"It could be like that again."

"We have to promise not to say anything to *anyone*."

"This is a pact, guys, and we're taking it to our graves."

"Oh man, oh man, oh man . . ."

"We have to do it."

"It's the only way."

So they found something to weigh down the body and dropped her overboard.

Sylvia Favero's corpse was never found. Stuart Clayton filed a missing person's report two months later, as if none of the band members had any clue as to her whereabouts.

And the secret had been kept for nearly forty years.

Berenger sat in his chair with tears in his eyes. It was such a sad—and reprehensible—story. Nance refused to look at him. He just stared at the floor and sobbed some more.

"I've never told anyone," the musician said. "I know we did wrong. But there's something else . . ."

"What?"

"I don't really know if we *did* dump her body overboard. We all talked about it a day later, when we'd come down. We all had the same impression of the events. We *think* she died on the boat. We *think* we put her in the water. Well, actually, at least three of the guys kept saying it never happened. They insisted that Sylvia was never on the boat in the first place!"

"How can that be?"

"I don't know. We were so messed up that weekend. The acid we dropped was the most powerful stuff I'd ever taken. Then there was everything else—the pot, the booze, the coke—we were out of our heads! Anything could have happened and I don't think we would have remembered it succinctly. What I've told you is the dream I keep having, over and over. Did it really happen? Spike, I'm telling you—I'm not exactly sure! It might have been some weird hallucination."

"But if you didn't do it, then what happened to Sylvia?"

"I don't know! She went missing!"

"Or she's dead."

"And if she is, that's why her ghost has come back to kill us all. Now you know."

"Joe," Berenger said softly. "I'm not absolving you of anything. Whether you guys were at fault in her death or not, I . . . I can't say. But I can assure you of this. Whoever is killing everyone is *not* a ghost. It's someone real and it's probably someone you know. Now think. Is there *anyone* who might have had a connection to Sylvia that could have found out about all this?"

Nance shook his head. "I've done nothing *but* think about it since the killings started. And I can't come up with anyone."

Berenger's cell rang.

"Berenger."

"Spike, it's Mike Case."

"Hey. What's up?"

"Well, I have some news. It's the suspect, Felix Bushnell."

"What about him?"

"He's dead."

"What?"

"Shot and killed by an undercover police officer."

"Why? How?"

"Caught red-handed in an armed robbery attempt in the First District, not far from Chinatown."

"No!"

"Yep. And guess what?"

"He was dressed—?"

"Yep. In drag. Blonde wig. Sunglasses. And carrying the Browning nine mil. Same caliber as the musician shootings. Could be a match, but we'll have to run the tests. But it's entirely possible that your case is closed."

Berenger sighed. "Maybe. Maybe not. Thanks, Mike. I'll get back to you." He hung up, stood, and went to the kitchen.

"Where are you going?" Nance asked.

"To get the Jack Daniel's."

Chapter Twenty-two

Ain't Wastin' Time No More
(performed by The Allman Brothers Band)

On Thursday, the day before the benefit concert, Berenger discussed the case with Prescott before phoning Rudy Bishop. As they sat in his hotel room, he related Nance's sad story to Prescott, who shook her head with pity.

"I suppose if I'd been born fifteen or twenty years earlier, that could have been me," she said. "I would have been sucked right in by the whole peace-and-love thing, just like I was influenced by Goth, punk, and new wave in the eighties. I was a bit of a bad girl, too."

"Yeah, but you straightened out," Berenger noted. "And besides, it's okay to be a little bad, and luckily you still are."

She punched him lightly on the shoulder. "Shut up, this isn't funny."

"I know." He then showed her that day's *Chicago Sun-Times*. "And now there's this." One of the smaller headlines on the front page proclaimed, MUSICIAN KILLER SLAIN.

"Oh, no," Prescott said. She picked up the paper and began to read.

"I think they're jumping the gun. They haven't finished the ballistics tests, they don't have the physical evidence to prove that Bushnell was the shooter . . . all they have is an armed robbery attempt totally unrelated to the musicians. The Chicago PD must really want to close this case."

"It happens all the time, Spike, you know that. The police will rush to close a high-profile case, even if they've got the wrong offender. You see it everywhere, especially in the big cities. Look what happened with that Central Park Jogger case in New York, for example."

"I know. What are you gonna do? It's out of our hands." He took out his mobile and started to dial a number, but stopped. "Oh, and I found out that Lucy Nance dyes her hair. A week ago it was blonde."

"Oh, really?"

"Uh huh."

"You think there's anything to it?"

"At this point, I'm not ruling out anything." He dialed New York and asked Melanie to connect him to Remix.

"Howdy-do, Spikers."

"How are you doing with collecting that music, Remix?"

"Got most of it. Spent all day yesterday in the Village haunting the vintage record and CD shops. I managed to get all of Red Skyez's stuff that you didn't already have, as well as Windy City Engine's. I'm still missing Joe Nance's solo album and Stuart Clayton's two records. But I have a lead on Clayton's that I should hear about today. I've started uploading the music."

"Thanks. I guess I need to start listening."

"You really think there'll be some clues in the music?"

"Well, I found out last night what the big mystery is about, so now I don't know if your efforts will be of any use."

"What? You mean I wore a hole in my tennis shoe for nothin'?"

"No. Stay on task. I'm still going to give everything a listen. Did you scan the album covers and upload them, too?"

"Not yet. I was doing the music first. I'll get on that today as well."

"Great. Thanks. Transfer me to Tommy, will you?"

After a few seconds, Briggs picked up the phone.

"What've you got, Tommy?"

"I was about to call you. Okay, I finally got the immigration records for Sylvia Favero, Joe Nance, and Stuart Clayton. Sylvia went back and forth from the U.S. to Italy three times in her lifetime. Once when she was young, in nineteen fifty-five. The next time was nineteen sixty-two. Then again in nineteen sixty-eight."

"That's when she went to have her baby."

"She left the U.S. in January of sixty-eight and returned in November. There are no records of her leaving the country after that."

"That's because she really was dead. I'm pretty sure about that now."

"Not a hundred percent?"

"No. What about the guys?"

"Joe Nance has a long history of traveling in and out of the country. Windy City Engine did eight European tours and three Far East tours over the years. All of those are accounted for."

"No other instances, not related to a tour?"

"Not that I can see."

"Okay, what about Clayton?"

"Other than one European tour that Red Skyez did in seventy-two, he left the country in nineteen eighty. Apparently he went to Italy, but as you know, that doesn't mean he stayed there. You can travel around Europe and maybe they'll stamp your passport when you enter a new country, and maybe not. The U.S. doesn't keep records of that—they just look to see where all you've been when you return to America. Unless it raises a red flag—like if you've been in a country that supports terrorism or somewhere that's on the State Department's no-no list—then usually Immigration doesn't give a hoot. But I've got a source that tells me that Clayton applied for a work visa in Italy, which he renewed a few times. So maybe he did plant some roots in that country. Anyway, he returned to the U.S. in nineteen ninety-two. Hasn't left since."

"Thanks, Tommy. I'm not sure what it means, but it just might be helpful."

Berenger wondered if the fact that Clayton went to Italy indicated that he had a connection to Julia Faerie. Was he Julia's father? Or was his residing there merely a coincidence?

"You do know that Clayton's parents were wealthy?" Briggs asked.

"Yeah. But I just have vague details about all that."

"His grandfather founded a ball bearing company in Chicago in the early nineteen hundreds. Made a fortune. Clayton's father took over the business during the forties. He and Clayton's mother died in some kind of boating accident in nineteen seventy-five."

"A boating accident?"

"That's what the death certificates say. There're a

few newspaper items about it. Seems there was a fire at sea and they didn't make it."

"Gee."

"Clayton sold the company soon after that. I would bet he used the money to live in Italy for those twelve years."

"Well, he's practically penniless now. He told us he has a trust fund that he depends on for income. I'd like to know where he was for the few years after his stroke in seventy-three."

"Hold on, I might have a lead for you." Berenger heard Briggs shuffle some papers. "I got hold of copies of his parents' death certificates. There's a family doctor listed—a Jeremiah Levine in Chicago. I have no idea if he's still in practice or not. Maybe you can find out?"

Berenger scribbled down the name. "Thanks, I'll look into it. Anything else?"

"Not right now."

"Okay, now transfer me to Rudy."

While he was waiting, Prescott's cell phone rang. She answered it and her eyes grew wide. "Oh, hello there!" She looked at Berenger and mouthed the name, Stuart Clayton! Berenger nodded enthusiastically, and then went across the room so he could have a private conversation.

"Hey, Spike."

"Rudy, we're staying until Saturday. That's my decision. I want to be here for the benefit concert tomorrow night at the very least. I think between now and then I'm going to learn something big. Just in the past twenty-four hours I've discovered a whole hell of a lot, and as you know, in this business when the dam breaks you get a flood."

"And you think the dam has broken?"

"I do. At least there's a big ol' crack in it. I'm getting close, Rudy, I can feel it."

"All right, Spike. Just keep me informed. I suppose we can write off your expenses."

"Geez, Rudy, if you want us to move out of the Drake and into a Motel Six, we will."

Bishop laughed. "Not necessary, partner. Just do your job and come home."

Berenger hung up and rejoined Prescott.

"Okay, Stuart, I'll see you then. Bye!" She hung up and smiled. "Okay, he said I could come over."

"Where's he been?"

"He didn't say. Didn't sound particularly coherent. You'd think he was about to drop dead any day. But anyway, I said I'd like to ask him some more questions and at first he hemmed and hawed and said he wasn't well, blah blah blah. But I mentioned that you were busy and it would just be me, so he warmed up to that idea."

"He has the hots for you, Suzanne."

"Yeah, but given his condition, I don't know what he'd be able to do about it."

"Sure you don't want me to go with you?"

"I'll be fine."

"Okay, then. Go on over there. Use that beautiful noggin of yours to draw him out. Use Nance's story if you need to. I'd like to get a confirmation from him that what Joe said happened really occurred."

"All right. What are you going to do?"

"I need to use your laptop. I'm going to sit here and listen to several hours of Chicagoprog music. I'm going to pretend it's not a waste of time. You never know."

225

She nodded, but Berenger could see that something was bothering her. "What's wrong?"

"What are we going to do about it, Spike?"

"About what?"

"You know, what happened in nineteen seventy. Are these guys liable for murder, or what?" she asked.

He shook his head. "I really don't know the legalities. We don't know if it was really murder. Negligence, yes. And I don't know if I should tell Mike Case or not. Would it make any difference after all this time? Would Joe and Stuart and Harrison be arrested? I doubt it. There's no body. There's no proof that Sylvia Favero died out there on that boat. There's no way they could pinpoint the location and drag the lake. There wouldn't be much left of her after thirty-nine years anyway. What would be the point in telling someone?"

She frowned and sighed. "I guess you're right. But it bothers me. Those guys *were* responsible, you know, in many ways. Seven adult men and one woman. They were really stupid. All those drugs. It's a wonder one or two of the guys didn't die, too!"

"If they're going to be judged then it's going to come from a higher power, Suzanne, if you believe that kind of stuff."

She shook her head. "You're forgetting something, Spike."

"What's that?"

"There might still be a killer out there who wants to judge—and sentence—them."

Chapter Twenty-three

Down In It
(performed by Nine Inch Nails)

Prescott left for Clayton's house and Berenger went online to try and find Dr. Jeremiah Levine. There was no practice with that name listed in any of the popular search engines. Googling it produced several hundred hits, none of which seemed to be located in Chicago. But he spent some time scanning the various entries and eventually found one with embedded text that mentioned a "Dr. Jeremiah Levine in Chicago." Berenger clicked on the link and found a website with a blog by a woman named Carol Hersh. He scanned the pages and finally found the reference. It was an entry dated two years earlier that described the traumatic experience of placing her father in an assisted living facility. Apparently her maiden name was Levine and she was the good doctor's daughter.

It was relatively easier to locate her telephone number. Berenger called it but reached an answering machine.

"Ms. Hersh, my name is Spike Berenger, and I'm a private investigator working with the Chicago police on a case." It was a lie, but a tiny white one. "I need to speak with your father, if he is the same Dr. Jeremiah Levine who had a practice in Chicago during the seventies. Please call me back. It's urgent." He left his mobile number and hung up.

Then he accessed Rockin' Security's server, found the folders where Remix had uploaded the music, and set about listening to the Red Skyez albums he wasn't familiar with. It was going to be a tedious job, but at least it was music he enjoyed.

Prescott drove the rental car to Clayton's house on Mango Avenue, parked in front, and got out. Curiosity got the better of her, so she walked around the side of the house. A separate garage stood at the end of an unpaved drive with a padlock securing the door closed. Prescott could plainly see tire tracks on the gravel leading to the structure, indicating that Clayton had recently driven his car. The backyard wasn't fenced, and Prescott noted that it was just as poorly cared for as the front. She had a mind to perform a good deed and hire a lawn service for a day as a gift for the invalid.

She went back to the front door and knocked, but the door was ajar and swung open on its own. Prescott took a step inside and called out, "Stuart? Are you here?" The house was eerily quiet. "Hello? Anybody home?" She went all the way in and closed the door behind her. The place smelled awful, worse than before. The hallway was dark and unlit, but she knew her way around. First she checked out the kitchen. Clayton wasn't there, but the sink remained full of dirty dishes and the pizza box from the other night—with uneaten pieces—was still on the table. She winced at the sight.

She retraced her steps back to the hallway, and then looked in the living room. It, too, was empty, and at first she thought nothing had changed since she and

Berenger had visited. But as she turned to explore more of the house, she noticed broken glass on the rug near the unused fireplace. Prescott moved closer to check it out and found that the framed photographs of the band had fallen. She picked them up and recoiled slightly when she saw that the pictures themselves had been mutilated. Someone had used a sharp object and sliced the faces of every band member in the photos.

"Stuart?" she called again. When still no one answered, she pulled out her cell and dialed Berenger. She cursed when his voice mail kicked in.

"Damn it, Spike, answer your phone. I'm at Stuart's house and no one's here. But *someone's* been here. I think he might be in trouble. I'm going to continue exploring to see what I find. Call me back."

She hung up and went back to the hallway. The bathroom was filthy and cluttered with toiletries—some empty and forgotten, and a few still in use. The shower curtain was moldy and gross. Prescott pulled it back to look at the tub. She couldn't imagine bathing in it.

Instinct prompted her to open the medicine cabinet. It was full of dozens of prescription medications, some dating as far back as the early nineties. There were antidepressants, antipsychotics, and tranquilizers, as well as standard over-the-counter painkillers. The most recent prescriptions were dated five years earlier and the bottles appeared to be untouched.

Prescott stepped out of the bathroom and went farther down the hall to the first bedroom. She knocked and carefully peered inside, fearful of what she might find. But there was nothing but an unmade bed and a room covered in discarded dirty clothing. The drawers on the bureau were partly open and contained underwear and socks. A closet contained a few shirts and pants on hangers.

A second bedroom, across the hall, was full of all manner of junk. Apparently Clayton didn't use it for anything but a receptacle for stuff he didn't use, such as a busted microwave, broken furniture, a rusty bedspring and uncovered mattress, and piles of old newspapers and magazines. A framed photo of Stuart Clayton in a high school graduation cap caught her eye. It was lying on top of an open carton. She took a moment to squat and examine the photo. Clayton was a handsome young man when he was seventeen or eighteen, whatever his age was when the photo was shot. She lifted the photo and found that the carton was full of artifacts from Clayton's high school years and earlier. There were a few school notebooks, a second-place science fair award, several track-and-field awards, and an old Boy Scout uniform. Clayton had reached First Class and collected a number of merit badges, but he must have dropped out before going further in the program. Prescott put everything back in the carton and stood. The rest of the stuff in the room was just trash. Lots of trash.

A firetrap waiting to happen, she thought.

She continued the exploration by making her way to the makeshift recording studio. There, she found several reel-to-reel tape boxes sitting on the mixing board, as if they'd recently been pulled from the storage room. The studio itself appeared untouched since their last visit. Prescott picked up the boxes and read the labels.

Trrrrans Sessions A. *Trrrrans* Sessions B. *Trrrrans* Sessions C. The box labeled Session A was empty.

Apparently they were the master tapes of Clayton's solo album from 1979. A reel was already threaded on the player, so Prescott reached out and pushed the Play button.

Clayton's fragile voice, accompanied only by piano, sang out through the speakers all over the house. The music was strangely beautiful, but there was something disturbing about it that Prescott couldn't quite put her finger on. The song was about an out-of-body experience, most certainly autobiographical. She wished Berenger were there; perhaps he would have more insight.

At one point, the music stopped because Clayton had made a mistake on the keyboard. A woman's voice said, "You did it again, Stuart."

"I know," Clayton replied. "Sorry."

"Try it again."

He picked up the song at a point prior to the error.

The woman's voice was familiar and Prescott was certain that she knew to whom it belonged. The person in the studio with Clayton during the recording was Sylvia Favero.

But if Sylvia Favero died in 1970, what was she doing in Clayton's studio in 1979?

The musician made another mistake.

"Stuart! You're never going to get the album finished if you keep fucking up."

"Sorry, honey. This is the first record I've made in a few years, remember?"

"I know, but you're a professional."

Clayton laughed a little. "Professionals make money doing this."

"Stop that, Stuart! We don't need bad vibes. Keep

thinking groovy thoughts, honey. Let your mind go free and soar in the sky. Just like we used to. I know you can do it."

"Okay."

He started again and this time he made it all the way through the song. Prescott found it profoundly moving, even though the lyrics were pretentiously obtuse.

"Take twelve. I'd say that's a good one," Sylvia said. "Want to try it again now or would you rather have your break?"

"No, no, I can keep going. Just let me drink some water . . . <sip> . . . okay. I'm ready."

And he started the song from the beginning.

Fascinating, Prescott thought. But who was listening to this earlier? Clayton . . . or someone else?

Berenger had turned the volume of Prescott's laptop as high as it would go. That way he could still listen to the music as he used the toilet, brushed his teeth, and showered. But as a result, he couldn't hear his cell phone. When he picked it up off the coffee table, he saw that he had missed three calls. One was marked as a Private Call, one was from Prescott, and one was from C. Hersh. He listened to the Private message first.

"Hey, Spike, it's Sandro here. I fo—" But a burst of static interrupted the message. The rest of it was broken up, probably due to bad reception when Ponti made the call. "—Julia—what was going on—with me—early morning flight from Milan, connecting through London—in Chicago by afternoon tomorrow. Okay? See you soon!"

What? Berenger replayed the message but still

couldn't make much sense out of it. He phoned Sandro back and reached the Italian's voice mail.

"Sandro, it's Spike. I got your message but you were breaking up. Couldn't understand a word. It sounded as if you're coming to Chicago, which is great. But I'd still like to talk to Julia if you find her before you leave, so please call me back when you can."

Next he listened to Carol Hersh's message: "Uhm, hello? This is Carol Hersh calling for Spike Berenger? You left a message that you want to speak to my father? Yes, he was Dr. Jeremiah Levine in the seventies. He's retired and lives in assisted living, but he's in pretty good health. If you want to call back, I'm at home now."

He dialed her number and she picked up.

"Hello?"

"Ms. Hersh?"

"Yes?"

"Spike Berenger."

"Oh, hello."

"Thanks for calling me back."

"You're welcome. What can I do for you?"

Berenger spent a minute explaining a little about who he was but not going into great detail about what case he was working on. The less she knew, the better.

"So, I'd really like to talk to your father about a patient he had in the seventies. Would he be in any shape to remember something like that?"

"Oh, gee, I don't know. He had a lot of patients. I suppose if he or she was a memorable one . . ."

"What about his records? Where would they be kept?"

"Another practice took over his when he retired. But

I imagine all the old records would be in storage somewhere unless the patients' files were still active. I work
in nursing, so I know how that is. If after ten years there
is no activity with a patient, that file gets archived.
Most of the time archives are kept in a completely separate office or maybe even a different building."

"I see. Well, then, I guess I'd like to speak with your
father and see if he remembers. Would that be all right?"

"Sure." She gave him the name and address of the
facility where the man lived.

"I saw your blog online," Berenger said. "I can re-
late to your experience. My mother is in an assisted
living home in New York."

"Oh, then you know how it is. It was difficult at
first, but it's a really nice place where my dad lives.
They treat him really well. And because he's a doctor,
he knows when the care is good or not!"

"Perhaps you could call over there and let him know
that I'm on the way?"

"I will. Let's see, what time is it? Oh, okay. He's up
from his afternoon nap by now. I'm sure you'd be able
to see him before their dinnertime if you go right now."

"Thanks. I can be there in half an hour."

"I'll call now."

He hung up, shut off the music, put the laptop in
sleep mode, and rushed out of the room. In his haste,
he forgot about Prescott's phone message.

Prescott turned off the player after the tape ran out.
The music had been extremely strange. Clayton seemed
to have intentionally set about creating compositions
that only he could understand. Nevertheless, there was

an emotion behind the words and music that was powerful and haunting. She felt a little odd that she had sat and listened to it without Clayton being there. It was as if she had pried into his personal things. But she told herself that she was a private investigator and it was her job to do such things. And it was time to continue looking around the house. If she didn't find anything else, she would leave and go back to the hotel.

She stepped out of the studio and noticed the storage room door. It had been closed and locked when she and Berenger had visited the other evening, but now it was ajar. Prescott pushed open the door to reveal shelving units full of record albums, tape boxes, and cartons of all sizes. It was a typical storeroom—

—except for the outline of a trapdoor in the floor.

She figured it went to a basement. Wouldn't the house have one? Where were the regular stairs?

Prescott backed out of the storeroom and returned to the kitchen. She hadn't noticed it before, but the table was butted against a closed door in the wall. She moved the table out of the way and tried to open the door, but it was either locked or stuck. She knocked on it and heard a hollow sound behind it. Surely the stairs to the basement were there . . . why was it inaccessible? Did Clayton never use his basement?

Prescott went back to the storeroom and took a closer look at the trapdoor. There was a ring attached to it so that one could lift up the panel—and that's what she did.

A wooden staircase led down into darkness.

"Hello?" she called. "Anyone down there?"

Quiet.

Wait—was there a flickering light down there? Could it be a lit candle?

What the hell . . .

She descended the steps and found herself in a small space surrounded by ceiling-to-floor white drapes. Sure enough, a tall, lit candle sat on a small table. The curtains created an anteroom effect, hiding the rest of the basement from her. The creepiest thing was that now there was no doubt someone was either still in the house or had recently been there to light the candle.

"Hello?" she nervously called again.

This was definitely odd.

The curtains appeared on two sides of the ante-room. Prescott slowly moved to the curtains directly behind her and parted them in the middle. As she peered beyond the drapes, her jaw dropped.

The space contained two Nautilus exercise machines—an elliptical trainer and a treadmill.

Who the hell uses these? Clayton certainly doesn't!

Prescott stepped past the curtains to examine the machines. They weren't new but they appeared to be used regularly. A towel was draped over the seat on the elliptical. Prescott tentatively reached out to touch it and discovered that it was damp. Definitely recently used.

Next to the machines was a small bathroom that contained a toilet, vanity, and shower. Remarkably, it was clean and spotless. A bath towel hung over the shower door. Inside the vanity were other toiletries—feminine ones, including a razor for shaving legs.

Holy shit, Prescott thought. What have I stumbled onto?

She went back to the trapdoor stairs and peered through the curtains on the other side of the anteroom. Prescott was just as astonished, if not more, by what she saw.

The basement obviously had as much floor space as the entire house upstairs. On this side of the curtains was one large room, tastefully furnished as living quarters for *someone*. Even though the lighting was dim, Prescott could see that the decor and colors were decidedly feminine. There was a large, round—and clean—Persian carpet on the concrete floor. On the far side of the room there was a queen-size bed covered with a flower-patterned spread. The dresser was white and pristine, and on top of it were trinkets and knick-knacks only a woman would keep. Next to the dresser was a set of oriental screens—the kind behind which a female would dress. Opposite that was a wardrobe with a large oval mirror on the door. There was a writing desk against one wall, and whoever used it was neat and organized. A small rack containing magazines and newspapers sat on the floor next to the desk. In the middle of the room were a table, three chairs, and an acoustic guitar propped on a stand.

Hanging on the wall near the desk was a cabinet with a glass door. Inside was an assortment of guns.

She pulled the curtains open as far as they could go and then stepped farther into the room. A shiver ran down her back as Prescott considered the implications of what she was seeing

My God, she thought. What is going on in this house?

She moved to the center to examine the guitar. It was a Gibson classical model with nylon strings. Prescott didn't have the expertise to determine its age, but it definitely wasn't new. She guessed it was at least twenty years old, maybe more.

Next she went to the gun cabinet. A Heckler & Koch PSG1 rifle hung on a rack behind the glass. Two handguns were also mounted inside and there was an empty space for a third. A padlock kept out anyone but the owner.

The rifle . . . a sniper rifle . . . probably the weapon that killed Axelrod?

She had to get out of there. Tell Berenger. Call the police. *Something.*

But Prescott wanted to see more. What was in the dresser? What kinds of clothing were inside the wardrobe? Would she discover the identity of the room's inhabitant if she searched the desk?

She slowly approached it and saw that a piece of paper was lying on top. Something was written on the scrap, but it was facedown. Prescott took the note by the corner and turned it over.

It was a list of names she recognized, and all but three had lines through them. The ones that didn't were "Joe Nance," "Harrison Brill," and "Stuart Clayton."

Sheer terror froze her to the spot as she dropped the scrap. Then she felt a sudden sensation of air moving behind her. Before she could act, a strong force grabbed hold of her and a cold and damp rag covered her mouth and nose. Prescott screamed but the cry was muffled. The cloth reeked of a horrible chemical smell that grew worse as she attempted to take in oxygen.

Her eyes focused on the wardrobe mirror. Prescott saw herself in the clutches of a tall blonde woman who had one arm around the PI's torso, and the other hand holding the cloth. The woman must have been hiding behind the oriental screen.

Then Prescott's vision blurred. The room tilted and spun.

Think! You're a martial arts expert!

Prescott managed to elbow her assailant in the stomach. There was a blunt cry of pain, but then a knee slammed into the middle of Prescott's back. Her knees weakened. The PI attempted a judo throw but her attacker resisted the maneuver with raw strength. Another blow in the back caused Prescott to drop to her knees. Whatever chemical was in the cloth, it was doing its job. She knew she was losing consciousness and there was nothing she could do about it. Prescott was aware of falling onto the rug.

The last thing she saw was that the blonde woman above her was wearing a floppy hat and sunglasses.

Chapter Twenty-four

Doctor Doctor
(performed by UFO)

Berenger took a taxi to the Meadowmere Southport Assisted Living Apartments on LaSalle, right across from city hall. He went inside, signed in at the front desk, and was shown to a comfortable sitting area where several elderly residents were watching the television, reading books, or playing cards. After a few minutes, a man of eightysomething came into the room using a walker. He was dressed in sweatpants and a sweatshirt that had a Chicago Bulls logo emblazoned on it. The man looked around, spotted Berenger, and approached him.

"You must be the young fellow my daughter told me about," he said.

Berenger stood and shook the man's hand. "Spike Berenger, sir. Glad to meet you."

"Jeremiah Levine." The doctor gestured to an empty sofa on the other side of the room. "Why don't we go sit over there where it's a little more quiet." Levine scooted the walker along at a reasonable pace and managed to lower himself onto the furniture without help. "It's my only real problem," he said once he was settled. "My legs have gone kaput. Especially the knees. I probably should've had the replacements done ten years ago, but I was stubborn and didn't do it. Now it's really too late to go through that kind of surgery at my age."

"You look like you're doing fine to me, sir."

"Thank you. You can call me Jeremiah. What was your name again?"

"Spike."

"Right. When my daughter told me your name, I expected I'd see a bulldog or something." He chuckled. "She said you're a private investigator. What can I do for you?"

"Do you remember a patient named Stuart Clayton?"

Berenger could have sworn that a shadow passed across the doctor's eyes. After a beat, he answered, "I do. His parents were good friends of mine. Lovely people."

"I was wondering if you could tell me about his . . . case. About what happened to him in nineteen seventy-three when he had his stroke."

"Stroke?"

"Didn't he have a stroke? Or a heart attack?"

The doctor's eyes narrowed. "Why do you want to know this, if I may ask?"

Berenger brought his voice down. "Mr. Clayton is the target of a killer who has been murdering rock 'n' roll musicians in Chicago. Several of his friends and former bandmates have already been killed. I recently learned about something that occurred in Mr. Clayton's past and it may be the reason behind the killer's motivation. Stuart—Mr. Clayton—is not well and has been reluctant to talk about it. In order to protect him, and perhaps figure out who the killer is, I need to understand more about Clayton's condition."

"You say Stuart is alive?"

"Yes, sir. Er, Jeremiah."

"He's still in Chicago?"

"Yes."

"I thought he'd moved to Europe."

"He came back in the early nineties."

"I didn't know that." The man shifted a little on the sofa. "You know, it goes against my ethics to reveal information about a patient—former patient or not—if he's still alive."

"I understand that. Perhaps if you spoke in general terms?"

"It's not that simple. I either tell you about him or I don't."

"What if I said that any information you tell me will be held in the strictest confidence, and that it's possibly something that could save Stuart's life?"

"I don't know . . ." The doctor shook his head. "If you had a court order or something . . ."

"Dr. Levine. There's a concert planned for tomorrow night featuring the remaining members of the band—and Stuart, too, if he agrees to show up—and we believe the killer is going to use that opportunity to strike. It's possible that anything you tell me will be totally useless, in which case I'll just forget about it and pretend we never spoke. But if it's something that has bearing on the situation and it can save some lives, then I have to know."

The doctor stared ahead for a few moments and then inhaled deeply. "Stuart Clayton did not have a stroke or a heart attack in . . . what year was it?"

"Nineteen seventy-three?"

"Yes. What happened was that he attempted suicide."

Berenger sat back. "How?"

"Drugs, of course. He had a long history with drug abuse. Especially street drugs. You do know that he's mentally ill?"

"Yes. That's fairly obvious."

"He was diagnosed as a schizophrenic when he was a teenager. Psychiatry in the sixties wasn't what it is today, you understand. His parents refused to take him to a psychiatrist. They thought there was a stigma attached to that. So I treated him for his mental illness. And I have to admit that I didn't really know what I was doing. Oh, I prescribed the correct medications, I'm sure of that. But the problem was that the boy began to experiment with those mind-altering drugs like LSD. And while LSD might not be harmful per se to the average person, for someone who already has an impaired mental condition it can be disastrous."

"I believe that."

"Stuart became bipolar as he matured, although that term was not used back then. He seemed to be fine when he was in a manic phase. He was productive, he was creative, he socialized, he played in his band . . . but during the depressive phase, he was pretty bad off. And in nineteen seventy-three, it got so bad that he tried to do himself in. He overdosed on LSD and another psychedelic drug, an herb that he grew in his backyard. I'd never heard of it at the time—"

"Would that be salvia divinorum?"

"That's it."

"So what happened?"

"I don't know who found him. He was down at the harbor where he had a boat—I forget which harbor—and he was lying on the pier, totally naked and unconscious. He was taken to a hospital. He was in a coma for two months. When he finally came out of it, he experienced several psychotic episodes. He had to be put in a psychiatric hospital for a year or so. I forget how long. He eventually recovered, more or less. But the experience left him disabled. Somehow the coma had affected his motor skills the way a stroke can—he lost some of the movement on his left side."

"I've noticed that."

"But he could still function. I thought he was rehabilitated as far as the drug abuse was concerned. So he was released."

"What happened after that?"

"His parents died in a terrible accident. It was a fire. On Stuart's boat."

"I heard that, but I didn't know it was on *his* boat."

"The story was that the whole family had taken it out on the lake—Stuart was with them—and somehow it caught fire. It sank, the parents were killed. Stuart suffered some minor burns but managed to grab a life vest and one of those lifesaver rings. The coast guard picked him up. After that, he wasn't the same. He was emotionally distraught. All the progress he'd made in the hospital went down the tubes. He came in to see me once or twice after that, and I discerned that he was abusing drugs again. I warned him about it." The doctor sighed heavily. "And I never saw him again. Sad case, really. I'm happy to hear that he's still alive. I was afraid he'd meet with a bad end."

The doctor looked away and frowned.

"Dr. Levine?"

"I'm sorry. I shouldn't have told you any of that. Stuart has a right to privacy just like anyone."

"Don't worry, Jeremiah. I won't tell—"

"Perhaps it's best if you go now. I said more than I wanted to say, but once I started talking, it just all came out. It's not your fault."

Berenger understood how the man felt and could appreciate the doctor's regret. But in the world of private investigation, secrets had to be unearthed and exposed by any means possible. In Berenger's mind, Levine had done nothing wrong. The man helped shed some light on one of the players in a complex and mystifying case.

"Thank you, Doctor." He stood and shook the man's hand. "Take care of yourself."

"I hope you solve your case."

"Me, too."

Berenger left the doctor on the sofa and headed for the front door. He said good-bye to the receptionist and went outside, where daylight was ebbing. The sun was low in the sky, blocked by the tall buildings.

From his pocket burst the strains of "21st Century Schizoid Man." He pulled out the mobile and noted that it was Remix calling.

"Berenger."

"Spike, there's something you got to see, man, like pronto, on the double!"

"What is it?"

"I got hold of those record albums—you know, Joe Nance's and Stuart Clayton's solo disks. I uploaded the music and the covers, just like you asked."

"Great."

"You need to take a look at the back cover of

245

Clayton's solo album, the one called *Trrrrans* with four Rs."

"I'm out and about and don't have Suzanne's laptop with me."

"Then go to a Kinko's and get online. Really, you need to see it."

"What is it, Remix?"

"It's best if you have a look yourself. I can't begin to describe it."

Berenger turned around and went back inside the building. Meadowmere's receptionist had a computer. "Okay, Remix. I'll take a look. I'll call you back if I have to." He hung up, approached the middle-aged woman, and asked, "Ma'am, pardon me, but is your computer connected to the Internet?"

"Yes, it is."

"Would you mind terribly if I just looked up something real quick?"

The woman frowned. "I don't know . . ."

"Pretty please?"

"Well, all right. But hurry. I don't want my supervisor seeing."

"I'll just be a few seconds." Berenger swung behind her desk, opened the browser, typed in the URL of Rockin' Security's server, entered his user name and password, and navigated to Remix's folders. The *Trrrrans* front cover consisted of nothing unusual—just a picture of Clayton, his back to the camera and looking into a blurred mirror. The reflection wasn't visible, but the words "Stuart Clayton" and the album's title were written across the top. Berenger then clicked on the link to view the back cover.

"Oh my God," Berenger whispered.

"Is something wrong?" the receptionist asked.

Berenger quickly closed the browser and moved from behind the desk. "No. Thanks very much."

He ran outside, pulled out his cell phone, and dialed Prescott's number. It rang twice but then went to her voice mail.

"Damn it, Suzanne!" He ended the call and then noticed that there was still a voice message he hadn't heard—from Prescott. He quickly connected to his mailbox and listened to what she had left him a couple of hours earlier.

A wave of dread surged through his gut.

He ran to the corner, whistled loudly, and hailed a cab. Once the taxi was on the way, Berenger phoned Mike Case and got voice mail—*didn't anyone answer the phone anymore?*—so he dialed 9-1-1. Not knowing exactly what he should tell the dispatcher, he merely said that there was a break-in at Clayton's address and to send a patrol car immediately. In a few minutes, the cab arrived at the decrepit house on Mango Avenue. The PI paid the driver, got out, started to run for the front door . . . and stopped.

Where's the rental car?

Prescott had driven it to Clayton's house, but it wasn't parked in front or anywhere on the street that Berenger could see. There was only a Chevy Malibu parked against the curb a couple of doors down. He pulled out his mobile and dialed Prescott's number again. Voice mail.

"Damn it, Suzanne!"

He went to the front door, and just as she had, found it ajar. Berenger knocked loudly and called inside, "Hello? Stuart? Suzanne?" There was no answer, but Berenger heard music coming from somewhere deep within the house. He wasn't sure exactly what it was, but it sounded familiar. He stepped inside and shouted louder, "Anyone home? Stuart? Suzanne?"

Berenger drew his Kahr and slowly walked to the kitchen. No one there—just a bunch of disgusting dirty dishes and the leftover pizza from the other evening still on the table. Yuck.

He searched the living room and found the broken picture frames and defaced photos, which caused his anxiety level to increase dramatically. From there he went back to the hallway, peeked into the first bedroom, then the second bedroom, and finally made his way to the studio.

The music was coming from the storage room. The door was open.

As he moved closer, he recognized the song that was playing. It was one of the tracks that the killer had left for him. Allegedly it was sung by Sylvia Favero, but it was really performed by Julia Faerie.

He saw the open trapdoor in the floor, something he hadn't noticed the first time he'd glimpsed the storeroom's interior. The music was drifting up from the basement. A light flickered down below. He knelt beside the opening and called, "Hello? Someone down there? Stuart?"

Berenger threw caution to the wind and descended the wooden staircase. Not realizing that he had followed in the footsteps of his partner, he found himself in the curtained anteroom with the lit candle illuminating the eerie chamber. He parted the drapes to reveal the subterranean living quarters. The music was coming from a CD player that sat on top of the dresser. No one was in the room, but there were several lit candles placed in various locations. The overall effect was macabre and funereal.

Then he saw her.

Prescott was lying on the bed at the other end of the room. She appeared to be asleep.

"Suzanne!"

Berenger ran across the Persian carpet, reached the bed, holstered his handgun, and leaned over to examine his partner. He touched her cheek—it was warm. He bent down and put his ear to her chest—her heart was beating. He rose and then lightly patted her face. "Suzanne, wake up. Hey. Suzanne!"

Perhaps it was the sixth sense he had developed working as a military investigator in Southeast Asia. Maybe it was the years of experience he held as a private detective. Whatever it was, Berenger's spine tingled and warned him that he was in danger.

He looked up and saw his reflection in the large oval mirror on the wardrobe. A woman with blonde hair, a floppy hat, and sunglasses was rushing toward him from behind. She had a sap in her hand, raised above her head.

Berenger whirled around and deflected a blow with his left arm. It hurt like hell and he yelped. The attacker screamed like a banshee and attempted to hit him again. The PI ducked and rolled out from under the woman's arm, but his assailant stuck out a leg and tripped him. He pitched forward and slammed onto the floor, facedown. Berenger twisted his body to avoid being pummeled but it was too late.

The sap came crashing down on his forehead.

Lights out.

* * *

The two patrolmen knocked loudly on the front door. When there was no answer, one of them asked the other, "Should we force it open?"

"Doesn't look broken into to me. I don't think anybody's home."

"Wait, I hear someone."

There was the sound of shuffling feet behind the door. It opened to reveal a tall, thin man with a cane.

"Yes?"

"Police officers, sir."

"I see that."

"We had a call that there was some trouble here. Is everything all right?"

Stuart Clayton blinked in confusion. "There's no trouble here."

The officers could see that something was wrong with the left side of the man's mouth. A stroke victim, perhaps?

"Is anyone else in the house with you?"

"No, I live alone."

"And everything's all right?"

"Everything is fine, Officers."

The two patrolmen looked at each other and shrugged. "Okay then. Must have been a false alarm. Sorry to bother you, sir."

"No bother. Thanks for checking."

The two officers walked back to their car. Clayton watched them drive away before he shut and locked the door.

Chapter Twenty-five

Down With the Sickness
(performed by Disturbed)

Prescott awoke nauseated and disoriented, with a massive headache and dry mouth. She was aware that she was lying horizontal on something comfortable— a bed, perhaps. But when she tried to move, she found that she couldn't. Her wrists were tied to the wooden headboard, which was made of two solid and decorative oak posts with several straight, vertical slats in between. Her ankles were tied to a matching footboard.

She was aware that someone was lying next to her on the bed. Prescott turned her head, attempted to focus her eyes, and realized it was Berenger. He, too, was restrained in the same manner. More troubling was the appearance of a wound on his forehead. The gray and brown hair on his frontal scalp was matted with dried blood. He was breathing heavily but was unconscious.

Her vision slowly cleared and she remembered where she was. With some effort, she was able to lift her head and scan her surroundings. The basement of Clayton's house was lit with several candles placed around the room. Strange music was playing from a CD player sitting on the dresser. She didn't see anyone.

Prescott turned back to her partner. "Spike?" Her voice was a hoarse whisper. She cleared her throat,

swallowed, and tried again. "Spike! Spike! Wake up!"
She attempted to bump her waist against his. Berenger
snorted with an intake of breath and made a throaty
gurgling noise. "Spike! Wake up!" She jostled her body
on the bed, causing the mattress to bounce on the
springs. *"Wake up!"*

Finally, the big man snorted again and moaned. His
eyes opened.

"Spike, it's me. I'm right here next to you."

He groaned in pain and confusion. Just as she had
done, he tried to move and discovered he was bound.
"What . . . what the . . . ?"

"Spike, we're tied up. We're in Clayton's basement."

"Su . . . Suzanne?"

"Yes! How do you feel? Are you all right?"

"Ohhhh, fuck. My . . . head. Fuck."

"You have a nasty bump on your forehead. What
happened?"

"I don't know. Wait . . . I remember. She . . . attacked me. The bitch . . . hit me . . ."

"She got me, too."

"Where . . . where is . . . she now?"

"I don't know."

He groaned louder. "Oh, my head."

"You might have a concussion. You need to stay
awake, Spike."

"I don't know . . ." His words were slurring. "I just
wanna sleep some more . . ."

"Spike! No!"

"Wait . . . wait a minute . . . I found out . . . something . . ."

"What? What did you find out? Spike!"

He mumbled and drifted away.

"Spike! Stay awake!"

"Huh?"

"What did you find out?"

"Trying to . . . remember . . . oh . . . yeah . . . she's not . . . she's not . . ."

"What? She's not what?"

"We're all . . . wrong . . . the . . . killer isn't . . ."

"Spike, what are you saying?"

But before he could answer, Prescott heard steps on the staircase at the other end of the room. She raised her head and saw the woman walking toward them. Their captor wore blue jeans, a baby-doll top, and the trademark floppy hat. Her sunglasses shielded most of her face from them.

"You're awake," the woman said. The voice was low and soft.

"My friend needs medical attention," Prescott said. "You hit him on the head. He's got a concussion."

The woman came closer, bent over Berenger and touched his head. The PI moaned, but didn't move. He was still dazed.

"It doesn't look so bad," the woman said. "It's a shame that you decided to work against me. He was going to produce my record. Now I see he was lying."

"Who are you?"

"You know who I am."

"You're not Sylvia Favero. She's dead."

The woman ignored her and moved to the wardrobe. She opened it and removed what appeared to be a Turkish hookah, but it was unlike any hookah that Prescott had seen before. There were four hoses protruding from the large water jar at the base of the contraption. An air mask that fit over the mouth and nose was attached to the end of each hose instead of the usual cylindrical mouthpiece. The hookah's single-stem body was tall, nearly four feet, and there was a large dish at the top. There appeared to be a motor underneath the dish.

"What the fuck is that?" Prescott asked.

The woman pushed the hookah across the rug and set it next to the bed. She then took a hose, placed the face mask on Berenger, and slipped the elastic band around his head so that it fit snugly over his mouth and nose. She then took another hose and mask and moved toward Prescott.

"Don't you touch me with that!"

Prescott rocked her head back and forth, struggling against the woman's strength. But the nausea returned and suffocated her, so she had to stop. Vomiting would not be a pleasant act, given that she and Berenger were restrained and lying on their backs. The killer got the face mask on her and tightened the elastic strap.

What was she going to do? Poison us?

The woman went back to the wardrobe and removed more items. She came back to the bed holding a large freezer bag full of what appeared to be oregano or marijuana. In her other hand was a butane lighter with a long stem. She carefully emptied some of the leafy material onto the hookah dish. Apparently there were several small bowls fastened to the top of the dish, placed around the inner side of its circumference. She filled each bowl with the substance and then flipped a switch on the motor. The dish slowly began to turn. The woman then attached an odd horseshoe-shaped object onto the stem beneath the dish. This "arm" stuck out beyond and over the dish so that its end pointed down at the moving bowls as they passed beneath it. Finally, the woman ignited the butane lighter and lit what appeared to be wick inside a container of oil that was built into the top of the arm.

She's going to make us smoke something . . . !

As Prescott watched with trepidation, she began to understand how the hookah worked. The dish was on a motorized timer. As the dish slowly turned, each bowl would align itself beneath the lit wick for a certain amount of time. As she and Berenger breathed, smoke would be drawn in from the bowl, through the hookah stem, and out of the hoses and face masks. There was nothing they could do to prevent themselves from breathing the smoke. After a few minutes, the dish continued to turn; the bowl and what was left in it would move away from the flame. But several minutes after that, a fresh bowl would line up with the flame.

One of the bowls was nearing the lit wick. The woman stood by the bed to watch and make sure the hookah was working properly.

Prescott's eyes grew wide with fear. What could possibly be in those bowls? If it was pot or tobacco, fine, she could handle it.

The bowl was almost there. Another few seconds . . .

Prescott smelled the smoke as it wafted into her face mask. She attempted to hold her breath as the mask filled, but the bowl stayed aligned with the fire for much longer than she could stand. Eventually she had to take a breath. It couldn't be helped—she inhaled the smoke into her lungs.

The effect was almost immediate. She felt a familiar rumbling sensation through her body and then she recognized the taste.

Salvia divinorum! Oh my God . . . !

And then she was tripping. Prescott felt her consciousness separate from her physical self and flatten into what seemed to be a membranelike plane. The room became a vessel filled with turbulence as she struggled against her binds, but her arms and legs were appendages with minds of their own. There was an impression of falling within herself, as if she were turning inside out. Then her body's molecules fused with the bed she was lying on and she became a part of the furniture—or she was the bed. She was aware of herself thinking, No! No! No! but at the same time there was a deafening roar in her ears that was the whirlpool of textures, lights, and sounds around her.

This unpleasantness broke away and developed into something new and more terrifying. Her free-floating consciousness was traveling at a great speed on a roller coaster of nerves, brain stems, blood cells, and veins. She was inside the membrane that was her only existence now—a living, breathing, fleshy layer of tissue that contained everything that was once Suzanne Prescott. The membrane was connected to the universe by stretchy tendrils of skin and hair. It was as if the cells of her body had gone through a blender and come out on the other side as *something else.*

Time was zero. Thoughts were oceans. She passed through a rip in reality and there was no way back.

And then . . . it began to wane . . .

Prescott had a human body again. Slowly, fluidly, gently . . . she became herself . . .

She didn't know how long the hallucinations lasted, but the trip was the most frightening thing she'd ever experienced. She had experimented with all manner of substances when she was younger. The salvia she had tried in the Far East was not as powerful as this. The woman was likely using the highest strength of extract possible. It was totally concentrated, pure, and dangerous.

Prescott was aware of the room once again. She turned her head and saw the hookah, which was now a totem pole of madness and evil. The dish was still turning and she understood that the bowl had cleared the lit wick. It would be some time before the next bowl aligned itself beneath the flame. Time enough to think . . . think . . .

Think! she commanded herself. Snap out of it!

She struggled and pulled her arms and legs against the binds.

Have . . . to . . . get . . . out . . . of . . . this!

She looked over at Berenger. What could he have just experienced? With a head wound, perhaps a concussion, what would the salvia trip have done to him? Sweat poured from his head. He breathed unsteadily. His eyes were closed.

Prescott tried to speak, but the face mask muffled her voice. She attempted to scream, but it was no use. Her eyes darted around, focusing on various objects in the room, and she realized that their captor was no longer there. The killer had left them alone with this . . . *torture*. Would it kill them? Or would it simply drive them mad? How long would it last? Prescott was unable to see how many bowls of salvia were on the dish. But several powerful doses of the stuff over an extended period of time could be disastrous.

She had to do something . . . but what?

* * *

By Friday at noon, Mike Case was worried. He had seen that Berenger had attempted to call him the night before but the PI hadn't left a message. Case tried calling Berenger on his cell three times that morning but got only voice mail. He had also learned that the PI had placed a 9-1-1 call to report a break-in at Stuart Clayton's house. The police officers who investigated the incident said nothing had happened. Case didn't go on duty until three o'clock, so on his own initiative he drove by Clayton's abode on Mango Avenue. He noted that there was nothing unusual. No cars were parked in front. The drapes were closed, which was typical of a shut-in like Clayton. As a last resort, he phoned Clayton's home number. The man answered, sounding as if he'd been wakened by the call. At first he didn't seem to know who Berenger and Prescott were, and then he recalled their visit. No, they had not been by since the other night, he told Case.

Since Bushnell's death, the Chicago Musician Murders Task Force was not as busy as before, but Doherty had arranged special details to work the benefit concert at the Park West that night. Case asked to be assigned to the detail, but the venue was in the Eighteenth District. Case worked for the Fourteenth. Even though the two districts were adjacent, Doherty said no. Rules were rules.

But Case figured that since he was an undercover Tac officer, he could maybe get away with "accidentally" patrolling across the district line.

The Park West was one of Chicago's most desirable and attractive venues for rock concerts. Touted as a "multimedia facility," the building had been around since the 1920s and housed various entertainment venues until it became the Park West in 1977. It was one of the few large spaces in Chicago that also had tables where patrons could sit, have beverages, and listen to live music.

Bud Callahan arrived at the venue early afternoon to oversee the setup. Rick Tittle and Harrison Brill were already there.

"It's been a while since we've played a venue as big as the Park West," Brill commented. "I'm looking forward to it."

"How's Joe doing?" Callahan asked.

"Okay, I guess. He went on a five-day binge after Charles's wake. He'll be here, though. We're a little spooked, I must admit."

"The stage manager said there will be plenty of police presence tonight. If that bitch comes anywhere near the venue, they'll get her."

"You can't catch a ghost, Bud."

"You don't really believe that, do you?"

Brill shrugged. "I don't know what I believe." His cell phone rang. He dug it out of his pocket. "Yeah? Oh, hi Joe. Yeah. What? *No shit?* That's fucking incredible. Okay, I'll let everyone know. When are you coming? Okay. See you." He hung up and said, "You're not going to believe this."

"What?"

"Stuart Clayton called Joe and said he wanted to play tonight."

"No shit?"

"That's what I said."

"I haven't seen Stuart perform in . . . what, thirty-five years?"

"Something like that. He'll be bringing his keyboards

in a while. We're to let everyone know. He might need some help unloading and setting up. He's disabled, you know."

"Yeah."

Tittle jumped off the stage and joined them. "Do we have an idea what ticket sales are like?" he asked.

"I've heard it's selling out fast," Callahan answered. "Two-thirds of the tickets sold within an hour after the concert was announced. The rest will be sold by showtime, I'll bet."

"Did you hear what I just told Bud?" Brill asked.

"No, what?"

"Stuart Clayton's playing with us tonight."

"No shit?"

Callahan and Brill laughed.

"Su . . . Su . . ."

"Spike?"

"Su . . . zanne?"

"Can you hear me?" The face masks muffled the words, but she hoped they could penetrate the miasma of the plastic and the chaotic mental cloudiness well enough to reach his ears.

"What's . . . what's . . . ?"

"We're in . . . trouble, Spike. We're in trouble!"

A fourth bowl aligned beneath the flame. Again smoke filled the face masks . . . and their lungs.

Chapter Twenty-six

Soul Sacrifice
(performed by Santana)

There was a lull in the intoxication, as the flame on the hookah was between bowls of salvia. Prescott was thankful that she knew something about the herb. Even though the effects came on quickly and intensely, they didn't last very long. Once the drug ceased being ingested, a person returned to reality within a few minutes. Subtle lingering effects could remain for an hour or more, but at least there was a sense of normalcy after the initial five-minute rush. A person could *think*.

She had lost track of how many bowls of the stuff they had smoked. Apparently the entire contents of a bowl were not burned while it was beneath the flame. The dish could spin around several times before the bowls would be empty. She knew hours had gone by, but it was difficult to measure time under the influence of the drug.

"Spike!" she called through the face mask. "Can you hear me?"

Berenger was having a tough time. She noticed that at times he was alert between inhalations, but he was confused and frightened. Perhaps the head wound was exacerbating his bewilderment. He hadn't completely comprehended what was happening to him.

So it was up to her. Prescott decided that if she had to sacrifice her soul to do it, she would free them.

If only she could get her arms out of the binds. The rope was tightly tied and the skin of her wrists was rubbed raw. But the headboard and footboard were made of wood. Surely the wood could be broken. Could she summon the strength to do it?

Once again, Prescott struggled by pulling and pushing with all of her might. Both the headboard and footboard rattled and shook along with the mattress, but she was unable to break anything.

She could smell the salvia again. Another dose was imminent. Prescott was determined not to let it mess her up, but she knew that was an impossible task.

Or was it?

Prescott would have kicked herself if she had been able. Why hadn't she thought of it before?

She was a practitioner of Transcendental Meditation! And she was good at it. She'd been doing it for fifteen years!

There was no need to concentrate. The steps were simple. She just needed to relax and repeat the mantra that her instructor had bestowed upon her during the seven-step course she had taken so long ago. The process would clear her mind, block out the external stimuli, and energize her.

Whether or not TM would block the effects of salvia—she had no idea. But it was worth the try.

She began. Slowly, quietly, she repeated the mantra and allowed herself to drift into the trance she knew so well.

The next bowl of salvia aligned with the flame. She was aware of the smoke entering the face mask.

Deeper . . . let the trance take you . . . deeper . . .

The words of her instructor echoed in her brain. When she had first learned how to meditate, the teacher gave her a set of simple instructions that put her into a trance. With practice, she was able to follow these instructions in her mind and do it herself. Her twice-a-day, twenty-minute ritual was now so habitual that Prescott could meditate on cue.

She began to feel the effects of the drug . . . but suddenly everything was different. Somehow she was now looking down on the membrane that was her consciousness instead of being inside of it, trapped by the drug. This was a new experience for her. She was more aware of her surroundings than she had been before, even though the salvia was surging through her system.

Deeper . . .

Fully into the meditative trance, Prescott was now able to completely ignore her surroundings. There was no longer a face mask on her mouth and nose, she was not tied to a bed, she was not a captive . . . she was free . . . her mind and body existed above and beyond the trappings of the physical world and the organic hallucinogen that threatened to drive her insane.

What she needed now was adrenaline. *Strength.*

She found that because she was outside of her consciousness, she was able to look inside her body with a new sense that wasn't one of the five customary ones. Examine the heart? No problem. It's beating fine. The lungs? Full of smoke, but who cares? The nervous system? A bit rattled, but it was nothing she couldn't overcome. The glandular system? Ah, that's where she needed to be. Squeeze some of the juice from the adrenal gland and get her muscles working. That's it. Feel the gush of energy flowing through her veins. Hear the roar of power filling those muscles. Her body was a machine, damn it, and she was going to make it work!

Prescott pulled hard with her arms.

Harder!

Again. The rope bit into her wrists.

Come on! Work those muscles! Feel that lovely chemical spurting from the glands!

Again! The wood in the headboard splintered.

Harder! Embrace the strength! Make it yours!

Again! The headboard post to which she was tied split in two.

Prescott pulled her arms down and immediately ripped off her face mask. She gasped a breath of pure, clean oxygen, and sat up. With her wrists still tied together, she reached over and removed Berenger's mask and threw it on the floor.

Using her teeth, she managed to loosen the knot around her wrists. It took another twenty seconds to free them, and then another forty seconds to untie her ankles.

She really *was* free.

Prescott set about untying Berenger and then sitting him up against the headboard.

"Spike! Wake up, honey. Come on." She slapped him lightly on the cheek. "Get that shit out of your system. Come on, it's Suzanne talking. Do you hear me? Make a noise if you hear me!"

Berenger moaned and his eyelids fluttered.

"That's it, come back to me, Spike. Come back to earth!"

She knew it would be a few minutes before the salvia effects would diminish. Nevertheless, she continued to lightly pat his face and speak to him.

"You're okay, Spike. You're coming back down. You're back in reality. Do you hear me, Spike? Talk to me. What's my name?"

He said something unintelligible.

"What? I didn't catch that. What's my name?"

"Su . . . Su . . . Suzanne . . ."

"Yes! Good boy, Spike! You're coming out of it. That's it! Breathe deeply. Come on, take some deep breaths."

He did as he was told. Berenger coughed but continued to inhale fresh air. His eyelids opened and he looked at her.

"Spike? You see me?"

Berenger nodded. "What . . . what the hell . . . happened to me?"

"Don't worry about it yet. You're still under the influence of . . . well, of a drug. You'll snap out of it soon."

"What . . . drug?"

"Never mind. Just concentrate on breathing. I'm going to find some water. We're both dehydrated. I'll be right back. Don't move!"

Prescott climbed over him and stood by the bed. She started to move away but found that she was too unsteady. She reached out and grabbed the hookah for support, but she lost her balance and fell, bringing the contraption down with her.

"Suzanne! Are you—?"

"Don't get up!" she commanded. "You're too uncoordinated right now, just like me. That's one of the effects of the drug."

"What drug, damn it!"

"Salvia, Spike. The bitch made us smoke salvia!"

Berenger put a hand to his head. "Ohhhhhh, no. Is that why my head hurts so bad?"

"Well, you were hit on the forehead, too." Prescott managed to pull herself up and sit on the bed next to him. "You probably have a concussion. Can you feel the bump?"

"Yeah." He winced. "Hurts like a mother—"

"How did you get it? Do you remember?"

"Uh, yeah. I came in here and found you on the bed. I was attacked from behind. Got hit with something."

He put his feet on the floor.

"Want to try standing?" she asked.

"Sure."

They held hands and pushed their butts off the bed. At first Berenger was very wobbly, but she held on to him until his equilibrium stabilized.

"Hey, success!" he said. He rubbed his eyes. "Man, I feel very strange. I'm still stoned, I think."

"You are. You'll feel that way for an hour or two."

"How come you're not?"

"Oh, I am, but I found a way to combat it."

"How's that?"

"TM, Spike. I keep telling you—you should try it!"

"Meditation? Are you serious?"

"That's how I got us out of this mess. Come on, can you walk? We need to get out of here."

"What time is it? What *day* is it? Oh, wait, I'm wearing my watch." He looked at it. "Shit, Suzanne, it's seven P.M., Friday. That benefit concert is going to start in an hour!" He reached for his handgun and experienced another shock. "Shit! My gun's gone!"

He began to move around the room, taking it all in for the first time. "Is it here somewhere?"

"I doubt it. But look at that cabinet on the wall."

Berenger walked carefully to the gun case and whistled. "I'll bet anything that's the sniper rifle that killed Jim Axelrod."

"That's what I thought, too." She found her handbag on the desk. "Here's my purse."

He looked around for a blunt object.

What the hell—He picked up the guitar and swung it at the cabinet. The glass shattered, leaving a sizable hole in the door. Berenger dropped the guitar, reached into the cabinet, and removed a handgun—a Browning 9mm. He checked the magazine, saw that it was fully loaded, and shoved it into his holster. It wasn't a perfect fit but it would do. He didn't care if it might have been the weapon used in some of the shootings.

"Come on." He headed for the staircase and started to climb, but he stopped suddenly and sat on one of the steps.

"Are you all right?"

"Yeah. Got dizzy for a second." He breathed deeply a couple of times, paused for a moment, and then slapped his knees. "I'm all right now." He stood and ascended to the ground floor. Prescott followed him. They emerged from the storage room and went straight toward the front door. When they were outside, Berenger raised his arms to the sky and shouted, "I love you, sky!"

"Spike! Geez!"

He looked up and down the street, and then he remembered. "Hey, where's the car, Suzanne?"

Her brow wrinkled. "I don't know. I parked it right there in front of the house."

"Did the perp take it?"

"Want to check the garage?"

"Good idea."

They hurried to the side of the house and saw the padlocked garage door.

"Oh, why not . . ." Berenger said as he drew the Browning from the holster. One shot blasted the lock off the door. Together they pulled the door up and, sure enough, the rental car was inside.

"Do you still have the keys?"

She looked inside her handbag and nodded.

"Can you drive?"

"I think so."

He felt his pocket and found his cell phone. "Lookie here." He opened it and saw that Mike Case had tried to call him several times. "Let's go. I'm going to call Mike."

They got inside the car; she started the ignition, and backed out. As he was dialing Case's number, Prescott said, "I'm gonna kill that bitch if I get my hands on her."

Berenger looked at her in confusion. "That bitch?"

"Yeah."

He slapped his knees. "Holy shit! Didn't I tell you what I found out?"

"No. What did you find out?"

"About the album cover?"

"What album cover?"

"The one Remix put on our server! I didn't tell you?"

"No, you didn't tell me! What? What?"

"Drive. I'll tell you on the way. Let me call Mike first."

Chapter Twenty-seven

In My Time of Dying
(performed by Led Zeppelin)

The Park West stage manager, Gus Watkins, was not in a good mood.

Five more minutes and he would make the call for places. The opening configuration of musicians consisted of Joe Nance, Harrison Brill, Bud Callahan, and Rick Tittle performing a Windy City Engine set. The plan was that Stuart Clayton would join the quartet after three songs and pleasantly surprise the hell out of the audience. Whether or not he would show had been the hot topic for days on prog-rock fan-site message boards. The trio would yield while the legendary recluse performed a short solo set of one or two pieces, and then the new quintet would present Red Skyez and more Clayton solo material. The second half of the show was to begin with the same five musicians on stage, joined by Sharon Callahan, Paul Trinidad, and Greg Cross for South Side and North Side tunes. Headliners Windy City Engine would close the show, but the encore would culminate in one big Chicago-prog jam session. It was supposed to be the wet dream of every progressive rock fan in the Midwest.

So far, though, things had not gone so well for Watkins. Stuart Clayton had arrived an hour and a half before showtime, which was also at least a couple of hours late for setup and sound check. That put every-thing behind schedule and Watkins was not pleased. Additionally, some of the lighting equipment failed to work and a union electrician had to run out to pick up some replacement parts. Nevertheless, in the eleventh hour the professional stagehands, music techs, and the bands' road crews, had everything ready to go—lights and all. Sound check went smoothly. Everything was cool.

The other band members made a big show of wel-coming the legendary recluse; many of them had not seen Clayton since his departure from Red Skyez in 1973. Joe Nance was the last one to peek out of the dressing room and greet the man with whom he had played in The Loop. He was shocked by Clayton's ap-pearance, but he did his best not to show it. Clayton was disheveled, frail, and pale, and he leaned on a cane. Nance presumed him to be very ill. He wondered if there was a possibility that his former bandmate might not be able to pull off the evening. After all, the rest of the band had rehearsed. Could Clayton smoothly fit in to the dynamics of what was happening onstage? What if he was terrible?

After the initial greeting and sound check, Clayton didn't speak to anyone. He went straight to his dress-ing room and shut the door, not wishing to be disturbed until his "places" call. Nance and the others looked at each and shrugged. They would make the best of it, but they weren't very happy about their old friend's demeanor.

As for Gus Watkins, he preferred country-and-western music.

* * *

The lingering effects of the drug continued to make Berenger quiet and introspective. Prescott merged into traffic on the Kennedy and then looked at him.

"You okay?"

"Yeah. I just feel weird."

She nodded and focused on the road. "I know, Spike. We were exposed to high doses of salvia for hours. I'm surprised we're not totally loony."

"If I close my eyes and think about it, I feel it all over again."

"That's one of the coming-down effects. You just have to think about the here and now, and don't day-dream."

"You saved my life, Suzanne."

"I saved mine at the same time, so consider it two for the price of one."

Berenger didn't smile. "How about you? You can drive okay?"

"I'm fine. Look, Spike, you've also got a concussion. I should take you to an emergency room."

"No!"

"Spike!"

"Just get to the Park West!"

Prescott exited onto North Avenue and turned east. They were ten minutes away.

King Crimson alerted Berenger that he had a call.

"Mike! Am I glad to hear you! Listen, I—what? Uh huh?" He passed on the news to Prescott, "Says he got my message, he's on his way to the venue, and he let the security team there know what was going on." Back to the cell. "Mike, listen to me. It's very important. They have to stop Stuart Clayton from going onstage."

*   *   *

The Park West was sold out, as Callahan had predicted. In fact, it had become the hot ticket in town, not to mention a major event in the world of prog rock. Ticket holders came from afar—not only from all over the U.S., but also the UK, Europe, Russia, and as far away as Japan. Scalpers were making fortunes on the street. Hundreds of fans swarmed the venue in the hopes of finding someone selling seats. As a result, people were still pouring into the theater when the clock struck eight. The audience was made up of a highly diversified mix of ages, races, and income levels (although 92 percent of the entire house was male). There were longtime fans of the original bands who were in their forties, fifties, and older. A younger crowd appreciated the historical significance of the music but also enjoyed the recent material by North Side or Windy City Engine. There were people who go to rock concerts regardless of who's playing, and there were the VIPs who attended, wanting to support the bands but also be seen. Just about every musical celebrity who had been at Charles Nance's wake was present. There were rumors that Pink Floyd's Nick Mason and The Moody Blues' John Lodge were in the audience. Excitement in the house was at a high. The diehards recognized the importance of the night's show and that it was most likely the last time these musicians played together. They were also aware of the recent tragic events, which placed another layer of tension on the proceedings. The large police presence was, for once, understood and welcomed.

Local hometown media had arrived in force. Even

though the musicians were not superstars, they were legends in the Chicago music scene. Print, radio, and television coverage was a given. At the last minute a deal was made with a cable channel to videotape the concert and broadcast it at a later date. The various record labels handling Windy City Engine and the other band members struck agreements to record and release a live CD documenting the evening.

Anticipation was at its highest when the stage manager announced over the PA that no photographs could be taken nor recordings made during the concert. When the lights finally went out, the crowd roared their approval. Follow-spots hit the stage as Nance, Brill, Callahan, and Tittle walked on from the wings. They waved to the standing-room-only audience, took a few bows, and then donned their instruments. Callahan had his own array of gear, including a Hammond B3 organ, a Leslie 145, a Mellotron M400, a Minimoog, a Sequential Circuits Prophet 5, an ARP Soloist, a Korg T2, and a Roland S550. Joe Nance used a Fender Strat, a Gibson Les Paul, and a Taylor six- and twelve-string acoustic. Rick Tittle played a Mapex Orion Series 7 kit and Meinl Byzance cymbals. Harrison Brill's equipment consisted of a Rickenbacker 4001 and a Korg Prophecy bass synth.

The two engineers at the soundboard had their work cut out for them.

As soon as the band was ready, Tittle began a syncopated 5/4 rhythm line that everyone in the house knew as the opening to one of Windy City Engine's more well-known songs, "The Mayor and the Player." Brill's bass line meshed into the drumbeat until it reached a crescendo, at which point the keyboards and guitar joined in. The audience was on its feet. They cheered again when Nance started to sing. He was in fine voice and the concert was off to a magnificent opening.

Prescott turned onto Armitage and discovered a mob scene outside the Park West.

"Where the hell am I going to park?"

"Damn," Berenger said. "Park illegally! I don't give a—"

They both screamed! A couple ran across the road in front of the car and Prescott had to slam on the brakes. The young man and woman just laughed and the guy made a peace sign with his right hand. "Peace, man!" he called.

"Careful, there are a lot of cops." Berenger scanned a side street and spotted a space in front of a fire hydrant. "Pull over there!"

"The car's registered to you and not me, right?" she asked as she made the turn.

"I'll pay the goddamned fine. Just park the car!"

She did. The two PIs jumped out and ran toward the building. They pushed through the crowd and made their way to the front doors, where two policemen stood guard.

One of them said, "Tickets." It was a command, not a question.

"We're private detectives working the Musician Murders case. Let us in!"

Berenger was obviously out of breath and still woozy from his ordeal. The ugly lesion on his forehead didn't look very pretty either. The cop nudged the other and said, "Oh, is that right? And I'm Humphrey Bogart. Who's she, Lauren Bacall?"

"Officer, you have to believe me—"

"Sure, sure, we've heard it all tonight. Every Tom, Dick, and Harry—and I do mean hairy!—wants in. Go on, get out of here!"

"But, Officer—"

The other patrolman, a much bigger man, stepped forward. "Look, Mac, did you hear him? Move along!"

"It's all right, Officers!"

Mike Case emerged from the multitude of people on the sidewalk. He held up his badge for the guards' benefit. "Officer Mike Case. These two are with me. I'm on the task force. Let us in."

The big policeman shrugged and gestured toward the door. "Be my guests."

"Thank you," Prescott said. She was beginning to feel the inevitable adrenaline crash. After expending so much epinephrine earlier, her body was dragging. She leaned on Berenger's arm as they slipped through the door, looking even more like stoned-out concertgoers. The first guard stared at them.

"It's okay," Case said again. "They've just been tortured and almost murdered with mind-altering drugs."

"Oh, all right then," the cop nodded. "No problem."

The trio entered the lobby and rushed to the center-aisle door. The band was playing hard and loud, the crowd was digging it, and the electrifying vibe was palpable. Berenger, Prescott, and Case stood at the back of the house, taking it all in.

"What do we do?" Prescott shouted at Berenger.

"I . . . I'm not sure."

"I should go find Doherty!" Case yelled. "Stay here!"

275

Berenger nodded.

The band was at the end of the intricate and epic-length "Funnel Cake Fandango," after which they rocked through a five-minute jam. The medley ended with "Cab Ride with Magritte," an impressive, techni-cally proficient riff that alternated between a 3/4 time signature to one of 7/8. They were surprisingly tight and dead-on for an underrehearsed group of musicians.

When the applause waned, Nance stepped up to the microphone and said, "Thank you. Now it's time for a little surprise for all you Red Skyez fans out there."

Cheers.

"And maybe for some of you fans who once liked a little band called The Loop, if any of you are still alive."

More cheers.

"He hasn't been onstage since nineteen seventy-three, folks. We managed to talk him into joining us tonight. So give a warm welcome to Stuart Clayton!"

The house went nuts. People screamed, whistled, cheered, stomped the floor . . . and then the noise abruptly fell away when a figure emerged from the wings.

It was a woman with long blonde hair, sunglasses, blue jeans, a baby-doll top, and a flowery floppy hat. The four musicians onstage all did double takes and stepped back, astonished. Nance's mouth dropped as the woman moved past him and took her place stand-ing behind Clayton's keyboards.

Someone in the crowd yelled, "That's not Stuart!" Laughter.

The woman spoke into a microphone. Her voice was soft, low, and sultry. "To start off my set, I want to sing you a song I wrote many years ago."

She immediately launched into a number that both Berenger and Prescott recognized as one of the tracks that the killer had left at the crime scenes. The musician played two keyboards at once, producing the kind of full, orchestral sound that Rick Wakeman would envy. The number was slow, haunting, and a complete change of mood and tempo from the previous set. Someone in the audience booed. There were some cat-calls.

Then she began to sing. The voice was the same as Berenger and Prescott remembered it . . . almost.

"Spike! What do we do?" Prescott whispered.

Berenger was frozen where he stood. It was a train wreck in slow motion. All he could was say, "Shhh."

Nance, Callahan, Brill, and Tittle remained onstage, staring at the newcomer with astonishment. Then, very slowly, Tittle and Brill managed to join with some rhythm and bass. By the last verse, Nance was also strumming the chords and Callahan filled out the sound with piano arpeggios.

When the song ended, there was scattered applause, more boos, and a few shouts of "Where's Stuart?"

The woman removed her sunglasses.

Nance, who was standing too close to his microphone, could be heard throughout the house when he said, "Oh my God. It's Stuart."

The other members looked closer at the musician onstage. Without the sunglasses, the keyboardist's face was visible. It *was* Stuart Clayton . . . dressed in drag and women's makeup.

He removed the floppy hat, and suddenly it was apparent to everyone. That was a man onstage, not a woman. The audience realized it was Stuart Clayton and the lull in excitement received a boost. The physical transformation was remarkable. Sylvia Favero was so dissimilar from the weak and fragile Stuart Clayton that it was as if an actor with the genius of Laurence Olivier had taken the stage.

Both Berenger and Prescott were astonished by how tall, broad shouldered, and muscular Clayton now appeared. He had walked onstage without a cane and played the keyboards with no noticeable handicap. The fifty-nine-year-old man was in perfect health. In fact, he was well enough to take down an adversary the size of Spike Berenger. That was the benefit of regularly training on Nautilus machines. It came easily to Clayton; after all, he had been a track-and-field star in his middle- and high-school years.

"I'll be damned," Prescott said.

"Told you so."

Clayton spoke into the microphone with the same feminine voice with which he had sung. "Thank you, everyone. And for my next number . . ."

The handgun appeared from nowhere. Berenger recognized his Kahr 9mm in Clayton's hand, and it was pointed at Harrison Brill.

Before anyone could react, the pistol cracked. Brill jerked and stumbled backward.

The audience collectively gasped. Someone screamed.

Clayton aimed the gun at Joe Nance. The guitarist had time only to open his eyes wide with fear.

The gun fired again. Nance twisted on his feet and dropped to his knees.

More screams. The audience panicked. A mass, uncontrolled evacuation ensued. Berenger and Prescott were caught in the onslaught of the stampede, but the sudden pandemonium was the catalyst for the PI to jump into action. He used his big body as a battering ram and thrust down the aisle toward the stage. Prescott followed in his wake.

Several policemen who had been on the outer aisles ran forward with their sidearms drawn. Someone yelled, "Freeze!" at Clayton, for the officers all trained their weapons on the musician. There were commands for him to drop the weapon.

And then Clayton pointed the gun under his chin with one hand and removed the blonde wig with the other. Right before their eyes, the man changed his body posture and exhibited a totally different physical language. With his left hand, he grasped the side of a keyboard to support himself, as if it were his cane. He had become Stuart Clayton again.

"Don't shoot him!" Berenger yelled. "Hold your fire!"

Doherty appeared next to the PI. "Throw down your weapon or we'll fire!" he yelled at Clayton.

"No! Sergeant! No!" By then, most of the crowd had trampled out of the theater except for the brave and curious. The media had stayed. Berenger made it to the apron and grabbed Doherty. "Tell your men to hold their fire!"

"Berenger! Get away, you fool!"

"I think I can talk him into surrendering!"

"Get out of here before I—"

Mike Case appeared from the side aisle and shouted, "Sergeant! Please!"

Doherty swung his head at Case.

Case whispered. "Let him try."

Doherty clinched his jaw for a moment, looked at

the man onstage, and then turned to Berenger. He gave the PI a curt nod.

Clayton spoke into the microphone again. "She said that Stuart Clayton would be the last to die. So here goes."

"Stuart, no. Don't do it," Berenger pleaded gently.

But a woman in the back of the theater shouted, "Father! No! Don't do it!" Clayton visibly reacted at the sound of it, but he kept the Kahr trained under his chin.

A man and woman hurried down the aisle toward the apron. Berenger recognized one of them as none other than his friend Sandro Ponti from Italy. The woman was an astonishing projection of what Sylvia Favero might have looked like at the age of forty. Berenger thought she was a dead ringer.

When they reached the edge of the stage, Berenger said, "Well, hello, Sandro." To the woman: "You must be Julia Faerie. You got here in time for the finale."

Chapter Twenty-eight

All the Madmen
(performed by David Bowie)

To Berenger, who was still a little under the influence of the salvia, Stuart Clayton's was the Face of Death. As the musician stood on the stage with the Kahr under his chin, he appeared extremely unwell and vulnerable—a man with one foot already in the grave. Clayton also looked truly pathetic in the drag clothing; now that he could be seen up close and personal, he was just an old man dressed in women's clothing and wearing poor makeup that ran with sweat.

Just as he had appeared in a photograph on the back cover of his 1979 album, *Trrrrans*.

What a sick fuck . . . It was all that Berenger could think.

The policemen remained in position with guns in outstretched hands, aiming at the killer. Doherty stood at the edge of the stage with Berenger, Prescott, Case, and the two newcomers. Reporters and photographers were videotaping and snapping photos of the entire thing. Nerves were frayed. People were scared. The situation was a powder keg, ready to explode any second. It was the ultimate in reality television.

Clayton's sad eyes moved to the woman who called herself Julia Faerie.

"Julia?" he called in his real voice.

"It's me, Father. Now put the gun down and then I'll give you a hug and say hello." She spoke with a distinctive Italian accent. The woman was attractive, blonde, and fit. She exhibited self-confidence and pride, even if the man on the stage was a blood relative and had caused so much heartache.

Clayton blinked. Realization dawned on his face, and his expression turned to one of guilt. There had always been pain in his eyes—seeing his daughter brought it to the forefront.

"Come on, Dad. You need to put it down. Please?"

"What . . . what are you . . . doing here?" Clayton stuttered.

"I came to see you. Can't I do that?"

Clayton didn't answer. His eyes darted around to everyone facing him, but the stage lights were blinding him. The only person on whom he could focus was Julia.

"Dad, if I ask these men to put down their guns, will you do the same and put down yours?"

Doherty said sotto voce to Berenger, "We can't be at a standstill all day."

"Wait," Berenger whispered.

Clayton slowly shook his head. He wasn't going to do what she asked.

There was dead silence in the house. No one moved. The tableau was a still photograph, frozen in time.

Then, from out of the quiet there came a soft and beautiful singing voice, humming a plaintive, beautiful melody. At first, no one realized it was coming from Julia until she opened her mouth and began to sing lyrics. Berenger recognized the song. It was one of the album tracks. The voice was identical. The album and its cuts were the work of the woman standing next to him.

Clayton reacted to her voice by closing his eyes and trembling. After a moment, a trickle of tears ran down his face. The pistol, however, never left the underside of his chin.

Berenger already knew that her music and lyrics were mesmerizing, but hearing her sing them live, a capella, was a revelation. He and everyone else in the theater were spellbound. It was the most surreal and dreamlike drama that Berenger had ever witnessed. He attributed much of his feelings of profundity to the lingering effects of the psychedelic drug to which he was subjected; nevertheless, the tragedy unfolding in front of him would be right up there in the Top Ten List of Strange Tales and Amazing Stories.

And then a movement on the left side of the stage distracted the PI. Someone was in the wings, not far from where Clayton stood. Berenger glanced at Doherty and saw that the sergeant was making subtle signals to men positioned there. Officers were ready to rush onstage and throw Clayton to the floor. All they needed was for Doherty to give them the go-ahead.

The song reached a climax and sent a chill down Berenger's spine. At the same time, he whispered, "Doherty, no!"

Julia stopped singing.

Doherty nodded.

Three officers burst onto the stage and headed for Clayton.

"No!" Berenger shouted.

Clayton saw the men rushing toward him and had the time to do one single act.

The gun went off, clearly demonstrating its power to blow the back of a man's skull and brains to bits. The officers, unable to stop their forward momentum, tackled the falling body and crashed onto the floor.

Julia Faerie cried out, turned to Ponti, and buried her head on his arm. He held her tightly as she began to sob.

Berenger hung his head. He felt Prescott take his hand. "Christ, Doherty," he muttered softly. But the sergeant had already jumped onto the stage along with other officers. Someone examining Nance called out, "This one's gone." The officer checking Brill on the other side echoed the statement.

Fuck! Berenger thought. I couldn't save any of 'em.

The hit list was complete. Sylvia Favero had her revenge.

Case left Berenger's side and stepped onto the stage. The PI had no wish to follow. He just wanted to get out of there. He turned to Ponti and the woman.

"I'm sorry."

Ponti nodded understandingly. The woman separated from him and wiped her face. She sniffed. "He was my father, you know."

"Her real name is Julia Favero," Ponti said.

Berenger gave her a kind smile. "I imagine you have quite a story to tell."

She sniffed and nodded. "I do. And I will. Later."

An officer approached them and said that they needed to make formal statements. Berenger sighed and allowed the uniforms to do their jobs. It appeared his immediate future was another long night with Chicago's finest.

But as he was being ushered out of the theater, Mike Case sided up to him and put something in his hand.

"They were taped to the back of one of Clayton's keyboards," he whispered.

Three compact disks. The final three tracks for the album. Berenger swiftly put them in his jacket pocket.

The big question was—who was the true artist behind the album? Sylvia Favero or Julia Faerie?

Chapter Twenty-nine

Brain Damage
(performed by Pink Floyd)

Berenger spent the rest of Friday night and all day Saturday at Northwestern Memorial Hospital. The concussion he had suffered was not terribly serious but bad enough that he be given treatment. The doctor on duty in the emergency room that day bandaged the wound on Berenger's forehead, ordered X-rays of his skull, and, after five hours, determined that there was no fracture. The PI was prescribed heavy-duty analgesics and twenty-fours of strict bed rest, followed by "taking it easy" for the next three weeks. The most important rule was not to drink alcohol for that period of time.

"For three weeks? No *alcohol*?" he complained to Prescott as they left the hospital Saturday night.

"Relax, Spike, it'll do you good."

"I think I'd rather opt for the brain surgery."

"You're lucky you're alive. I'm taking you back to the hotel, you're going to take your pain pills, and you're going straight to bed. And you're going to stay there until Sunday night—and then you're going to sleep again all night and not leave the hotel room until Monday morning. Got that?"

"Who are you, Florence Nightingale?"

"No, but I play her on TV."

"Do you have one of those little nurse outfits?"

"Don't get kinky."

"You brought it up."

And true to her word, Prescott made sure Berenger never left his room until Monday morning. She fielded all phone calls and took notes. She made the reports to Bishop in New York, talked to Briggs and Remix, and checked in with Mike Case. Sandro Ponti and Julia Faerie remained in town because the singer insisted on telling Berenger her story. Prescott had told her she'd have to wait until Monday, but that was all right with her. She needed some decompression time for herself. In the meantime, Prescott meditated, caught up on her reading, did work on her laptop, and took care of the patient in the next room.

She was finally able to peruse the material Remix had uploaded to Rockin' Security's server. The *Trrrrans* record album cover was just as Berenger had described. The front cover portrayed Clayton looking into a mirror with no reflection. The back cover was the same photo, except that the image in the mirror was his drag characterization of Sylvia Favero. The man was telling the world what his ailment was. Didn't someone know about it or care? Prescott now realized that both voices she had heard on Clayton's *Trrrrans* session recording belonged to him—his own and the Sylvia's. They had been working on the recording "together." Was Stuart Clayton a Norman Bates, the Anthony Perkins character from Hitchcock's *Psycho*? Was he the Michael Caine cross-dressing killer in *Dressed to Kill*? Prescott figured Clayton was both, plus much more. The exacerbation of his affliction had to be

Clayton's guilt over Sylvia Favero's death, combined with the excessive ingestion of hallucinogens on top of preexisting schizophrenic tendencies. This triumvirate catapulted the musician into a twilight zone of dual identities. What was truly remarkable was that when Clayton was "Sylvia," he no longer experienced the paresthesia that weakened the left side of his body. As "Sylvia," he could walk, run, shoot, and fight with the strength and ability of a trained athlete—which "she" was. Only when he assumed the Clayton persona did his body tend to shrink and become frail. Psychosomatic, perhaps? She didn't know.

It was certainly weird.

On Monday morning they met, of all places, at the Cook County medical examiner's office building on West Harrison Street, not far from the University of Illinois at Chicago. Clayton's autopsy was scheduled for eight thirty. The morgue was overcrowded on Saturday, closed on Sunday, and Monday was the soonest it could be done. Mike Case had arranged for Berenger and Prescott, the "out-of-town law-enforcement officials," to witness the postmortem. Faerie still needed to officially identify the body, so she and Ponti were going to arrive in a little while.

The trio observed the procedure along with several other interested parties, including other Chicago PD, someone from the D.A.'s office, and a psychiatrist. Unlike what one sees in movies and television, there were no cubicle freezers in which individual cadavers are kept. At the Cook County morgue, all the bodies were kept in a large refrigerated room as big as a warehouse. Bodies were stacked horizontally on shelves, lying in plain sight, some completely covered, some half out of body bags. There must have been a hundred corpses. Most had already been autopsied, while others waited for a turn on the stainless steel table. After Clayton's procedure, Berenger, Prescott, and Case stepped into the cold, gray space. Two familiar toe-tag names belonged to a couple of cadavers that had been recently added to the "Done" pile.

"Here's Joe and Harrison," Berenger said.

Prescott gasped, "Oh, gee." She grasped Berenger's arm.

"You've been in a morgue before, Suzanne."

"I know. It still creeps me out."

Berenger had to agree. A morgue was a place that, no matter how well it was lit, still had a dark side. He had never been in one he liked. First of all, they all had a foul, distinctive chemical smell that clung to one's clothing for hours after a visit. Even shoes absorbed the odor. Secondly, a morgue's employees developed a gallows-humor objectivity that protected them from the more unpleasant aspects of their jobs. They became so clinically oriented that the slabs of flesh on the autopsy tables were no longer individuals. While Berenger appreciated the necessity for black humor, he didn't care for the way bodies were treated so cavalierly. The proceedings only served to drive home how compact and intricately constructed human beings are, and yet how useless the machines are after the souls have departed. Perhaps the most surreal things, in Berenger's mind, were the numerous fly traps hanging from the ceilings of every room in the building. Every trap was covered with dead flies.

They met Julia and Ponti in the reception area at the

front of the building. Julia filled out the appropriate paperwork, and then they were all taken to a small viewing room. She commented that it wasn't what she expected.

"Another misconception about morgues is that people identify bodies by looking directly at the corpse in the flesh, so to speak," Case explained. "Not so." In actuality, a camera is pointed at the cadaver's head and shoulders and the image is broadcast to a wide, flat-screen television on the wall of the viewing room. In a way, the space reminded Berenger of a chapel. There were comfortable chairs and a couch, a piece of art on the wall that symbolized Christianity, Judaism, and Islam, and an Extenda-Barrier in front of the television to keep distraught family members from touching the screen.

Stuart Clayton's head had been draped in white to cover the gunshot wounds, but a good portion of his face was visible.

Julia stood in front of the screen and stared at the man. Berenger, Prescott, Ponti, and Case respectfully kept their distance but had a close eye on her in case she had a case of waterworks. Berenger got the impression that Julia was a tough lady, for she showed little emotion and seemed to take the death of her father in stride.

"I thought he was already dead," she said. She turned to the group. "I was very surprised when Sandro told me what was happening here. I am sorry. It could have been prevented."

Berenger quietly asked, "How?"

Julia turned back to her father and began the story.

"I was born in Milan in nineteen sixty-eight. As you

know, Sylvia Favero was my mother. She was a selfish person, I think, to have me like that and then just run away. She left me with my grandmother, who raised me. My grandfather went to prison when I was one year old and he died there, so it was just my grandmother and me. I never met my mother—saw only photographs. She went missing when I was two, but I didn't find out about it until I was much older—when I was twelve." She indicated Clayton on the screen. "And it was this man—who I knew as my father—who told me."

"So he knew about you and knew where you lived?"

"Apparently so. To tell you the truth, I'm not totally positive he's my father. He always said he was. Now I understand he might have been one of the other men in the band. But Stuart was convinced he was my father. He sent money every six months after my mother's disappearance. Quite a nice sum of money, too. He had inherited wealth from his family and he spent most of it on me, as I understand it."

"Did you know where the money was coming from?"

"My grandmother put it in a bank for me until I was old enough to know what money was. She told me that money was coming from America for me to use when I grew up. She didn't say it was from my father. She said it was from an anonymous relative. Perhaps she didn't know."

Prescott asked, "And then one day he just showed up in Italy?"

"It was nineteen eighty. He had released his solo album, *Trrrrans*, and then decided to move to Milan to be near me. He showed up one day and introduced himself to my grandmother and me. Needless to say, we were taken aback. And suspicious. For one thing, we could see that the man was not well. It was evident on first sight. I was only twelve, so I didn't completely understand what was wrong with him, but my grandmother did. She told him to go away. He explained that it was he who was sending the money. My grandmother still made him leave. So he did . . . but he rented a flat not far from ours. He kept watch on me as I grew older. I'd see him on the street, watching me. And then . . . when I was sixteen, my grandmother died. I had no one. But I was smart and resourceful, and I had money. It was then that I reacquainted myself with the man who claimed to be my father. I never got to know him very well, but we were . . . friendly. Yes, he was a very strange man. But I felt sorry for him."

"What was he doing in Italy?"

She laughed a little. "For a while he worked in an alternative nightclub called Plastic where drag queens perform. He was totally into it, too. There really was a transformation when he dressed in women's clothing. The afflictions he normally suffered—having to walk with a cane, a weakness on the left side of his face— they just disappeared when he was a woman. It was only . . . later . . . that I realized that the woman he was becoming was meant to be my mother."

"So that's how he was supporting himself? Working as a drag queen?" Berenger asked. The thing just got stranger by the minute.

"I suppose he still had some of his family's money left. He stopped the payments to me once I was eighteen. I'm pretty sure he ran out of money, and that's one of the reasons he left Italy in ninety-two. He wanted to make music again and he felt that the only place he could do it was in Chicago. But that's skipping ahead."

Berenger suddenly felt a chill. He involuntarily shivered at the bizarre notion that they had just been standing in the autopsy room, watching the dissection of the woman's serial-killer father. The story of her relationship with the man suddenly made that lifeless slab of flesh and vessel of organs seem more human.

Prescott said, "So, Julia, if I may ask . . . I don't mean to embarrass you . . . but your father, did he ever think about having transgender surgery or anything like that?"

"I understand your asking the question, and I think it's important that you know that my dad wasn't into the cross-dressing thing for sexual reasons. By that, I mean he wasn't getting off on it like some men do when they're into that particular fetish. And, no, he wasn't a transgender candidate. He didn't *want* to be a woman. He had no plans to have a sex change or anything like that."

"He just wanted Sylvia Favero to still be alive, didn't he?" Berenger asked.

"His problem was that he had a split personality. And he knew it, too. He could talk about it rationally, as if he were standing outside his own body and could analyze what was happening."

Case added, "We've learned that he could do things for Sylvia while he was Stuart Clayton and vice versa. For example, Clayton drove a ninety-eight Chevy Malibu with a hole in the tail end for the sniper rifle. On the evening you two were trapped in the house,

Clayton parked his Malibu on the street and put your rental car in his garage. He had the cognizance to do that."

"I remember seeing that car parked a couple of houses down from his," Berenger said. "And he must have been following me in it the day I was shadowing Bushnell on Clark Street. That's how 'Sylvia' knew I was following someone when she called. He was watching me the whole time."

"And you know how she got your unlisted number?" Case asked.

"My number's on my business card, and I gave one to Stuart. And he gave it to . . . Sylvia." He nodded to Julia. "Go on."

"As time went on," the woman continued, "he explained it all to me, leaving out the part about my mother dying on his boat. The way he told it was that he felt terribly guilty about my mother's *disappearance*. And I'm afraid this was also the theme of several acid trips he took in those days."

"We know about the drugs, Julia," Berenger said. "And we know he was already being treated for mental illness. I spoke to his family doctor. The onset of Stuart Clayton's schizophrenia was when he was in high school."

She nodded. "My mother's death, the drugs, the stress of being a musician—all that contributed to my father's digression into a pit of hell. I understand that he tried to commit suicide shortly after that."

"That's right."

"He tried it again in Italy. The drag queen job at the nightclub had got him into some trouble with some gay-bashing thugs. They thought he was a homosexual since he worked as a drag queen. They beat him up pretty badly one night after a performance, outside behind the building. So he stopped performing. He overdosed on drugs again. I don't know where he got the psychedelics from—they are very hard to obtain in Italy. At any rate, he went over the edge. He spent longer periods of time as Sylvia Favero until he was her twenty four-seven. The doctors couldn't get him to change back to his real self. He was in a Milan hospital for three years."

Julia turned to them again. "I'm glad you're not laughing. I know it sounds like a bad comedy."

"No, it doesn't," Prescott answered. "It's sad."

"Anyway, I didn't think he was violent—that is, violent toward other people. I knew he was a danger to himself. But something happened that brought him out of the ditch he was in."

"What was that?"

"He heard me sing."

"Tell us about that."

"I had been singing all my life. I joined the church choir and sang in the choirs at school. When I was on my own as a teenager, I started performing with an ensemble that traveled the country and sang church music. It was good experience, but I wanted to write and sing my own songs. So I did. It was a very difficult life. For a while I lived in Rome and tried to make it in the music scene there, but eventually I came back to Milan. And then Stuart gave me a tape. He said it was some demos that my mother had made before she . . . disappeared. He urged me to learn them. And I did.

They were a perfect fit for me. I loved the songs. In fact, they inspired me in my own writing, and I could say that my songs are very similar in style to hers.

"Anyway, Stuart became obsessed with my making an album. He was convinced that my studio recordings were great. Mostly I did my own original songs, but I covered a couple of my mother's. But, I don't know, Father somehow mixed up everything. He called me Sylvia at times. He forgot I was her daughter. And then *he* was Sylvia at times, and she was telling him that it was her album and that he owed it to *her* to get it made." Julia gave them a sad smile. "My friends . . . my father had a very, very troubled mind. By the time he left for Chicago in nineteen ninety-two, he didn't know if I was Sylvia or Julia, or if he was Stuart or Sylvia. I feared for him. I tried to keep in touch, but he stopped writing. He moved and changed his contact details. It was as if he cut me out of his life. After a while, I was afraid that he may have died. I had no way of knowing."

"I think I understand what happened," Prescott said. "The Sylvia persona was so strong in him, that he couldn't accept *you* as a surrogate Sylvia. There was only one Sylvia, and she was within him."

"I think you're right."

"But why did he start killing his former band members?" Case asked.

"I don't think we'll ever know," Julia answered.

"I can guess," Berenger said. "It was the guilt. All the guys contributed to Sylvia's death. They all covered it up. He lived with that horrible secret and it tortured his weak and sick mind. Finally, after so many years, it culminated in murder. It was the only way he could live with himself. He had to fulfill two goals. One was seeing that your album was made because in his mind it was some kind of tribute to Sylvia. Atonement. The second was avenging Sylvia's death, and that including killing Stuart Clayton—himself."

Everyone was quiet until Ponti said, "*Mama mia.*" That brought a few chuckles of relief from everyone in the room.

Berenger thought of the two familiar names he saw in the large body-room. "I wonder how much guilt weighed on Joe, for instance?" he asked. "How much did it trouble any of the other guys? Surely they had nightmares about it. Surely they were haunted by Sylvia's ghost."

Prescott said, "It's probably why they were all so ready to believe that it was her ghost that was killing them all off."

Then they were all quiet for a moment. Case eventually asked Julia if she was finished. She nodded.

"I'll tell the attendant," Case said. "Then I guess we can get out of here."

Julia turned to them. "Thank you for listening. I've never told that story to anyone."

"You're welcome," Berenger said. "It had to be told and I'm glad you trusted us enough to do so."

She smiled. "Are you still going to try and get the album made?"

He nodded. "It's a good record. I think I know some people who can get it in the right hands at a major label. Credited to you, of course. I figure the songwriting credits will be shared by you and your mother. Is that fair?"

"Yes, thank you. I would be very grateful. It's been

a long, hard road for me. It will be ironic that I make my first album when I'm in my forties."

"Stranger things have happened."

She looked down at her father. "That's certainly true."

Chapter Thirty

Lucky Man
(performed by Emerson, Lake & Palmer)

Berenger and Prescott returned to New York that evening, having said their good-byes to their friends in Chicago, officially informed the kind folks at the Fourteenth District and Area Five of their departure, and paid the parking ticket they had received on the previous Friday night. Berenger was warned that his headache may worsen while he flew—and it did. By the time they had picked up their luggage at baggage claim, the PI truly felt like crap.

The couple shared a taxi from LaGuardia. Since Prescott lived in the East Village and Berenger lived on the Upper East Side, it was more practical to drop him off first. The cab pulled up to his building on East Sixty-eighth Street and he turned to Prescott.

"I'll call you?"

Prescott wasn't sure why he felt the need to ask that question. "Sure." She gave a little shrug.

Berenger nodded.

"You rest," she told him. "You know, you're a lucky man."

He nodded again. "See ya." He got out, closed the door, and walked away.

Berenger picked up the week's worth of junk mail

and took the elevator to his apartment. He unlocked the door, stepped inside, and dropped his luggage on the floor, went to the kitchen, and placed the mail on the counter. The red light on the answering machine was blinking. He punched the button and heard Linda's voice.

"Hi, Spike, I'm calling you from the hotel in Chicago. I tried to reach you while you were still here, but they said you'd checked out. I, uhm, wanted to let you know that Richard and I have decided to just go ahead and take the plunge. We're going to get married this week. I know it's kind of sudden, but it's what we feel like doing. We're flying to Las Vegas tonight— assuming it's still Monday when you get this message— to do the deed. I know, it's pretty crazy and you probably can't believe *I'm* going to get married in Las Vegas. Well, it's true. Unless I get cold feet at the last minute, which I don't think will happen, I'm going to do it. So, even though you didn't have to be, I wanted you to be the first to know, Spike. I'm going to call Michael and Pam now and tell them. So now you can't say I let your kids know before I told you.

"I also wanted to say it was a surprise seeing you and Suzanne in Chicago, but it turned out all right. It was actually kind of nice to see you. Richard liked you a lot. I had to suffer through him going into the Virgin Megastore to find some of the bands you mentioned. I hope you haven't corrupted him, Spike, I really do.

"Anyway, we'll come back to New York after a short honeymoon in Vegas. I didn't want you to wonder where I was. I hope you solved your case, whatever it was. Bye."

And that was it.

That was it? She tells me she's getting hitched in Vegas and that's it?

Berenger played the whole message again to make sure he didn't miss anything. Nope, she didn't say "hope to see you again soon," or "love you," or "I'll talk to you later" . . . not that she was obligated to do so. He wasn't sure if she had been flaunting her decision to get married immediately, of if she was simply informing him. The latter was, of course, the right thing to do. He supposed it could have been both, but Linda wasn't the type to say, "nyah nyah nyah, look what I'm doing and you're not." They had moved past hurting each other for sport a long time ago.

He supposed he wished her well. But how could he send flowers or a card if he didn't know where they were getting married? Maybe Pam would know.

Funny thing, that. Linda was marrying Mr. Clean. His new best friend.

Berenger sighed heavily and took a look at the mail. He then went back to the entry hall, picked up his suitcase, and took it to the bedroom. Thirty minutes later, he had unpacked, watered the two plants he kept in the living room, and then went back into the kitchen for the phone. He dialed a number he knew by heart.

"Yeah?"

"Charlie, it's Spike."

"Hey, Spike. What's up?"

"I just got back from Chicago."

"Chicago? Were you on a case?"

"Yeah."

"How'd it go?"

"Not so good."

"Oh. I'm sorry."

"You want to come over and jam?"

Berenger could hear Charlie Potts stretch the way he did—like a cat waking from a nap. "Oh, I don't know, Spike. I'm kind of settled in for the evening. It's a Monday. I'm watching TV."

"Okay. Some other time."

"Some other time."

He hung up, stared at the phone, and dialed another number he knew from memory.

"Hello?"

"Suzanne?"

"Yeah?"

"You made it home all right?"

"Sure. Why wouldn't I?"

"Oh, I was just calling to make sure. Hey, you feel like going out for a meal or a drink or something?"

"Spike, you can't have a drink or something."

"Oh, yeah. I keep forgetting."

"Well, remember. It's important."

"So how about a meal? Split a pizza or something? I hated that Chicago pizza we ate. New York will always have the best pizza, don't you agree?"

"I do agree, but Spike, I'm exhausted. I just got home and I am dead. Really, I can't imagine how you've got the energy to want to go out."

"I don't know, I just walked into my apartment and it felt strange. Like I needed to get out of it for a while."

"You were just out of it for a whole week, Spike. Geez. Listen, you still have a head injury and, face it, you went through some serious psychological torture the other night. You can't take it for granted or poo-poo it. That was some heavy shit Stuart Clayton did to you—to us—and I think it's okay that you feel strange.

I feel strange, too. But I also feel very tired. So I'm going to hang up, and I'll see you at the office tomorrow, right?"

"Yeah, I guess so."

"Spike?"

"Yes, Suzanne. I'm fine."

"Okay."

"Okay."

"Bye."

"Bye."

Berenger hung up, opened the cabinet, removed the bottle of Jack Daniel's, grabbed a glass from the cupboard, and poured himself a couple of inches. He set down the bottle, picked up the glass, put it to his lips . . .

. . . and remembered that he wasn't supposed to drink alcohol for three weeks.

"Shiiiiiiit," he groaned.

He tried to pour the whiskey back into the bottle, but ended up spilling most of it. He cursed again, washed his hands, put the Jack away, and opened the refrigerator. There stood a carton of Minute Maid pulp-free orange juice. The expiration date was still good, too.

He rinsed out the glass and filled it with juice. He took the glass and went straight to his music room, a space that he had converted into a small recording studio and practice room. It's where he and Charlie always jammed. It's where he spent many a night laying down guitar solos or pieces of unfinished songs with a glass or two of Jack or bourbon or beer or wine or vodka . . .

Berenger turned on the mixer, the amplifiers, the microphones, the recording equipment, and then moved to the middle of the studio. He sat on his stool, placed the drink beside him on a small table that was there for that purpose, and picked up his DBZ acoustic guitar from its stand.

It had been an extraordinary, frustrating week and he felt very unsettled about it. It was possibly the most disturbing case he'd ever worked on and its closure was far from pleasant. Berenger wasn't sure if he could call the job a success simply because the perpetrator was dead. Eleven other people were also gone—ten men and a woman who were talented musicians. And then there was the legacy of what happened to Sylvia Favero and everything it wrought. It was almost as if a curse really had befallen the members of The Loop and its two offspring—Windy City Engine and Red Skyez.

Had he failed? Could he have stopped Stuart Clayton from killing the final few? Had he not worked hard enough or fast enough? He didn't know the answers to those questions, but he also figured there was nothing more he could have done to identify Clayton sooner.

Prescott was right. They had been through something remarkable and possibly significant. Perhaps the biggest question Berenger needed to ask was—had the experience changed him in any way?

He didn't know the answer to that one either, so he strummed an A minor seventh chord, held it, and then played a D minor seventh. The combination had enough of a melancholic quality to suit his mood, so he continued to alternate between the two. It eventually worked its way into an old prog ballad that he had written with The Fixers—it had been their attempt at something similar to one of ELP's vocal numbers like "Lucky Man" or "In the Beginning." The song was called "I Crossed to the Other Side," and it was a personal favorite of Berenger's repertoire. In his low, gravelly, Beefheart-like voice, the PI sang the tune.

And then he sang another.

HAGGAI CARMON

Author of *The Red Syndrome*

The master criminal and con man known as the Chameleon has eluded international law enforcement for twenty years. Dan Gordon was sure he finally had him, but he was left empty-handed. Now he won't rest until the Chameleon is stopped. The Chameleon is actually more than a mere criminal — he's an undercover sleeper agent. But Gordon is more than he seems, too. He's an experienced hunter, trained by the Mossad, working now for the CIA.

The trail leads Gordon to unforeseen locales and surprising alliances. His hunt for the slippery Chameleon will send him undercover to Iran, surrounded by danger and betrayal on all sides. What he learns could affect the world's balance of power . . . if he makes it out of Tehran alive.

THE CHAMELEON CONSPIRACY

A Dan Gordon Intelligence Thriller ®

ISBN 13: 978-0-8439-6191-1

To order a book or to request a catalog call:
1-800-481-9191
Our books are also available at your local bookstore, or you can check out our Web site **www.dorchesterpub.com** where you can look up your favorite authors, read excerpts, or glance at our discussion forum to see what people have to say about your favorite books.

✂

☐ **YES!**

Sign me up for the Leisure Thriller Book Club and send
my FREE BOOKS! If I choose to stay in the club, I will
pay only $4.25* each month, a savings of $3.74!

NAME: _____

ADDRESS: _____

TELEPHONE: _____

EMAIL: _____

☐ I want to pay by credit card.

☐ **VISA**   ☐ MasterCard   ☐ DISC VER

ACCOUNT #: _____

EXPIRATION DATE: _____

SIGNATURE: _____

Mail this page along with $2.00 shipping and handling to:
Leisure Thriller Book Club
PO Box 6640
Wayne, PA 19087
Or fax (must include credit card information) to:
610-995-9274

You can also sign up online at **www.dorchesterpub.com**.
*Plus $2.00 for shipping. Offer open to residents of the U.S. and Canada only.
Canadian residents please call 1-800-481-9191 for pricing information.
If under 18, a parent or guardian must sign. Terms, prices and conditions subject to
change. Subscription subject to acceptance. Dorchester Publishing reserves the right
to reject any order or cancel any subscription.